The Secret Life of Sandrina M.

ALSO BY JESSICA DEE ROHM

Make Me an Offer
Sugar Tower

OLIVICAS PRESS
New York

JESSICA DEE ROHM

The Secret Life of Sandrina M.

A Novel

2010 Olivicas Press Paperback Edition

Originally published in hardcover in the United States in 2004.

ISBN 1453754083

PRINTED IN THE UNITED STATES OF AMERICA

www.jessicadeerohm.com

This book is dedicated to my husband, Eberhard Rohm,
who taught me everything I know about love.

Chapter One

Sandrina had come by the house that day to pick up the cats, but since they were hiding from her under sofas and chairs, she sat alone in the quiet room simply waiting for them to come to her. She closed her eyes and listened to the silence, sensing Joshua Baum's spirit lingering. Here was where she had first met him 19 years earlier, on the evening that changed her life.

The enormous limestone mansion where Joshua and Esther lived sat on the corner of Sutton Place, capturing views of not only the river to the east but New York's jagged cityscape to the south.

The memories evoked by the now familiar wood-polish scent of the furniture and the tangy taste of the river carried in on summer breezes made her dizzy with recollected emotion.

So much in the world and her had changed since that night, but the house was the same. The thick nest of dark leaves that smothered the façade had once been a young growth of ivy cascading over the limestone house like a waterfall. And she had been young too, alive to possibility.

With her eyes closed, alone in the room, she could still picture Stewart, the Baum's houseman, in a tuxedo and white gloves as he opened the door to her, and behind him, her friend and colleague,

Cameron Finn, from *Journey* magazine. It was Cameron who had invited her there that evening; he smiled as he offered her his hand and swept her into the cavernous front hall.

Cameron Finn, long dead like Esther and Joshua and a part of herself, looked to her then like a water reed, tall, thin, and slightly bent. Sipping sweet vermouth, which many parties later she learned was his trademark drink, he led her deeper into the house.

The grand salon had two sets of double height French doors, which opened onto a private field of new grass that sloped to the FDR Drive. The lawn was bordered then, as it still was now, by flower gardens of pink peonies and white rose bushes, with beds of irises, phlox, and catmint below. All those colors, which she remembered so vividly, looked paler now as she opened her eyes and looked around.

The walls of the room itself were upholstered in a muted peach-and-cream patterned silk that blended with the luxuriously cut draperies. The line of the drapery valence fed into thin moldings with invisible hooks from which the most spectacular paintings Sandrina had ever seen outside of a museum were hung.

The paintings were astounding, she now knew, thanks to Joshua, because it was he who had taught her what they were.

There was a Seurat over the sofa in an elaborate gold frame, flanked by beveled Murano glass sconces. There was a Monet, hanging over a lacquered chinoiserie commode inlaid with ivory and mother of pearl. Beside it was a Louis XV loveseat. The first time she had seen these treasures she had no idea how important they were.

Along the wall across from the French doors hung a triad that she learned that first night were a Picasso, a Degas, and a Corot, by inspecting the little brass plaques that were discreetly nailed to the bottom of their frames.

Then she heard Cameron's voice, transporting her back to that earlier time, saying: "I'm glad you're here," as he handed Sandrina a glass that he lifted from a tray being passed around.

It was the best champagne Sandrina had ever tasted. It was rosé, which she later learned was Taittinger Comptes de Champagne, and the icy bubbles slid down her throat.

"Cameron, whose house is this? A maharaja?" she asked.

Cameron laughed. "The house belongs to Joshua Baum—he's over there."

She recognized only the name at the time. The buzz on Joshua Baum was that he had invented the modern public relations profession. "Didn't he come to America from Germany in the early thirties? He didn't speak a word of English, had no money, no family, no education?"

"That's him," Cameron replied.

Over the course of their long relationship, the facts of Joshua Baum's saga changed from time to time, fueling Sandrina's later speculation that his own history was his primary piece of spin. Regardless of the means, the end could not be denied: Joshua Baum elevated the pursuit of publicity from favors exchanged over three martini lunches to corporate image building and artful power brokering—and he became very wealthy along the way.

Perhaps it was the 25-room urban mansion with its private garden, Stewart the butler, the priceless antiques and famous paintings. Or maybe it was all that plus the magnanimity of the person himself. But the first time Sandrina met Joshua Baum, she was in awe. Portly and bald-headed, with the dove-gray handlebar mustache of a carnival barker, he was small, no more than five feet tall. Despite his size, he was the biggest person she would ever know.

She approached him impulsively, without waiting to be introduced, her heart racing with uncertainty. "You have some amazing art here," she said, not knowing what else to say.

"Are you a collector?" he asked.

She smiled. "Rather a connecter, I'd say. But I'm very interested in learning more. Did someone teach you how to select such beautiful pieces, or do you just have a natural eye for quality?"

"I like to think that I know a good thing when I see it," Joshua said.

"I imagine, Mr. Baum, that's true. It takes one to know one." And so intent was she on impressing him she forgot to tell him her name.

If only she had been privy to what everyone said that night, she would have been flattered and embarrassed by the conversation that ensued:

"Who is that charming girl?" Joshua asked Cameron Finn minutes later.

"Her name is Sandrina Favonian," Cameron replied. "She's been at *Journey* a bit over three months—mainly covering the New York scene, getting her feet wet."

"What's her provenance?" Joshua asked.

"She went to Smith on an academic scholarship, won the Magazine Fund Award her senior year—" Cameron said.

"So that's how she got to *Journey*?"

"It should have been, but we were too slow. *Glamour* snatched her first, but for her looks, not her brains. They were scouting college campuses for models, saw Sandrina, wanted to photograph her for an article on "Overcoming Your One Physical Imperfection.""

Joshua Baum looked sidelong at the comely twenty-two year old girl sitting poised on his Louis XV loveseat in a flowered dress and scuffed shoes with the heels worn down. He appraised her as he would an artwork — objectively.

"What imperfection was that?" he asked.

"Exactly. The editor interviewed Sandrina and offered her a job as a writer, not a model, as the scouts had intended."

The two sexagenarians, who had been friends for thirty years, exchanged knowing looks.

"So she's smart and beautiful," Joshua observed. "What else should I know?"

"She's tireless and determined. Self-starter and shrewd," Cameron said.

"Sounds like my kind of girl," Joshua said.

"Don't you mean she sounds like you?" Cameron asked.

"That too," Joshua chuckled.

"I've taken her to fundraisers, ribbon cuttings, and social events at various clubs. You know, The Circuit." He took a draw on his vermouth, the way one might a cigarette. "Her modest upbringing shows —" Cameron said, reverting to his Locust Valley intonation.

Joshua raised an eyebrow and his champagne flute in perfect unison, "How so?"

"Well, for one thing, I've seen her eat from the wrong bread plate."

Joshua smiled. "Well, that can be fixed—"

"Yes, certainly, with a little training and experience," Cameron said. "Funny thing, though. Her lack of polish is blatant, but no one seems to mind. Adrian von Bachmaier was smitten. Even Phyllis Marcus finds her charming. And Phyllis has nothing nice to say about anyone." He followed his friend's fixed gaze. "She's charismatic, Josh. Look at her."

Both distinguished arbiters of interesting people, as different as a longsword and a battle flail with spikes, Cameron and Joshua turned once again to face Sandrina.

Sandrina saw them watching her. She lowered her eyes with reserve. Something about Joshua's attention gave her pause. It wasn't sexual, what men gave attractive women whom they had designs on, but more proprietary—as if he were appraising a piece of real estate that he felt he could improve upon with a modicum of care.

Sandrina could see that he projected an air of quiet authority, as if he could be the most knowing person in any room. Despite her independence and confidence, Sandrina found his air of superiority enticing. She instinctively knew she could learn so much from someone like him.

What she had not realized then was that Joshua Baum was equally fascinated by her.

On days in her life now, when she was being reflective and thought back to those early years of her apprenticeship, a sad smile crossed her lips. What, she often wondered, had she lost along the way? During the early phase of their relationship, Sandrina's job at *Journey* became the excuse for their continued friendship. Joshua began by inviting her to his power luncheons, after which she would supply tidbits to her *Seen in New York* column about his fascinating guests.

Gradually, she became his eager protégé, enthusiastically imbibing his wisdom and enjoying his joie de vivre. She learned many things by observation, like the fact that one's bread plate is found on the left, and other lessons by design. Joshua fed Sandrina information in measured doses, like Rose Tone to a bed of American Beauties, fearing, he told her, that if she received too much at once she would peak and fade, rather than blossom over time.

At least once a week she went to the Sutton Place house to dine with Joshua's carefully assorted mix of clients, journalists, artists, and financiers. These gatherings were her fieldwork—for the ritualized lessons that took place every week on Sunday afternoons at three. Over chamomile tea in china cups, accompanied by fudge brownies and sugar cookies, the education of Sandrina progressed.

As Joshua became her Pygmalion, transposed from ancient Cyprus to modern-day Manhattan, Sandrina became his Galatea. Carefully absorbing his instructions on which parties to attend, whom she should get to know, and how to spot phonies, she learned to navigate the treacherous waters of New York's social scene. This included lessons on: how to know who had money and looked as though they didn't and who didn't but looked as though they did; to arrive late at every party and leave early; and, to be gracious and generous even when no one else was.

Joshua focused Sandrina's reading habits and helped her decide whose op-ed pieces were worth repeating and whose were not. The list of where to shop in London and Paris for antiques that Joshua provided came years before she had earned enough money to buy a single chair. Potential interior designers for her apartment were introduced long before she even had a place to decorate. Then Joshua arranged for her to meet Betty Halbreich, Bergdorf Goodman's most discriminating personal shopper, who chose Sandrina's outfits and accessories for years, pinning Polaroids of the complete ensembles to transparent garment bags and shoe boxes, until Sandrina learned how to fashionably dress herself.

Over time she could have written a book from the notes she took.

Arriving early to Joshua's on Sunday afternoons, she would study the collection of drawings that lined the stairwell facing the front door while she waited for him in the reception hall. The wall was blank now, but then there were dozens of masterpieces, including Cézanne's *Mercury* and Matisse's *Girl with Tulips*, which she learned to appreciate through Joshua's eyes. Not one failed to enthrall her, but Sandrina's favorite was *Woman in Profile* by the Austrian artist Gustav Klimt. The small drawing, not much larger than one foot square, was sketched in blue pencil; the hint of mystery on the subject's face, hidden behind a cascade of hair, took her breath away every time she saw it.

It was at one of these teas, after they'd known each other for six months, that Joshua had become uncharacteristically grave as he unveiled his plan for her in the form of three pieces of advice. As she remembered, she could feel his presence next to her, as if he were there in flesh and blood.

"Sandrina," he began. "I've been thinking about your life: You are twenty-two, beautiful, charming, smart, and independent. It is time we make some lasting plans."

"Josh," she had scolded. "You make me sound like the subject of a press release!"

Ignoring her reprimand, he continued: "First, I've noticed at my table that you eat with gusto.

This must stop. From now on, always eat before lunch."

Sandrina's mouth had been stuffed with a large bite of brownie, which she chewed quietly as she listened.

"Second," he persisted, "marry once and marry well."

"Uh oh," she interrupted, "is this about that stuffy banker William Stokes again? He's definitely not my type."

"No, no, but you should reconsider him, he's a Mortimer on his mother's side. Anyway, just listen." Joshua paused for effect before delivering his coup de grace. "I want you to start a public relations firm—"

She was so surprised that she practically broke the teacup as she inadvertently clapped it down on the saucer with force. "Josh, what do I know about PR? Or business, for that matter? Why would anyone hire a novice like me?"

"You've got the energy, talent, and poise. The market is begging for a new leader in the PR business. No one has emerged to fill the shoes of the founding fathers like me." He paused and contemplatively twirled his mustache. "Pick a niche—like travel or fashion—to differentiate you and limit the competition. I've even got your first client in mind."

Relaxing into the down cushions, she let his suggestion sink in. "You know, Josh, my mother is an entrepreneur of sorts. She owns Jewel Beauty, a small line of costume jewelry that she designs herself."

"That's how Jolie Gabor started," Joshua said.

"Mom's always discouraged me from the pursuit of money, saying that independent women attract the wrong kind of men," Sandrina said.

"Hogwash," Joshua replied. "You don't want to end up like Zsa Zsa, poor thing. Look what happened to her."

Sandrina had heard of the Gabor sisters but she knew about as much about them as she did about Eleanor of Aquitaine. She made a mental note to Google them when she got home.

"I'm not sure, Josh. Remember what I told you about my father."

She thought about her father now as she had then, with a longing approaching desperation. Sometimes she thought she was so driven toward perfection in an effort to make him love her in the ways he never had.

"No man will take advantage of you, Sandrina. You're too smart," Joshua said.

"It's not about intellect, though, is it?" she asked.

Then, as now, she suppressed the feelings of rejection by her father and smiled at her fatherly friend. Knowing how successful Joshua had been at the art of public relations, she was flattered and intrigued that he thought she could follow in his footsteps. So she accepted Joshua's offer to set up a meeting with Jason Rothstein and Max Sharf, who, he offered as an afterthought, "Were recently out of jail and about to open a hotel."

"Jail?!"

"Just trust me," he said. "You will be the jewel in their crown."

True to his word, the following week Joshua arranged for Sandrina to meet Jason and Max, former comedy club impresarios and recently released convicted tax evaders. She went to the meeting more out of curiosity than with any serious intention of starting a business with them as her clients. Why would they hire her anyway, without training or experience?

Jason and Max were entrepreneurs themselves and had a need for strong PR, but she later learned that the true reason for her shot at the account was that no established firm would touch them after their incarceration.

When Sandrina called Joshua and told him that Max and Jason had offered her their business, she could hear the excitement in his voice.

"Grab it," he said. "It's a once in a lifetime opportunity!"

"I've never done this before, Joshua. I'm only twenty-two. Shouldn't I go to school? Columbia's got a great MBA program. Or work for one of the biggies, like Dale & Seaton or Polk & Raymond? You know, to learn the business?"

"Sandrina, all you will learn from those firms are bad habits, and an MBA takes too long. Besides, in a few years you'll probably be teaching there."

Intuitively, she knew he was right. "I must admit, Josh, I felt empowered in that meeting. I thought to myself, 'I can do this.'"

"I *know* you can. Trust your instincts."

The next day, Sandrina gave her boss at *Journey* two weeks notice.

At lunchtime she leased an office at 515 Madison Avenue. She was exactly one block from her first client, another piece of advice from Joshua, and just across town from Jean-Georges, where, by the time she was 25, she had her own table at lunch.

From the time Sandrina's doors opened for business, she seemed to have the golden touch. After a year she needed larger office space, a loft-like, open landscape floor on East 56th Street. With seven accounts and twice as many people working for her, she started to spend most of her weekdays jetting around the world for clients. However, no matter how far away from New York she might be, she always made sure she was back in time for Sunday tea with Josh.

Sandrina's love life during those years were just as busy but not so fortuitous. Sometimes she liked men with a dark side, shades of her father, just beyond reach. Like the art dealer she nearly married until she discovered he was an art thief. Or the Wall Street stock specialist who was mad for her until she realized that the high energy she admired was a cocaine addiction. Then there was the empire builder, whom Joshua introduced her to and approved of, until he stood her up for lunch because he was busy, and she realized she would always be an also ran to his business. Finally came the con man from Italy, who ran up $16,000 on her American Express card to pay off his previous mark.

That Italian threw her for a loop, and she was about to give up on men altogether, at the age of 25, when Joshua invited her to dinner on April Fool's Day. Seated next to her was Michael Morgan, at 31 an heir to Morgan Paper, one of the largest privately held family-owned businesses in America, and Joshua's newest client.

What Joshua had actually told her on the phone was that Michael had an MBA from Harvard and a degree in chemical engineering from the University of Mannheim, and that he traveled around the world negotiating complex transactions to buy pulp and to sell paper products, ranging from corrugated cardboard to specially treated and coded paper used for printing currencies.

The patriarch had recently passed away and left the shares unequally to his two sons, with 51 percent going to Thomas, the eldest, who ran the mills and manufacturing arm, and 49 percent to Michael, the more genteel of the two, who managed to develop the high-margin currency paper market due to a special chemically treated paper he had invented and patented for the firm. The two siblings wanted the business to expand, which was why Thomas and Michael had retained Joshua to manage the media coverage of their empire.

Michael Morgan was tall and slim, with a runner's build, and chestnut curls. Expensively dressed, in a dark gray suit and a blue shirt, he wore no tie, so that Sandrina could detect just a few tight coils of hair springing out from above the top button of his shirt. There was a boyish energy about him, and she could tell by the way he smiled that he was smitten with her.

The conversation from that night came back to her as if the words were immortalized in a book:

"Joshua mentioned that you own your own business, and that you're very successful," Michael said, over the lobster bisque.

"He embellishes."

"I don't think so," Michael said.

"Well, in any event, success at work is the easy part."

"Isn't everything easy for you?" he asked.

"Not everything. What about you? Josh told me you're in your family's paper business."

"Family business has its pros and cons. But what I really love is tinkering—inventing compounds and chemical treatments for papers, to make them water resistant, fire retardant, wrinkle-proof—"

"How about a chemical for stationery that makes the recipient fall in love with the sender?"

"I can't believe you'd need that."

"I guess I'm just destined to be a career woman."

"I take it you haven't met Mr. Right?"

"Right, no Mr. Right."

"It will happen. Maybe sooner than you think."

Sandrina remembered that she'd found Michael so charming and easy to talk to that evening. How carefree and full of expectation their lives had been when they first met.

"I'm hopeless," she told him that night.

"Would it be okay if I called you? We could go out to dinner," he said urgently, just before the last dessert plates, smeared with the remains of blueberry pot de crème, were cleared.

"Please call me," Sandrina replied. "But if you don't mind, I'd rather not go out. I feel like I spend my life in restaurants, entertaining clients, meeting new strangers. You can come over. I'll throw together a meal."

"Wow," Michael was impressed. "You cook too?"

Michael called her that night and five times the next day. On their second date he told her that he loved her. He fought hard against his brother Thomas, who considered Sandrina beneath the Morgans socially and just the type of independent woman he'd always despised. But Michael prevailed, and although Joshua really hadn't known Michael Morgan well, he considered Sandrina and Michael's marriage a year later to be one of the best mergers he had ever had a part in making.

Over the next several years, Sandrina's business continued to grow and her life with Michael became as complete as she could have ever dared to imagine. And, she owed so much of it to Joshua.

A glance at her watch snapped her out of her reverie. It was time to go. As she sprinkled a trail of catnip from the living room to Joshua and Esther's front door, herding the cats the only way she knew how, she found it hard to believe that back then she'd never thought meeting another person would transform her life. Now she knew it could…again and again.

Chapter Two

Baby pictures in silver frames, a pink satin jewelry roll and a decoupage tissue box, all of which sat on Sandrina's dressing table top, eclipsed the 15-year-old wedding portrait of Sandrina and Michael Morgan. A love poem Michael had written to her, curling at the edges, had been tucked behind the frame, propping up the newlyweds with long forgotten words.

Sandrina snatched a tissue out of the box and gingerly patted her upper lip, making the beads of moisture that gathered there disappear. She tossed the damp Kleenex in the wastepaper basket and drew in a deep breath as the old photograph caught her eye. The image in the picture beamed in comparison to the one she saw in the three-way mirror of her antique vanity. Twelve blazing lightbulbs gave the tableau the wattage of a Broadway marquee, and left every detail of her unhappiness exposed.

As Sandrina began the routine she could perform in her sleep, she noted that since the miscarriage her laugh lines had been getting deeper and her skin had gotten dryer. Recently, even the briefest exposure to the sun caused a discoloration of the pigmentation along her jaw and upper lip, making her look as though she needed to wash. "It's just the hormones," she said to herself, but she didn't believe it. The loss of the baby represented the loss of fertility — and she feared it had been her last chance.

As she reached over to pick up the ringing telephone, she toppled the box of Q-tips, which spilled in random array like pick-up sticks. Behind her, in bed, Michael was still asleep. He snored loudly, and Sandrina marveled at the way he could sleep through anything.

Sitting in front of her reflection, Sandrina repeated for the thousandth time everything the girl at the make-up counter at Bergdorf's had taught her how to do. Every skin imperfection was dotted with cover-up and blended in with a sponge. Using a magical combination of foundation and tinted pressed powder, she made as many flaws as she could disappear. A gold-dusty powder lightened her eyelids, while a pencil colored her brows fawn, a crayon painted her lips caramel-candy, and a bristled stick stroked her eyelashes blue-black. The ceremony ended with a cursory blow-dry to her thick ebony hair.

Scanning the rack in her closet the way some people flip through their address books, Sandrina decided to dress all in black, multi-purpose, for the office and then the plane. Size six jeans, a tight sweater, and a short leather jacket; her earrings were black enamel with diamond crosses. Michael had recently had them made for her after the originals were stolen.

Glancing sideways in the full-length mirror, she loathed the flat stomach she once had worked so hard to achieve. It looked so...denied. Black seemed to be her uniform recently, most likely reflecting her mood, and she vowed to try soon if wearing bright colors would help it change.

In the kitchen, Sandrina ate breakfast, slowly sipping her coffee, before returning to the bedroom to get her bags.

"All packed?" Michael asked. He had wakened and showered while she was downstairs. Twelve minutes from start to finish, and he was almost ready to leave for work.

"Ready to go."

"You look great."

"I never know who I'll sit next to—could be my next big client." She smiled, trying hard to appear convivial although she felt anything but.

While Michael patched up a shaving nick on his chin, Sandrina stole a glance at her husband.

Still dashing in his silver-gray suit, which matched the hair near his temples, and the cerulean blue shirt, which was the exact color of his eyes. Those eyes were light and open, with tiny white pinprick moons that only Sandrina noticed. When Sandrina had been 25, and first discovered them, she had hoped that they would be an entrance to a deeper world, one full of magical surprises, like the world Alice enters when she steps through the looking glass. How idealistic that seemed now.

The late May lushness of Central Park outside their window seemed a harsh contrast to their perfectly manicured rooms. Those full and vibrant branches had been bare just weeks ago. Why couldn't people renew each year the way nature does?

Michael noticed her admiring the view, although she knew he hadn't guessed what she was thinking. "I still love our apartment," he said.

"So do I," Sandrina agreed. "As soon as I saw how bright and cheerful the rooms were, I knew we should live here." There was an extra one, a nursery, which would most likely never be used. An abortion. Michael had actually proposed an abortion, claiming that he liked their life together exactly as it was.

"How many apartments did you drag me to before we settled on this one? A hundred at least." Michael shook his head.

"Yes, back then we had a family in mind," she said pointedly.

"Think the *Finance Journal* is here yet?" he asked. "Let's see what innuendo they've planted today," Michael said with heaviness in his voice. "Wonder why they're targeting us."

"It's a sign of the times." Thinking about the baby she'd lost had made her forget Michael's problems for the first time in days. An image of her brother-in-law, Thomas, intruded. It was hard to believe how easily Thomas had taken a bad situation and made it worse. She looked at her husband with concern.

"You need to exercise damage control now, early. Bring in Joshua; he knows the company and the players, I've brought him up to speed, he's the master of this game—" she said.

"Thomas won't allow it. Says, 'Joshua's too old.'"

"I'm sure Thomas won't go to Joshua because he knows Joshua won't do what Thomas tells him to."

"Sandrina, Josh has been officially retired for a decade—"

"He'll never retire; you know that. And, he is the world expert in damage control."

"Well, to be honest, even Joshua would find it hard to control Thomas these days. He always thinks he knows better than the experts, which is why Josh resigned the account the first time around. Remember?" But she had lost interest in the conversation and didn't respond. "Hey, 'Drina, you look glum. What's wrong?"

She was angry, at Michael for not wanting their baby, and angry about something else. Loss, yes, she was angry about loss. But whom could she blame for that? "We've both been feeling the pressure lately. I'm tired of constantly traveling. I'm always tired..."

"Just think how much worse it would have been if we'd had a child," Michael said.

Sandrina did her best to ignore his comment. "I've been thinking about grooming Isabel to take over more of the travel. She's the most promising person I have right now. Young, bright, eager—"

"More promising than Lucy?" Lucy had been Sandrina's lieutenant for years.

"Lucy is great. Really great. Intelligent, reliable, loyal—"

"But?" Michael asked.

The question forced her to compare the two women and examine the differences between them. "Lucy's not...hungry. That's it. I see the same hunger in Isabel that I had when I was her age. Channeled properly, that kind of drive can forecast success." In fact, Isabel reminded her of herself in more ways than one, convincing Sandrina even more that, with the right mentoring, someday Isabel would surprise them all.

Michael looked at his watch. "'Drina, I've got to go. I'm meeting Thomas in ten minutes—to debrief yesterday's interview. Ha!"

Once again pushing down feelings of anger, she put her arms around her husband's neck in an embrace filled with sympathy, familiarity, and comfort. She wanted him to surprise her, to share her desires and to quash their troubles for good.

Michael looked at her with a questioning expression in his eyes. Then he walked out, gently closing the door behind him.

Sandrina sat back in the yellow taxi and observed how beautiful the May morning was. People hurried by on their way to work as the cab crawled through traffic. As much as she felt burned out on travel, and concerned about Michael, she had to admit she was looking forward to a change of scenery. Although she had seen many places in the 19 years of owning a public relations agency specializing in tourism, she had never been to Brazil before. The brief vacation promised a welcome break from reality.

Flavio and Beatriz Gaspar, Sandrina's clients of ten years, had suggested that she attend the conference sponsored by Brazil's tourism agency in Rio de Janeiro. The idea of possibly picking up another client or two—the tourist board or Varig Airlines—appealed to her. And, the conference theme—the impact of potential terrorist attacks on the international tourist industry—interested her.

The newest offices of Sandrina's company, TravelSmart, were located on the seventh floor of a converted warehouse building on lower Fifth

Avenue. During the boom years just before Lehman went bust, Sandrina made so much money that she had hired Eve Houseman to decorate the new space. Eve had apportioned a large part of the 22,000 square foot floor, formerly a dress factory, to be a glamorous reception area, which she then had paneled in imported African mahogany.

Art collector Ray Jagger, whom Sandrina had met at one of Joshua's soirées, had lent her three sculptures to display prominently in the sitting area. They were Venuses, with a rich green patina of verdigris, like moss; they stood tall and bold, albeit headless, proudly guarding her professional domain.

Once past the museum-like reception area, TravelSmart was one huge open space surrounded by floor-to-ceiling windows. Sandrina passed Isabel Riley on her way in, which pleased her but was unusual, since Sandrina was almost always the first to arrive. She passed several other empty cubicles on the way to her corner office.

On her desk were pictures of Michael, beaming in his tennis-pro pose, and several of them together. They looked healthy, happy, and smiling. Sandrina wondered if her whole life was really like these photographs; in hundreds of discarded snapshots she was frowning, or Michael's eyes were closed, but the world saw only the perfect ones she chose to show, professionally printed and cropped, decorated by precious frames.

Isabel knocked softly on the door. "Busy?" she asked.

Sandrina swiveled in her chair to face her rising star. Isabel looked fresh and pretty, with flowing, wavy strawberry-blond hair and freckles. The expression in her eyes was knowing, in jarring contrast to the rest of her innocent demeanor. She needed no makeup, for her skin had the natural healthy glow of youth. It impressed Sandrina that she had apparently been at work for some time.

"You're in early. What's up?" Sandrina asked.

"I need your help. Max Sharf called after you left on Friday. They're thinking about launching their first resort," Isabel said.

"He told you that? Why didn't you call me at home?"

"I thought only in emergencies," Isabel replied. Odd, thought Sandrina, that Max would tell Isabel, but isn't that what she had wanted to happen? She wanted her clients to trust her staff, not to rely solely on her for strategic advice. It was all part of letting go.

"They're really excited. They have a big meeting with the bankers next week while you're in Brazil. He wants to see us today to discuss strategy."

"It'd be nice if he'd given us more notice."

"You know how they are," Isabel said. "They're spontaneous—"

"I know," Sandrina said, as she regarded the packed agenda her executive assistant Beth had left for her. She had to leave for the airport at three.

"I told him you were free from two to three," Isabel said.

She'd have to bring her luggage to the meeting, and make sure it didn't run late. "This is important, Isabel. If they're talking resort, that represents a major strategic shift...I feel I need more time to prepare."

Isabel shoved a Power Point deck under her nose. "I took the liberty of preparing this."

Sandrina skimmed the color presentation. It looked familiar. "Where did you get these ideas?"

"From you. I went through your old presentations, for other clients, old press clippings. I found them in your files."

"Isabel, that's not how we usually do things around here."

"I know that. But given the time constraints, and your going away, what else could I do?"

Sandrina recognized the pressure. Clients had put her in tight spots before. She reminded herself that if she wanted to groom Isabel to take on more responsibility she needed to be patient, and to give up some of the control. Shifting hormones, her irritability had to do with hormones; she'd have to chalk it up to that.

"I suppose you're right. I'll read this and let you know before lunch if I have any changes."

As Isabel was walking out, she stopped and turned. Sandrina said: "Anything else?"

Isabel flashed a smile as sweet as a sugar-coated fruit slice as she walked out of Sandrina's office, bumping into Beth on the way: "Yup. I helped myself to an Altoid from the tin on your desk. Hope you don't mind."

Sandrina reminded herself that she had picked Isabel precisely because she saw so much of her younger self in her — pluck and all.

"Not at all," she replied.

The day flew by with phone calls and debriefs. Somehow the SH deck Isabel had prepared never got read. Preparing for her trip to Brazil was uppermost in her mind. At 1:30, Isabel came to get her. Beth and Sandrina hauled the suitcases out into the hall.

"Mind giving me a hand?" Sandrina asked Isabel.

"Sure," Isabel said, as she picked up the lightest bag.

In the car on the way to the meeting they had a chance to talk. "You know, Isabel," Sandrina said.

"I've known Max and Jason longer than I've known my husband. They were my first clients."

"I know how important they are to you."

"It's not just sentimental...they believed in me before I believed in myself. They once prepaid an entire year's fees so I could cover my overhead while my business grew."

"I never knew that."

"TravelSmart has grown so much that I can't service them the way I used to, but they're still top priority to me. They've resisted senior management on the account before. But I think you've got so much going for you, and they seem to have confidence in you—"

"Thank you for believing in me, Sandrina," Isabel said.

"It was a good sign that they spoke with you Friday evening. In the past, they would have called me over the weekend at home. I've been thinking of creating a new position for you—Vice President of Client Services. There'd be a lot of travel involved, and the clients are very sharp and demanding—"

"And Lucy?"

Sandrina was taken aback. "Initially, you'd be reporting to her."

Isabel frowned, but this time as the car stopped outside Sharf and Rothstein's office she helped with the bags without being asked.

In the SH Hotels waiting room, they looked through the presentation together. "Isabel, where did you get these statistics about declining resort occupancy rates."

"Mostly from the Internet."

"Are you sure about your hypotheses?"

"Absolutely. Between the economy and fear of terrorism, no one seems interested in swimming pools and piña coladas any more."

"I suppose you're right," Sandrina said.

Jason and Max were still dynamic entrepreneurs, but they had lost some of the humility that had initially endeared them to Sandrina. They had become clients who always kept her waiting. True they were busy, and in demand. But now Sandrina knew they kept her waiting for effect. Since becoming the hotel mavens of North America, every single interaction they had was driven by power. The extensive publicity Sandrina had garnered for them had gone straight to their heads.

Although the two men had become more difficult to work for, SH Hotels was her biggest client, still growing every year, and she considered them to be the foundation of her business.

At 2:30 p.m., Max opened the door to the office he and Jason shared. Sandrina stood a head taller than Max, who was thin and sallow, with lips shaped like a violin on its side, and deep green-gray shadows under his eyes. Max was wearing his "uniform," worn chinos and a white shirt, sleeves rolled up to just below his elbows. Jason, who was all muscle and energy, a weightlifter, wore a dark suit. Jason was handsome, his sharp black eyes aggressively surveying every movement around him as he stood up behind the partners' desk.

"Jason," Sandrina said, proffering a kiss. "How are you?"

"Busy as always." He waved them in.

Max's kind eyes were smiling. "I was about to order up a malted from the corner deli. What can I get you?" He picked up the phone to dial.

"Nothing, Max. Thanks but no time. I'm sorry, but as Isabel may have told you, I need to leave at three sharp for the airport." Isabel looked sheepish as she set up her laptop on Max and Jason's desk.

"Don't we pay you enough to get her highness's attention for more than half an hour?" Jason said. He was in an extremely foul mood.

"Jason, you have had my constant attention for 19 years. It's just—"

He preempted her before she could finish her sentence. "Well, then we don't have a moment to lose. Let's hear what you have to say." He sat down and folded his arms across his chest in expectation. Sandrina observed that a little white foam had gathered in the corners of his mouth. He looked rabid.

"Our recommendation is that you go to your investors next week with a plan for making SH Hotels an urban only, market-driven company. Your position in the marketplace is as a downtown trendy boutique hotel developer." She was talking fast and pointedly because she was afraid she would run out of time. "Expanding into resorts now would be plain dumb." Max looked as though he wanted to interrupt, but she asked that he let her finish the presentation first.

He interrupted anyway. "Sandrina, the decision is made. We are opening our first SH Resort on the island of Oahu in Hawaii. We are closing on the property on Friday," he said.

Sandrina looked at Isabel in confusion.

"Didn't you tell her?" Max directed the question to Isabel.

Sandrina couldn't lay the blame on one of her staff. She considered herself ultimately responsible for everything at TravelSmart. "Isabel did tell me that you were thinking about opening a resort," Sandrina replied.

"So?" Jason asked.

"We just thought you might reconsider based on our findings." She was winging it.

Max looked at Sandrina sympathetically. Jason glared as he flipped through the presentation.

"For every number in your report we have ten that contradict. Sure, things are down now; that's why we were able to buy the beachfront property so cheaply. But the long-term consensus is for occupancy rates to trend upward, as soon as things recover. Business is cyclical. You know that," Jason said.

"Renovations are being fast-tracked. We've lined up the whole executive team—general manager, food and beverage VP, marketing exec; we've even hired a local PR person to give you more regional support," Max said. "Great time to be hiring."

"We're looking at a soft opening before Christmas," Jason added. "That's why the advance publicity is so crucial; that's why you're here! Not to give us business advice."

"Jason—" Max interrupted.

"Why don't you stick to what you know, Sandrina—namely PR—and leave the strategic development decisions to us?" Jason said.

They all looked up at the young man in the white apron who had come to deliver Max's chocolate malt.

It was 3:10. Sandrina felt as though she had been ambushed. For the first time in many years, she felt genuinely uncomfortable in front of a client.

She regained her composure while Max paid the deliveryman. "I'm sorry if it appears that way to you, Jason. Isabel can stay and continue the conversation in more depth. I promise to readdress it as soon as I return. I guess I misunderstood the purpose of the meeting. With the big Millennium Universal opening in just a couple of weeks, I never thought this project could be so imminent."

Jason seemed unmoved.

Sandrina sighed. She looked again at her watch for dramatic effect. Despite her clients' unhappiness, she had to leave. She hoped that Isabel would be able to pacify them, at least a bit.

Forcing a smile, she said: "I'm sorry to leave in the middle of all this, but I really do have to rush. I have complete trust in Isabel."

Isabel gave her a confident smile. Sandrina looked at her uncertainly, and then left, awkwardly dragging her suitcases behind her as if they were two sand bags in snow.

Chapter Three

Problems in life have a way of snowballing.

The devastating effect that world events had had on Sandrina's sense of well-being, from the meltdown of the global economy to the wars in Iraq and Afghanistan, was compounded by Michael not wanting the baby, by Morgan Paper's threat of an exposé, and now, it seemed, by another business problem of her own. The sour meeting with Jason plagued her as her car snaked through traffic along the Long Island Expressway toward JFK. Jason was always under pressure in advance of a big opening, but never quite like this. He had been frothing like a rice cooker about to explode.

At the airport, Sandrina waited 40 minutes in the security line, patiently listening to babies squalling and businessmen swearing, and being displaced by passengers feigning flights about to depart just so they could cut the line.

"Take off your shoes, jacket, and jewelry," said the female security guard. "Open your computer and give it to Mr. Henry over there." She then inspected the inside of Sandrina's shoes, the lining of her clothing, and even the reading glasses on her nose, before scanning her entire body with a metal-detecting device that resembled a branding iron.

The security area was packed, with a bottleneck forming where the hand luggage emerged. Sandrina thought about her morning interaction with her husband while she waited for her items to appear. True, things were difficult between them. She found it hard to forgive Michael's objection to a child and his obvious relief when she miscarried, making the problem no longer his to resolve. A man has all the time in the world but the opportunity for a woman to be a mother slips by as silently and as surely as sand in an hourglass.

Underneath the illusion she created about her value, by the brand names she wore and by the clients she served, it had been only her fleeting pregnancy that gave her a feeling of true purpose. And knowing that Michael held this power over her full realization of herself, made her feel toward him something close to hate.

To be fair, this rift between Michael and herself had probably made her less sensitive to Michael's needs. Was it possible that the threat of losing Morgan Paper was as devastating to him as the reality of losing the baby had been to her?

In her mind, she replayed the conversation with Michael the night before, during which he told her the little he had learned about his brother's latest blunder.

"The reporter told him his paper was investigating the company, so Thomas invited him over for lunch. He thought he could buy the guy's silence."

"Thomas should have told us about the *Finance Journal* call before talking to the reporter. Then maybe I could have intervened. I talked to Josh, who called the editor after the incident. Josh said it doesn't sound good—"

"That's all he said? What does that mean?" Michael had asked her.

"What it means is that by Thomas lying and wheedling—and trying to buy the reporter's cooperation—Thomas has made things worse. If only he had been open and honest, laid the facts out on the table, I believe the eventual article would be more balanced."

Michael had been perspiring as he considered her statement.

"Actually, Sandrina—honesty might not have been the best policy in this case," he confided. "There could be circumstances under which it would be advisable to lie. To lie...and deny." Sandrina remembered staring at him in amazement as he continued. "It's common practice, and almost impossible to do business abroad, without paying kickbacks to foreign government officials. Morgan's global activities fall under my responsibilities... I could be implicated."

"Michael, I know you wouldn't have authorized kickbacks. I know you—you're not capable of bribery."

At that point, he had walked over to shut the bedroom door. "Sandrina, I'm in the middle. I never approved such methods, but technically the heads of sales in the countries in question report to me, so even if I didn't know what went on behind my back, some would say I should have."

He looked so forlorn. Michael only did what she would have done—he made excuses for a family member's shortcomings—but even in sibling loyalty there had to be a line drawn somewhere.

"Over the line, step over the line!" she heard someone shout at her. It was the TSA agent, who smiled a toothy grin as he placed her laptop back in her hands.

Even at the crack of dawn, when her flight touched down in São Paulo, Brazil, the airport there was a hub of disorder. There were people milling everywhere, and she stood adrift in the human sea until she heard the familiar voice of Beatriz Gaspar above the din of the crowd.

"*Alô, alô*! Sandrina. I am here. It is Beatriz."

Flavio was by her side. "Welcome! How was your flight?" he asked, as he warmly embraced her.

Flavio Gaspar, a tall, stately man in his mid-fifties, was impeccably attired, despite the early hour. He wore flawlessly cut slacks with a perfect press down the middle of each leg, a light-blue and pearl-white checkered shirt, and a sports coat with a yellow handkerchief cheering-up his breast pocket. Flavio's image contrasted sharply with that of his talkative wife, who had been a fashion model once and followed a life-long regimen of self-starvation. She was a bundle of brittle sticks in a designer sack, with a warm and sparky personality that made one wonder if the whole package would ignite.

"Fine. It's good to see you both," Sandrina said. "It wasn't necessary for you to get up so early."

"It's your first time in Brazil. We want you to feel welcome," Beatriz said. "Such a shame you can't come down to the farm for the weekend, but I agree the trip is too long for just two days."

"I have a folder for you with the agenda for the tourism conference, as well as a letter for the hotel's general manager, Rafael Sotto. We have arranged a car and driver for you. The city can be dangerous, especially at night. The driver is very good, Afonso Silveira, he is a native of Rio—a *carioca*," Flavio explained.

"How do I find him?"

"He will be at the airport in Rio. He will find you. Since you can't come to the *fazenda*, why don't you stay in Rio for the weekend?"

"Actually, I was planning to do just that," Sandrina said.

"Excellent. You will be our guest, at the Copacabana Palace. The driver included." Flavio led them to a small café that had just opened for breakfast. He ordered strong black *cafezinho*, sugar-laced espresso, and a sweet coconut tart called *quindim*.

"Would you like one?" he asked.

"Too sweet for so early in the morning," Sandrina said.

"Ponte Aerea, the São Paulo-Rio shuttle, to Rio de Janeiro is boarding now," boomed an accented male voice over the loudspeaker, first in Portuguese and then in English. Sandrina bade her good friends farewell.

"We'll call you from the fazenda," they promised.

"And Sandrina," Flavio added. "Try to have fun."

It was midday when Sandrina emerged from the terminal of Rio's Aeroporto Santos Dumont. The city twinkled from sunlight reflecting off surfaces as if it were midnight and all the lights of the buildings were on. It was the beginning of winter in Brazil, but since Rio de Janeiro enjoys reverse seasons it was a steamy, tropical 82 degrees. Everything smelled sweet and acidic, like oranges.

Leaving the airport, the Mercedes passed through chaotic, run-down neighborhoods reminiscent of third-world capitals she had visited in places as disparate as Haiti and Thailand. The jarring poverty jammed up against the gates of the homes of very wealthy people in an uncomfortable proximity, reminding Sandrina of how close and how far apart people could be at the same time.

As Afonso drove up to the front entrance of the Copacabana Palace Hotel, Sandrina thought it looked exactly as her wedding cake had. It was painted marshmallow-white, with balconies extending from the setback façade like ten layers of confection. The plantings were thriving and abundant, an explosion of color and lushness. On a terrace of an upper floor she saw a man and woman kissing. They looked just like the plastic bride and groom from her cake of long ago.

In the vast marble-floored lobby sat a lone piano, atop an Oriental carpet. On every tabletop surface, there were white and purple orchids that floated on nearly invisible stems, bifurcated wings fluttering, like butterflies about to take off.

The sitting room of the lavish penthouse suite that had been reserved for her faced the ocean. The colors were tangerine, taupe, and saffron. And orchids, more orchids, everywhere.

A bottle of Taittinger Comptes de Champagne rosé, courtesy of the Gaspars, sat chilling in a silver bucket on a center hall table in the foyer. A box of chocolate truffles, imported from Switzerland, rested on an ivory napkin folded to look like a hand bestowing a gift.

The bathroom countertops were mahogany, with inlaid lapis lazuli forming a continuous trim, like a racing stripe. The plush ivory-colored towels even had her monogram, *SM*, embroidered in white.

She undressed and stepped into the enormous porcelain tub to bathe, marveling at the contrast between her luxurious surroundings and the modesty of her first hotel account. Sandrina recalled walking into the shell of a former welfare hotel that was to become Max and Jason's first project and the construction foreman handing her a hard hat, not with her own initials, or even those of SH Hotels, but TC—for Townsend Construction.

Joshua had prepped her on Max Sharf and Jason Rothstein before the meeting, to assure her that they were smart and hard-working, despite their bad luck with the law. It seemed that Max and Jason had a nose for talent, the rumor mill giving them credit for providing Chris Rock and Steve Carell with their first breaks, in the partners' original comedy club.

"So, what do you like to do on your day off?" Max had asked her as she stood with them amidst demolition debris in her TC hard hat.

"I rarely take a day off," she had replied.

"I bet you go to lots of parties, clubs, that kind of thing," Jason said, in a leading way.

She was embarrassed to admit that she had never been to their club, or any club for that matter, because the action started too late for her. "Actually," she said. "I love movies. Especially old movies. Give me a bag of popcorn and a Humphrey Bogart double feature and I'm in heaven."

"Have you ever seen <u>Casablanca</u>?" Max asked. He loved old movies too.

"Are you kidding? Twelve times. That scene when Ilse walks out on Rick—"

"I love the souk scene—you know, where she's buying the lace," Max said.

"Oh, I know. He's so…troubled and strong. And, the ending. It always makes me cry," Sandrina confessed.

"Yeah," Max said. "Me too."

"Sandrina, we've read your clips, so we know you can write. What about media contacts?" Jason had asked.

"I do know press people through Joshua. And my friend Cameron Finn. And, of course, I know everyone at *Journey*. But do you really think that's what matters? Isn't it the story, not just who you know? If you create worthwhile and interesting news and I present it to the media in a creative and attention-getting way, won't the reporters all be interested—no, make that obligated—to cover you?"

Back then, they listened attentively.

She didn't know it at the time, but she was intuiting a new approach to the way public relations was starting to be done.

"I've got a PR joke for you," Max said. Jason rolled his eyes.

"I love jokes," Sandrina responded.

"What did Moses's public relations guy say to Moses as he was leading the Jews out of Egypt?"

"What?"

"Moses, if you part the Red Sea, I can get you six pages in the Old Testament."

"Exactly," Sandrina said, laughing. "That's what we have to do — part the Red Sea!"

"I like you," Jason said. "You're different."

"I'm no different from you," Sandrina replied. "You've never built or run a hotel before, but I just know you're going to do it in an original way, vastly different from the way it's been done before."

"Financing wasn't easy to come by," Jason admitted. "So our budget is limited."

"This place is small, the rooms will be compact, the décor smart but certainly not opulent. We were thinking about budget pricing..." Max said.

"We'd have to think about that carefully. You may be right, but — " Sandrina hesitated.

"But what?" Jason asked.

Joshua had always told her to trust her instincts. "If you launch your brand under a discount banner, my intuition tells me that you'll forever be stuck there. You may be leaving money on the table before you get off the ground."

"Interesting," Max had said, clearly processing her comments.

"But we need to find a niche of some kind," Jason said. "Otherwise we'll get creamed by the more established hotel chains."

Sandrina had then applied another of Joshua's lessons—one that would help define the rest of her career. "How about coining the term 'boutique hotel'? Boutiques have an image of being small, exclusive, and unique," she said, picturing Madison Avenue in her mind. It was, after all, the same principle that Joshua had insisted she apply to her own life.

Jason and Max looked at each other. The human electricity in the room went up a watt or two. "You're on to something, Sandrina. Can you give us a minute to talk?" Max said.

When Max Sharf and Jason Rothstein called her back in after ten minutes they were sold.

"It's unanimous!" Max said. "The proxies are in. If you start your own business, we would be proud to be your first account."

As she toweled the water out of her hair, she realized that what had happened in New York 19 years before was the fire that launched the rocket that brought her here to Rio de Janeiro. As she changed into an indigo-blue suit and her shoes, exactly one shade darker than her outfit, she wondered where the rocket of her career would land next. She switched purses, choosing a silk clutch from India with azurite stones encircled by fine thread-like chains. In lieu of perfume, she crushed a few orchid petals and rubbed them on her neck and wrists.

Afonso drove south from the Copacabana Palace Hotel to the conference along the broad avenues of Rio, allowing Sandrina to soak up the steaming street life around her. The coastal drive passed the beaches of Copacabana, Ipanema, and Leblon in the *zona sul*. There were lots of sexy girls in multi-colored thong bikinis cajoling and coquetting with locals and tourists alike. The boys were playing beach *futebol* and flying *papagaios,* kites that looked like voodoo spirits in the sky.

Rio juxtaposed sultriness with verve. It had a sleepy, slow-moving attitude that seemed to mask an underlying force, not unlike the still wait preceding a tornado. She felt the contrasts in her own body as well—tired and excited, heavy- and light-hearted at the same time. She felt Michael and Thomas and Jason—her problems and cares and concerns—all slipping away, far away, as if they were unreal.

As Afonso crossed the Jardim de Alah canal, into Vidigal, where the Rio Grande Luxe Hotel was located, her dreaminess disappeared as her curiosity was piqued.

"How does anyone concentrate on business here?" Sandrina murmured. "So much stimulation, so many distractions."

Afonso smiled at her in the rear-view mirror. "It is not easy, Senhora. This is why I moved to São Paulo."

The enormous lobby of the Rio Grande Luxe was somber, especially in vivid contrast to the bright sunshine outside. Colored flags of different Brazilian states and South American countries occasionally punctuated the bronze monotone of the walls. There were half a dozen front desk managers, neatly dressed in crisp cadet-blue uniforms, efficiently checking in conference attendees and other guests. Sandrina saw several people she knew, including John D'Angelo from the Hotel Association of America and Christoff Peipers, director of tourism for the German spa town of Baden-Baden.

"I was going to call you, Sandrina. I am so glad you are here! The Brenner's Park-Hotel in Baden-Baden is looking for a PR firm. I suggested you. Did they call?" Christoff asked.

"Not yet," she said.

"Are you free for dinner tonight? I'll tell you everything I know," Christoff said.

"Love to," she said, turning to John D'Angelo. "John, why don't you come too?"

"You know, the Brenner's uses our reservations system. Maybe I can help," John said.

"It's settled then. I know just the place. Brazilian barbeque," Christoff said.

"Catch you later," she said, blowing them kisses.

The crowd was chatting amiably as they entered the Rio Grande Luxe auditorium. At four p.m. sharp, Reginald MacIntyre, designated master of ceremonies, opened the conference. He was affable and blustery, a life-long bachelor with a keen sense of humor. Sandrina knew Reg from Columbia Business School in New York, where she taught public relations from time to time in the Executive MBA program, and he was on the faculty full time.

"Good afternoon, everyone! Welcome to Rio," he began in his raffish Scottish accent. "The purpose of this marketing session is to explore ways to identify underserved markets during times of economic and political hardship. Most of you know me as an irreverent old business school professor, but in order to afford the luxury to teach I first had to make some money of my own."

Sandrina noticed the audience furiously scribbling; she craned her neck to see what her neighbors thought Reg was saying that was worthy of note-taking.

"In every downturn," Reg explained, "be it caused by economics or fear, there are people who have the need and opportunity to travel. All you have to do is find them. During my heyday after the 9/11 terrorist attack in New York most Americans were canceling vacations left and right. So we bundled a crocodile hunter with a nurse and a bridge instructor and sold our Australian outback 'Down FUNder Tours' to elderly ladies with a lust for life."

When Reg had finished his opening remarks, Sandrina noticed that on her own pad she had jotted down only two words: Need and Opportunity. It seemed to her that she'd heard those words used together before.

The first panel discussion involved four participants, and the topic was "Overcoming Fear of Travel Due to Terrorism." The panelists included a kinetic, red-haired, Dutch tour operator named Ineke de Ridder, who specialized in tours to South Africa; Harvey Blotter, dean of the Cornell Hotel School, whose eyelids, cheeks, mustache, and lips all drooped, as if his face were made of melting wax; Kathleen McFadden, the never married but often engaged director of sales for Apollo Hotels; and,

Warren Waterhouse, owner and CEO of Chaucer Suites, a representation company for luxury, privately owned hotels throughout the U.K.

Sandrina settled into her seat on the far left in the next to last row as the panelists took their chairs on the dais. Reg had just finished introducing the first three panelists in his usual jocular way, and then he looked affectionately at the last speaker before launching into a description more like a roast than a biographical sketch. It hit Sandrina that they must know each other well.

"Warren C. Waterhouse, our last speaker on this afternoon's panel, was born in London. The C. stands for Churchill because his mother was an ardent Anglophile. His mother hates England now, almost as much as Warren hates his middle name."

The subject grimaced uncomfortably while the audience howled in laughter. Sandrina got the feeling that he didn't want to be there.

"It is not without a touch of irony, and perhaps filial rebelliousness against his mother, that Warren now owns Chaucer Suites, a company he founded ten years ago. It already has over two hundred independent properties throughout the United Kingdom for which it provides proprietary reservations and marketing services."

Warren thanked Reg and assumed command of the panel. His strong voice served as a natural megaphone to keep the attention of the audience focused on him.

The panel discussion was lively with two participants, Warren and Kathleen McFadden, almost getting into a fistfight over whether chain hotels or independent inns were more immune to threats of terrorism.

Warren C. Waterhouse projected a self-assuredness that forced Sandrina to notice he was there. His hair was thick and wavy, the color of burnt sienna right out of the tube of paint when it is still glistening, with a few spirals of gray, as if airbrushed in as an afterthought. He was wearing a slightly rumpled beige suit that was baggy around the elbows. He really wasn't handsome in a conventional way, like Michael. He had dark eyes that appeared intense and curious. Something about him electrified her, and she became suddenly aware of the linen of her suit pressing against her thighs and breasts.

When the session broke, Sandrina sought out Reg.

"You're one of a kind, Reg. How do you get away with being so outrageous?"

"It's old age, my dear. They humor me."

"You and Mr. Waterhouse seem to be old friends. Just how well do you know his mother?" she asked.

With a glint in his eye, Reg said, "Very well."

"She's American I take it?"

"Yes. A New Yawk-er. She married a Brit," he said. "He was a Joseph Conrad scholar from Oxford."

"Sounds like an unlikely match," Sandrina said.

"It was. But opposites have been attracting since the caveman days I'm sure. It may be the genesis of many marriages, like Warren's parents, but I suspect it is also the root of many divorces," he continued, attempting to change the subject. At this point Ineke and Kathleen wandered over and joined the conversation.

"Funny you should mention that," said Sandrina. "My friend Joshua Baum was just telling me about a book written by a well-known New York psychiatrist on this very subject — opposites attracting. He apparently crafted these thoughts into a highly acclaimed new relationship theory."

"I'm sure I know who your friend's talking about. His name is Dr. Avi Goldstein, and his book is called *The Opposites Track*," Ineke said. They gaped at her. She did not seem the type who read self-help books about relationships.

"That's right…Avi Goldstein."

"So, Reg," Sandrina asked. "Did Warren's parents get divorced?"

Reg glanced around nervously to make sure Warren wasn't within earshot.

"Who are you talking about?" asked Kathleen.

"Warren Waterhouse," whispered Sandrina. She could spot his broad back at the bar across the lobby.

"Should we be talking about him like this?" Ineke asked. She had seen him too.

"Why else do we come to these conferences?" said Kathleen.

Kathleen moved on and Ineke left too. Sandrina and Reg were alone again. "Did his father end up coming back to teach at Columbia? Is that how Warren ended up in America?" she asked.

"No, no. He stayed at Oxford, but…Lorita returned to the States. Why are you so interested in him, my dear?"

Regaining her composure after Reg's embarrassing question threw her off guard, she said, "He reminds me of someone. I just can't recall who."

Chapter Four

Sandrina could see Warren's face reflected in the smoky mirror behind the bar as she walked in his direction. While his colleagues were prattling on about him at the cocktail reception, he had been sitting at the bar, alone. Sandrina approached softly and sat on the stool next to his.

"I'll have a glass of white wine," she said to the bartender.

"I wouldn't order white wine in Brazil if I were you," Warren said to her.

"Why not?"

"They serve it warm here," he said just as the glass was placed before her.

She took a sip. He was right.

"I'm Sandrina Morgan," she said, extending her hand.

He ignored her gesture. "I'm Warren Waterhouse."

"I know," she said.

"I spotted you talking to Reg over there. Do you know him?" Warren asked.

"Yes. From Columbia Business School."

"Did you go there?"

"Actually, I teach there."

"I'm impressed."

"How do you know him?" Sandrina asked. "You two seemed on familiar terms."

"I've known him since I was a kid. He was a friend of my parents. They met in New York when my father was guest lecturing at Columbia."

"So your father was a professional colleague of Reg's?"

"At first. But then my parents moved to England. When we returned to the States, Reg was the only link from before...and after." He motioned for the bartender to bring him another drink.

"What was your father's field?" she asked.

"He was a Joseph Conrad scholar."

"How interesting. I love Conrad. Dark, very dark."

He snorted. "You're the first woman I ever met who loves Conrad. What have you read?"

"College stuff. *Lord Jim* and *The Secret Agent*. A couple of the stories," she recalled. "The ones set in Africa."

"That's how I got into the travel business," he said. *"Heart of Darkness,"* *"Falk,"* and *"The Secret Sharer"* were all set in the Belgian Congo. I was intrigued, so I went there. Of course, now it's Zaire."

"Did you find what you were looking for?" she asked.

He looked at her in a way that made her wonder if he would burn holes in her linen suit. "I never said I was looking for anything," he said.

"I know. But did you find it?"

His finger traced the rim of his glass. "No," he said.

"Oh, my God. What time is it?" she asked, suddenly uncomfortably aroused.

Looking at his watch, Warren asked: "It's getting late. Do you have dinner plans?"

"Yes," she said, glad to have a legitimate excuse to get away from this man as fast as possible. She tossed a few reais on the bar and left, feeling his eyes on her back as she quickly walked away.

As soon as she stepped outside the hotel she took out her phone to call home. Michael was home, eating dinner in the kitchen.

"What's Brazil like?" Michael asked.

How could she describe it to her husband? It was sensual, exotic, unreal. "The beach is to them, the cariocas, what Central Park is to us. Everyone's out on a beautiful day — enjoying the weather, carefree." Carefree...it sounded so enticing as she said it. "But I'm stuck in an over air-conditioned hotel without windows."

"Don't you get time off?" Michael asked. She heard the rustle of newspaper pages being turned.

"We'll see...I'll call you tomorrow and let you know."

"OK. Thanks for the call," Michael said as she heard his chair push back and scrape the floor.

Back inside she easily found John and Christoff in the thinning crowd. They talked about whom they knew and pretended to know. Then Sandrina asked if John knew the speaker who owned the hotel rep company. She couldn't control her curiosity.

"He's one of our competitors," he said. "Not very social, but very successful. Waterhouse's approach is to take on only U.K.-based, privately owned properties, some with as few as six guest rooms, but he represents them globally. It helps the small innkeeper to have only one contact working on his behalf worldwide. He's amassed a virtual monopoly in his niche in just ten years."

"Sounds like he's reinvented the business," Sandrina said.

"He has. He's very smart and charming. When he wants to be," John added.

As if on cue, Warren walked past them on his way from the bar just as they were talking about him.

"Warren. Warren. Over here," John said. "You almost got in a fight up there with that McFadden woman from Apollo didn't you?"

"Everyone knows you don't challenge a fellow panelist like that. Anyway, she's dead wrong."

"Warren, do you know Sandrina Morgan?"

"We've met." He smiled.

Sandrina was usually as smooth and as cool as a freshly watered ice-skating rink, but Warren made her nervous. She behaved so out of character, coquettish and coy, that John and Christoff and Harvey Blotter, who had joined them, were dumbfounded. Warren just laughed out loud, a laugh like a lion's roar. Sandrina felt heat rise up her neck and spread across her face.

"I'll be right back," she said, as she excused herself.

Bracing herself on the marble countertop, she stared at her reddened reflection in the ladies' room mirror. After her color returned to normal, Sandrina took five deep breaths before returning to her group, only to find that Warren had moved on. John had invited Harvey to join them for dinner at Churrascaria Copacabana, the restaurant Christoff had been raving about.

"Did you invite Warren too?" she asked.

"No, I try not to fraternize with competitors," John replied. She was both disappointed and relieved.

The Copacabana Churrascaria had a cavelike atmosphere with textured stucco walls. To the right of the entrance was an enormous display of every type of salgadinhos, Brazilian appetizers, imaginable. There were linguica and lombo, local pork dishes, bacalhau, salt cod grilled in a black-bean sauce. There were salads and stews, sausages and local specialties such as vatapa, a pureé of shrimp, ginger, and Brazil nuts. Through a large glass window one could catch a glimpse of the open fire pit where the chefs, dressed like gauchos, were cooking different types of meat on spits.

A waiter with a machete-like knife sidled up to Sandrina and carved the meat right off the skewers onto her plate with great fanfare.

Early in the evening, they drank and laughed a lot and talked, mostly about business, the Brenner's Park-Hotel, and a French movie that Sandrina thought was too neurotic to be appealing but that everyone else loved. They were all comfortable with one another, having been friends since their twenties.

It was nearly midnight by the time they left the restaurant. Sandrina instructed Afonso to drive Harvey home because the Copacabana Churrascaria was right across the street from her hotel while the others were staying at the Rio Grande Luxe. She arranged for Afonso to pick her up at a quarter to nine the next morning and, after taking one long, last look at this new city, she entered the Copacabana lobby and retrieved her key and messages from the concierge.

She stood to the side of the lobby, near the darkened bar that was concealed by a russet velvet curtain, reading what she had retrieved. Michael had called, to say good night, "Nothing important, don't call back," the message said. Beth had called twice. There was no news from Isabel about the meeting with Max and Jason, which she interpreted as good news, and the Gaspars had called to see if she was comfortable.

As she began to read a fax forwarded by Beth from a new client in France, a strong hand with thick rectangular fingers grasped her arm, pulling her slightly toward the bar, startling her and thrilling her at the same time.

"Hello," said a faceless voice. "Are you staying here too?" Warren slightly slurred his words.

"Yes, I am," she said. "One of my clients made the arrangements."

He had been sitting at the bar, alone except for two men and a woman smoking with abandon. The cigarette haze was thick and white, reminiscent of another era, or an episode of *Mad Men*. Warren was drinking a martini, with a twist.

Warren had changed out of his wrinkled cream-colored linen suit into a lightweight gray cashmere collared sweater that was buttoned up to the neck, and a pair of light charcoal pants. The little bit of silver in his hair swirled around behind his ears and blended into the collar of his shirt. His eyes weren't black after all but deep brown, and as Sandrina got closer she could see flecks of gold in them, floating.

"Can I buy you a nightcap? You'll sleep sounder."

"Why not?" she said, feeling that if she tried to sleep she wouldn't be able to.

Warren ordered her a caipirinha made with crushed lime, sugar, and sugarcane liquor called cachaca. Seated on a comfortably padded bar stool, she crossed her legs. Their limbs touched; she kept hers there. "That feels really nice," he acknowledged. She watched him watch her for a few moments. His eyes were lustful, his smile was gentle, and his body language was wary. She was confused as hell.

"Where did you go for dinner?" he asked.

"Across the street. Gruesome." He laughed. "And you?" she asked.

"I've been sitting here. Thinking."

And drinking, she thought. "What about?" she asked. God, he was attractive.

"About you."

"Me…?"

"What are you doing here in Rio?"

"Same as you," she said. "I'm here for the conference, hoping to cultivate some new business. It would be nice to have more than one client south of the border."

"I thought you were a business school professor."

"I own a public relations agency; my company specializes in travel and tourism accounts. I only spot-teach—the occasional marketing module. My 'clients' own this hotel. Flavio and Beatriz Gaspar."

She could see that impressed him, probably because he worked in the hotel industry and knew who they were. "I've never met them, but I know of them, of course." He studied her a while. "How did you get into this business, Sandrina? Obviously, you're very successful to have clients like the Gaspars... and shoes by Manolo Blahnik," he said looking down her long legs to her designer-clad feet. He noticed that her glass was empty and ordered another round.

Now she was impressed. Not too many men would recognize Manolo Blahnik.

"Have you been to Brazil before?" Sandrina asked.

"Yes, many times. A couple of years ago I explored the possibility of expanding beyond the U.K. In fact, I tried repeatedly, and unsuccessfully, to get in to see the Gaspars, because landing their hotels would have solidified a plum position in the South American market."

"Would you like to know about them?" she asked.

"Not tonight. I want to know about you," he said.

"Ask away."

"Where do you and your husband live?"

She hesitated at the mention of Michael. "New York City."

"On Park Avenue?"

"On Fifth."

"I live in New York, too. In the Essex House."

"So you're divorced?"

"Yes. How did you know that?"

"No ring, for one thing. And, only divorced guys live in hotels. Any more questions?"

"How long have you had your business? Do you have partners? Where were you educated? Miss Porter's?" Miss Porter's, Sandrina knew, was a very snooty finishing school for not very bright young ladies from places like Greenwich, Connecticut. He machine-gunned questions at her.

"Do you want to hear my life story? How far back do you want me to go?" she asked, taking the bait.

"How about the beginning? You can start with the silver spoon." That gentle smile again.

"I wasn't born rich, no silver spoon. My early years weren't so easy. In fact, they were pretty tough." She looked directly at him. "Do you think, as I do, that adversity molds the person we become?"

"I wouldn't know any other way. But...go on. I want to hear more."

Sandrina took a deep breath and continued. "My earliest memories are of...my father, but it's always hard to remember specifics. Sometimes I'm not sure if I remember anything at all or just think I remember based on what others have told me."

"Ah, to not remember, Sandrina, could be a blessing."

"I don't know—"

"Can you remember what you felt, if not the incidents themselves?"

She was astonished. She couldn't remember the last time anyone had asked her how she felt about anything. Not even Michael. Especially not Michael. He'd treated the episode of her pregnancy as if they'd had a temporary infestation of mice.

"Yes, sometimes I remember the feelings."

"Are your parents still married?" he asked.

"Not any more."

"Go on," he said.

"Until I was seven, when my parents divorced, I remember feeling scared all the time but not much else. My father left us broke, taking all his and my mother's money with him."

"Hard for you, I imagine. Not easy to trust men, I suppose."

She thought about his comment but decided to ignore it. "Well, if adversity makes you strong, maybe mine has made me who I am."

Sandrina was becoming uneasy confessing the intimate pain of her childhood to an attractive stranger in another hemisphere in a bar owned by her client. They had crossed the invisible line of appropriate social distance. She diverted her gaze from Warren's eyes to the opening in the bar's entryway and briefly considered bolting. A nearly full moon shone through the picture window in the hotel's lobby. The Southern Cross bore down on her and the high white moon seemed to glower with disapproval. Still, she didn't want to leave.

"Are your parents still together?" she asked.

"My father is dead." That sad look again, that stare into the rows of liquor bottles.

Warren gulped his drink. They sat without talking for several minutes. Sandrina delicately plucked his lemon peel from the empty martini glass and chewed on it slowly. She broke the silence.

"I've got a line from Goethe that just about sums it up."

"Goethe? Do you always quote German poets?"

"It's a habit I picked up from my mom. This one she had blown up as a poster and taped to my wall. 'Whatever you can do, or dream you can, begin it. Boldness has genius, power and magic in it.' " She was challenging him. They both knew it.

"That's pretty powerful. A bit optimistic for my taste." After a thoughtful pause he asked, "So how did you use it?"

"I guess I overcame adversity, you know, driven to succeed. The power came from accomplishment. Success gave me strength and courage, boldness and power, and a life filled with magic, just as Goethe promised. It seemed to work like a charm...until recently."

"What happened recently?"

"Never mind... here in Brazil it seems like a dream anyway."

Warren stared at Sandrina. He seemed to look through her just as he had looked through the transparent bottles behind the bar. Despite her evasion, she knew he saw her demons, 100 percent proof and completely clear, just like a bottle of vodka. She was unhappy and unfulfilled, just like him.

"So you've read Conrad and Goethe. Have you read C.S. Lewis as well?

"Well, that's a bit condescending. Of course I read everything...if it strikes my fancy, that is," she retorted.

He was leading her into a trap. "What have you read of his?"

"Well, he's a children's author, isn't he?"

"Hardly. Have you ever read *The Screwtape Letters*?"

"No, I haven't." She forced a smile, hating it when someone had read something that she hadn't, hating feeling intellectually usurped. "What is it about?"

"It's about Our Father...Below. You're in it. We all are. I almost went mad the first time I read it." That's as far as he would go though, for the moment, on *Screwtape*. "Speaking of Our Father Below, is your father still alive?" Warren asked.

"He died five years ago, at the age of sixty-four," she shook her head from side to side, sadly.

"What killed him?" Warren asked.

"Who knows? He smoked and drank. I hadn't seen him in years."

You remind me of him, Sandrina thought. *Run, Sandrina, run,* a voice inside screamed.

"Okay. So not all beautiful women are stupid, and you didn't go to Miss Porter's. Where did you go to school?"

"At first I went to public school, near where my parents and aunt lived. When my parents divorced I got into Brearley on scholarship. Have you ever heard of it?"

"Yes, I know where that is. I have two daughters," he said. "Smart girls go there."

"Are you sure you're interested in all of this?"

"I'm sure," he said.

She felt as though she was being intellectually X-rayed but continued anyway. "Then I went to Smith College."

"So how did you get from Northampton, Massachusetts, to the Copacabana Palace in Rio de Janeiro?"

"It was a journey," she said. "You know how it goes. I never thought about starting a business. Or about public relations. I just fell into it."

"So is the business yours, or yours and your husband's?"

It seemed to her that men always thought a successful business had to be male run. "I owned it before I married, and my husband, since you ask, has nothing to do with it."

"Where does your husband fit in then?"

By this time it was two a.m. and Sandrina was working on her third cocktail. Her elbows were up on the bar, as were Warren's, and they had drifted so close to each other that she could feel his warm breath on her cheek. She knew he had an erection even before she saw it. She was shamefully more interested in how that would fit into her than how Michael fit into her story.

"Were you ever in love with him?" Warren said.

"Are you assuming that I'm not now?" she asked.

"If you were, you wouldn't be here with me. What I want to know is...were you ever?" They were both really drunk.

"I wonder. But he was in love with me, and he was so different from my father. I was ready to get married." She thought about her conference notes: Need and Opportunity.

"Marriage," he said, "is ridiculous."

Without elaboration, Warren turned to face Sandrina at the exact moment she felt pulled toward him. She noticed how heavy his eyelids had grown from the alcohol. His nostrils flared and he had a light lick of moisture on his full lips; his mouth was sensual and beckoning.

They were oblivious to the bartender and the few stragglers who had wandered in during the last hour. Sandrina drank in the scent of his neck as if she were dying of thirst. His hands explored her smooth legs, soft pubic hair, and firm buttocks.

"God, look at you. Look at you," he murmured in her ear as his hands roamed freely all over her body. They probed and kneaded. She pressed closer against the bulge in his pants. She pushed hard against him until she was practically riveted between his legs, toppling the stool over and both of them with it.

Strewn on the floor, looking like fools, they were laughing at themselves. Sandrina, whose propensity for intoxication was tipped over the edge by the spill on the floor, started to see the room spin. All of a sudden the lights everywhere went out.

She wondered if she were dead. She couldn't be or she wouldn't be thinking. The feel of Warren's body pressing against hers confirmed that she was conscious.

"What's happening?" she asked. "Is it a terror attack?"

"I don't know," he said.

"I feel sick. Woozy."

"Stay still, love. I'll take care of you."

She watched the room spin even in the pitch black, confirming to herself that perception was far greater than reality.

Warren never let go of Sandrina's beautifully manicured hand, the left one with her wedding band and the diamond engagement ring, which had belonged to Michael's mother. Warren held her hand while he lifted her from the floor and simultaneously tried to find out what had happened.

"*Com licença, Garçon! O que é isto?*" he asked the bartender in Portuguese. He even spoke Portuguese, something that registered on Sandrina's radar screen even as her head swooned.

"It is a blackout, Senhor. Quite common," the man answered in English. But then in Portuguese, "*Como é Senhora? Chamo um medico?*"

"No, no. I don't think she needs a doctor," he said while feeling her head. *"Uma garrafa de agua mineral... me de a conta, por favor."*

The mineral water and the bill were passed through the darkness immediately. Warren felt for her lips so that she could drink from the bottle in his hand. He told the bartender to make it a room charge since he couldn't read the bill anyway. Then Warren guided Sandrina out of the bar and into the Copacabana's lobby.

By this time the hotel staff had illuminated the lobby with torches. All windows and doors were locked, the night manager explained, because looting during blackouts was common. The elevators were out too, so Warren and Sandrina stumbled toward the stairwell. With a candle in one hand and Sandrina in the other, Warren led her up the stairs to his suite on the fourth floor.

Sandrina weighed only 118 pounds. Three *caipirinhas* sent her reeling toward the bathroom as soon they entered Warren's room. He followed her in with his candle, which he leaned against the soap dish as he discreetly closed the door. The vanity in the bathroom of his suite looked so masculine, with dark paneling and inlaid agate. Four thick royal blue towels, without a monogram, she noted through her alcohol haze, were neatly stacked on a stool in the corner. Warren used one of these towels to wipe her face with cool water when she emerged from the bathroom.

He escorted her to the sofa in the living room of the suite. Candles that he had found in a drawer were lit, and he had melted the bottoms so they'd stay upright in the ashtrays. How he had managed this feat in complete darkness she couldn't imagine, but she was happy, at least, that the darkness had prevented him from seeing her retch. If he was repulsed, he hid it well, because she lay down on the sofa and he stroked her hair until she fell asleep. It was three thirty in the morning.

When Sandrina woke up four hours later it was to an empty suite that was not hers and a room service breakfast delivery that she hadn't ordered. She was disoriented and confused; her head pounded, her clothes were wrinkled, and she noticed her shoes positioned parallel near the mini-bar. The bacon and eggs that Warren had forgotten to cancel sat congealing on the plate, evoking a renewed surge of nausea. The power had been restored while she slept so that every light in the suite was blazing as the sun glared into the room; she felt as ashamed — and then she remembered how tenderly taken care of she had felt the night before.

Thinking Warren was asleep, she tiptoed into the bedroom. The king-size bed was untouched. She knocked on the bathroom door. No answer. He was nowhere to be found. She pulled herself together and returned to her own suite upstairs, just in time to catch the phone ringing. Expecting it to be Warren, she leapt for the phone, brutally stubbing her toe on the metal bed rail along the way.

"Hello?" she answered. She was out of breath.

"Sandrina," Michael sounded exasperated. "Where the hell have you been? I've been worried sick. It's not like you to stay out so late. I was calling until midnight."

"You must have just missed me. I was with John and Christoff and Harvey. There was a blackout. Very dramatic. We were under house arrest in the hotel and cocooned in the bar for comfort." Half-truths. Sandrina had never lied to him before.

"Well then, I'm glad you're okay," Michael said.

"Yes." They were both quiet. "Michael, there's something I want to share with you...I mean I want to tell you how I feel...about a baby—"

"Christ, Sandrina. Not that again. Not now."

She swallowed her words with her emotions; clearly Michael wasn't interested anyway. "Is anything wrong?"

"I'm anxious as hell. Just as we feared, the *Finance Journal* has called our auditors. They're asking them all kinds of questions about our accounting practices. Specifically, about cash transfers to private accounts abroad," Michael said.

"What did your auditors say?"

"For now they're claiming client confidentiality. They've referred the reporters to Thomas."

"Oh, Michael, I don't know what's worse. Giving them carte blanche to examine your books or unleashing your brother on them."

"We have to buy time. 'Drina, we could lose everything."

Gnawing at her for months was the feeling that she already had lost everything; she knew what he was going through. "Promise me you will finally call Joshua. He's got some connection to Ken Larkin, the lead reporter, that goes way back. He's our best hope."

"I'll think about it, Sandrina. Thomas is dead set against it. In fact, he's forbidden it. I've got to get—"

"Going..." she completed his sentence. The line went dead and she realized he hadn't said goodbye. Maybe it was just as well. Anyway, Afonso would be picking her up in half an hour and she needed a serious overhaul.

Chapter Five

After showering, Sandrina dressed in a butter-soft cream-colored skirt with a slit up the side and an eggshell-white silk and cotton T-shirt. Fortunately, she had brought with her a pair of open-toe lizard sandals, because the toe she'd smashed into the bed rail was already too swollen for shoes.

Just as she was about to leave her suite she heard the piercing crash of pistol fire. By the time she rode the elevator down to the lobby, a swarm of police and hotel guards were on the premises.

"Mrs. Morgan. Please accept my apologies—I am so sorry for all the trouble this morning. We had an unfortunate accident because of the blackout. I hope you were not disturbed," said Rafael Sotto, the general manager.

"I did hear a noise that sounded like shooting—"

"It was nothing important. No need to worry or to mention it to Senhor Gaspar."

"Don't worry. I won't say anything." She never imagined that someone could have been killed. "Have you seen my driver?"

"Please, let me escort you personally to your car."

She spotted Afonso through the picture window.

"Thank you, but that won't be necessary. I need to do something first."

Despite the chaos, Sandrina still thought to check with the concierge, hoping that Warren had left her a message. Nothing.

Would he be at the conference today? All the way to the Rio Grande Luxe, she tried to rationalize why she had let it happen, whatever *it* was anyway: She had been drunk, she was having a mid-life crisis, whatever, it was wrong.

I'll never see him again, she lied to herself, honestly.

At the conference, several other people whom she had never met or who looked vaguely familiar approached her, business cards in hand, compliments and conversations glibly rolling off their tongues. Sandrina was a pro. She smiled, and chatted, and shook hands. Her mind was on him — on his smile, the sad one, expressing what the Brazilians call saudade, and his hands all over her body.

Thinking about the night before brought back feelings she had long abandoned — freedom, loss of control, disregard for her responsibilities. The pure sexual heat was addictive. It wasn't just physical attraction; she knew that feeling. It was something much more complicated, and threatening. He had pierced her, a clear entry, and now that he had withdrawn, there was an even larger void than the one he had discovered.

Balancing her coffee cup in one hand and her notebook in the other, Sandrina found a seat between a beautiful Indian woman from Oberoi Hotels and an older goateed gentleman from the Bermuda Tourist Office. The screeching of a microphone signaled that the session was about to begin.

In addition to his talent as master of ceremonies, Reg McIntyre had a creative teaching style. To underscore the gravity of the impact of terrorism on the travel industry, he and his associates had written an opera in three parts. With the lights dimmed, the actors and musicians performed for an unsuspecting and delighted audience.

The opera singers agonized about whether or not they should fly or take a vacation; they fantasized about exotic adventure and beautiful beaches; and they confronted the drudgery of staying at home.

While the diva sang the first two acts in Italian, local musicians crouched by the stage playing authentic samba music to accompany the lyrics. Reg had employed four lovely girls to dance the samba de morro, an undulating variety that translated means 'samba of the hills or the favelas.'

The last act was sung in German to a tropicalismo beat; "Tropicalismo music, as it is known in Brazil, focuses on social injustice and political tyranny," Reg's voiceover explained. The opera, sung in Italian and German, to only percussion instruments and accompanied by samba dancers, took Sandrina's mind off Warren, momentarily, and lightened her mood.

At the break, a slightly panicked Reg pulled her aside. "Sandrina, dear. I've just had a call from Felicity Fogwell, you know, the author of a series of travel books on vacationing with children. She was scheduled to be our afternoon speaker but canceled at the last moment. Could you fill in?"

"I really haven't prepared anything, Reg. I'm not sure…"

"Please, Sandrina. I'm stuck. Just ad-lib. Talk about how to combat the negative publicity associated with traveling. Tell them about successful campaigns you have done in the past. Anything…just say yes."

"Of course I'll help out, Reg. By the way…fantastic production this morning! Wonderful idea."

The speaker after the break was incredibly dull. Barry Garone gave an unconvincing fifty-minute Power Point presentation on the statistical evidence against recurring terrorist attacks. Not one person was convinced.

"Are you worried about the future?" Sandrina asked Reg at lunch.

"It's senseless to worry more than one day at a time. At my age, if I wake up in the morning I'm happy."

Sandrina reapplied her lipstick, straightened her skirt, and got ready to speak.

Despite being exhausted, she managed to enliven her audience. Talking about travel as a life-broadening experience, she pointed out that it was one Americans were unlikely to give up. In the back of her mind, she remembered Isabel's hypotheses from the meeting with Jason and Max, and they angered her because she believed what she was now saying to be true.

To make the crowd laugh, she reminisced about several funny or challenging experiences she had come upon in her work.

There were a few high-profile editors and reporters in the audience, including H.P. Weinstock from the *New York Times* and Randi Rothschild from the *Chicago Tribune*, scribbling away. If she impressed them, they might give a plug to TravelSmart.

The woman from Oberoi raised her hand. "Do you have any examples of how you have changed a negative perception through public relations?" she asked.

"We were hired by The Tides in La Jolla to help them create a more youthful image to attract a younger clientele. For those of you who don't know, The Tides was called 'the waiting room to heaven' just a few years ago; occupancy was way down because the clientele was so old its members kept dying off.

"We invented travel packages" — at this she caught Reg's eye because he had given her the idea, "for young families, things like 'The Mind-Your-Manners Summer Camp' to teach children proper behavior and 'The Off-the-Wall Street Money Program' with investing tips for kids. Now even I can't get a reservation."

After the closing cocktail party, at about seven p.m., she declined a dinner invitation from the handsome head of Hilton's advertising agency and had Afonso drop her off at the Copacabana Palace. She felt badly about keeping him from his family on the weekend, so she told him to pick her up on Sunday at four o' clock to take her to the airport for her overnight flight home, giving him Saturday off.

After checking for messages at the concierge desk, and learning that there were none, she lingered longer than she knew was prudent, pondering what to do. Then impulsively, she jotted a note to Warren:

"I'll be alone this weekend, and in Rio for the first time," she wrote. "I'd appreciate your advice on some other highlights I shouldn't miss."

There, she thought, perhaps they could be friends.

After a room service order of a chef's salad and an iced tea, Sandrina called home. Michael was solicitous, asking her how her day had gone.

"Today they had me sub for a speaker who didn't show. From now on I think I'll always present unprepared; I've never had such a positive response. The guy before me was so boring. Maybe that's why they liked me."

"No, it's because you are a terrific speaker."

Had Michael ever seen her speak? "Anything new on the *Finance Journal* investigation?" she asked.

"Thomas met with our senior auditor and the reporter this morning."

"Weren't you invited?"

"No. I was assigned the meeting with the lawyers, a mistake on Thomas's part. They told me things I doubt he intended for me to know."

"Did you call Joshua?"

He hesitated. "I broached the subject, but I think Thomas wants you to handle the PR—he said something about 'keeping business in the family.' On this note, I agree with him." While mulling over ways that she might help quell the *Finance Journal* damage, Michael asked: "Are you already in bed?"

"Bathed, fed, and under the covers. I'm dead tired."

"The weekend is supposed to be hot."

"Try to relax."

"I will. Listen, I need you. We've been invited next Saturday—and I use that word loosely—to Thomas and Pamela's, in Southampton, for lunch. He says it's urgent, says he wants action on this *Finance Journal* matter once and for all."

"Should I wear armor?"

"Does Chanel do chain-mail these days?"

"Very funny. No, seriously, how contentious are things?"

"They're bad, really bad. I had a surreal meeting with the lawyers today. I'm still shaking."

"What did they say?"

"Well, for one thing they advised me to get our apartment appraised—"

Sandrina froze. "Could we lose it?"

"Anything is possible."

"How could you not see it coming?"

"I've been thinking about that myself. It reminds me of what's happened to all those guys at Bear Stearns and Lehman back in '07 and '08. We were all just conducting our business as it'd always been conducted before when—wham!—the rules changed. If you heard the allegations this morning, you'd have thought that Thomas and I are the worst sort of criminals for doing what our father and grandfather taught us was par for the course."

While she waited for Michael to say good night, she tried to assuage her guilt. The experience in the bar was so out of character for her. She had many men friends and clients but had remained completely faithful to Michael. It hadn't been hard to keep her clothes on all these years. She hadn't been interested in having an affair or, worse, a one-night stand on a business trip.

What she did want, what she thought was missing, was to feel as alive as one could ever feel — to be in love.

"'Drina, are you there?"

"Umm. Just dozing off I think."

"Well, sleep well."

The conversation with Michael was like a dose of caffeine. Sandrina was sitting in her hotel bed at ten p.m. with her newly prescribed reading glasses on her nose and her iPad on her lap, cleaning up her e-mails for the week. "Hi, Beth," she wrote, "Tell the Gaspar Hotels team that the new lobby renovation is fantastic. I e-mailed them a description and attached photos. Make sure they don't delete."

Beth had forwarded a Request For Proposal from the Brenner's Park-Hotel. "Check my calendar to see if I'm available the dates of the pitch. Get Lucy and Maria started on the presentation."

"No, unfortunately we can't participate in the Monarch Hotels pitch. Conflict of interest with Mandarin. Dash off a 'thanks, but no thanks' letter on my behalf."

"Set up a lunch with Gary Brent. Tell him we'll work out the billing problem when I return."

"Send back the printing job if it's too green. We should never accept sub-standard work. Just make sure we don't pay the bill until we're satisfied."

From her mother: "Stay out of the sun! It damages the skin."

To Michael: "Forgot to ask. When's the lunch with Thomas?"

To Isabel: To Ms. V.P. of Client Services:

How did the meeting with Max and Jason go after I left?

The phone rang. "Hi, again," she said, thinking it was Michael.

"It's me," said that deep voice, the one she knew she'd never forget.

Chapter Six

"I got your note," Warren said.

A total of four words and every hair was standing on end.

After her bath she had massaged soothing aromatic oils into her skin. The residue made her silk and lace nightgown adhere ever so slightly to her bare thighs and stomach. Without realizing it, she put aside her iPad and started stroking her smooth legs as they spoke.

"I thought you might have gone," she said. "You weren't at the conference today. What did you do instead?"

He ignored her question. If some people listened selectively, he answered selectively. "How was it? Did I miss anything?"

"Well, there was a fabulous opera set to samba music in the morning."

"An opera? Sounds like Reg. He's very imaginative, isn't he?"

"So what did you do?" She didn't give up easily.

"After I left you, I went for a swim," he said.

She was thinking about the noises she had heard. "Were you still outside early this morning? Did you hear anything?"

"I heard voices in the distance—"

"Anything else?" Sandrina said.

"Then I heard a loud noise, like a shot."

"That's what I was wondering. I heard it too. The manager said it was nothing—did you see anything?"

"No. It was all over by the time I got to the lobby, but the night manager told me what happened. Apparently a kid from the favela near the Estadio Maracana had been looting during the blackout. When the power returned, he tried to hide behind some foliage in the hotel garden. The police found him and shot him without even a warning. He had stolen only a TV and a waffle iron," Warren reported.

"How awful." The irony—that those two items that cost him his life required electricity to enjoy—struck her deeply.

"What a waste of life. I started to get depressed, that's partly why I didn't come to the conference today. I buried myself in work."

"Tell me. Tell me about your work," she said, trying to get her mind off the senseless shooting.

"If I told you the crap I had to deal with this morning, you might not find me very engaging," he said.

"I doubt that. Try me."

"When I got back to my room there were nine faxes waiting there, all with problems I had to solve. I booted up my computer and scanned fifty-seven new e-mails. Did you ever notice how the red color makes them look angry? Or maybe it's just that they always are. I spent four hours working."

"On what kinds of things?" she asked.

"For example, there was an urgent message from Malcolm Broadbent. He's the manager of Middlethorpe Hall in York. It said, 'Dreadful Americans have arrived with five children and two French poodles, despite our published policy of no children and no dogs.'"

Sandrina laughed. "I have clients too," she said. "What did you recommend, Milk-Bones?"

"Move them to the Intercontinental, I told him. We'll pay the taxi."

"More!" she begged.

"You asked for it," he replied. "The agent of a famous German rock star, Udo Lindenberg, sent an angry fax that the cash-only Plumber Manor in Dorset refused to accept Udo's Black American Express card. Udo's luggage is being held hostage until the bill of 11,420 pounds, half of it for telephone calls, is settled."

"What did you do?"

"I had my London office run the card through and forward the cash to the Plumber Manor."

"Do you spend a lot of time in London? I mean, I know you live in New York but it seems that if all your clients are over there you would have to be there at least half the year," Sandrina said. It surprised her that she hoped he would say no.

"The Chaucer Suites headquarters is in New York, since seventy percent of bookings for the hotels we represent originate in the United States. So while we're not close to our clients, we're close to our clients' clients. We also have sales offices in London, Tokyo, Berlin, Toronto, Sydney, and Johannesburg."

They talked like two old friends. Not a word about the night before. She mentioned that she had eaten lunch with Reg. She described her own session and the accolades she had received, but not the fact that she had spent the entire day waiting for him to call.

"So you never left the hotel?" she asked.

"I did actually. I just got back," he said.

"So where else did you go?"

"Do you always ask so many questions?"

"Only when I'm interested in the subject."

"I left the hotel before lunch and took a taxi to Final do Leblon on Rua Dias Ferreira; it's a casual restaurant favored by local Brazilians and journalists—a good place for you to know, come to think of it. I never got dinner last night, or breakfast this morning, so I was starving and ordered a black bean and pork stew called *feijoada*, which I ate at the bar, and washed down the meal with three ice-cold local draft beers called *chopp*."

Simply describing what he ate made her want him. "And, then?"

"Then I went to a soccer match, at the Estadio Maracana. They take soccer, or futebol, very seriously here. The Flamengo were playing the Vasco da Gama."

Somewhere in the back of her mind she knew Pele was Brazilian…and that he played soccer. But that was all she knew. "What was it like?"

"It was crowded. At least a hundred thousand people. Horns were blowing, and streamers were tossed from the stands. Instead of throwing popcorn, like in America, they threw talcum powder everywhere."

They were both quiet on the line. She could hear him breathing. She was thinking about how male he was—heavy food, cold beer, soccer. Her heart was racing.

"Who won?"

"I didn't stay to see the game end. I walked around the neighboring *favela* for a while—I needed to think."

"Did it work?" Sandrina asked.

"What?"

"You know what."

"Was I able to blot out what happened between us last night? No, damn it, it didn't work."

"Warren, when will I see you again?"

Silence again. "Listen," he said. "We need to talk. I've got the whole day free tomorrow, and it's supposed to be gorgeous. If you like, we can take the ferry to an island off the coast. You'll need a bathing suit. I'll arrange everything else. What do you say? Around ten in the lobby?"

Something told her not to go. "Sure. I would love to see the islands. I hear they're wonderful. I'll be in the lobby at ten."

"Sleep tight," he said.

That was the last thing Sandrina could do. During the brief phone conversation her hand had gravitated to the moist nest between her legs. She dimmed the lights near the bed and closed her eyes. Her sensory memory was on high alert. She could smell his spicy scent in her nostrils. She could taste the martini on his lips. She could feel his enormous erection pressing against her pelvis through their layers of clothing. She could hear him breathing heavily in her ears, whispering, "I want to be inside you."

As she remembered all of this, she rubbed and stroked herself in an ever-quickening tempo until her whole body stiffened and she came with the taste and smell and sound of him in her mind.

Repeated orgasms did nothing to release her from her fantasy of being penetrated by Warren. The uninterrupted movement, the back-and-forth motion of her fingers between her legs, made her want him even more.

The little sleep that she did manage to get was permeated by wild dreams where she was falling from a skyscraper, surrounded by diaphanous sheets of sheer fabric like mosquito netting, the edges lapping at her naked body, trying to catch her as she plummeted, but just missing every time.

Chapter Seven

For her outing to the island, Sandrina chose a pale pink sheath and threw a cashmere sweater of almost the same color over her shoulders. She wore closed-toe sling-backs because they matched the dress, even though her stubbed toe, now purple and red like an over-ripe cherry, was killing her. In her ears she wore translucent pink intaglios surrounded by tiny unmatched seed pearls that she had bought for herself last month after signing the Hotel du Cap on the Cote d'Azure.

Into her travel bag, she threw a red bikini with a color-coordinated scarf that she usually tied around her like a sarong. She packed sunglasses, sunscreen, make-up, a hairbrush, and a bottle of perfume.

When Sandrina emerged from the north elevator into the cool marble lobby at three minutes after ten, Warren was standing at the front desk, looking stunningly male, and very relaxed. He had on a pair of sunglasses that hid his eyes, and a pair of loose khakis that hid nothing.

"Good morning, gorgeous." His smile wasn't sad today, but charming. There was something boyish about him that, when combined with his masculinity, made him irresistible. He was strong and open, self-confident and naïve, all at the same time.

It wasn't easy for her to walk, with an aching toe, but she persevered. Warren took her bag and handed it to a porter, who had already loaded the towels and lunch into the trunk of a rented fire engine red car.

Warren drove the way she had expected — fast and defiantly. The sunroof was open because it was an unseasonably hot day with the temperature already topping 77 degrees. The humidity made Sandrina's black hair full and wild. They drove in silence most of the way, interrupted from time to time by Warren pointing out scenery.

She was grateful for the lack of conversation because it gave her an opportunity to study his face. He had a glorious profile, noble really — with complicated lips that looked full and pouty when he gave his sad smile but thin and taut when serious.

The 75-minute motor launch ride from Praca Quinze through Guanabara Bay passed under the Niteroi Suspension Bridge alongside the imposing Pão de Açucar, what Americans call Sugarloaf Mountain and the image on many postcards of Rio.

"Where are we going exactly?" asked Sandrina.

"A place called Ilha de Paquetá in the middle of the bay," he said. "There are eighty-four islands in Guanabara Bay, and another three hundred or so in Angra dos Reis, the Bay of Kings, about ninety miles southwest of here."

"With so many to choose from, why did you pick Paquetá?"

"I picked Paquetá for today because it is the loveliest of the islands I've visited over the years. It has a wistful beauty. I don't think it could ever be copied. It's unique," he said. Then, as an afterthought, "Like you."

The ferry was larger than she had expected, with passenger seating on the top deck. It moved slowly through the water, creating a gentle splashing sound as they moved farther away from the shore. Sandrina and Warren were leaning on the teak railing, with the mist of the bay cooling the sun on their faces. He looked at her unusual face, into her uncommon green eyes, and through her in a way that gave her a chill, despite the heat.

"That episode in the bar last night was, well, incredible."

"I know," she said.

"But it was crazy," he continued. "You're married; it was irresponsible and reckless."

"This is a different you from the one last night in the bar."

"After I left you sleeping there I felt so guilty," he said. "I thought if I went for a swim it would clear my head so that I could think straight."

"Perhaps you shouldn't think so much."

"Sandrina, I kept thinking about your husband."

"I'm the one who should feel guilty, not you," she said.

"Do you?"

"I'd never have a casual affair, but this...is different."

"Sandrina. You are beautiful, and you are desirable, but..."

"But what?"

"But I don't want to fall in love with anyone now, especially not a married woman, no matter how unusual she may be. It just doesn't fit into my plan."

Sandrina closed her eyes and measured the time between gusts of humid air that rolled over her bare shoulders like the fingers of a masseuse. "What plan?" she said.

He looked into her eyes. She could see him wavering. "After my swim I returned to my suite. I took a long hot shower and stared in the mirror for what seemed an eternity while I shaved. I knew I felt something for you the night before. Something deeper and tenderer. First, I thought it was just sex, because you are an incredible woman, and you excite me—but so do lots of less complicated, and unmarried, girls."

His comments flattered her and stung at the same time. "Go on," she said.

"I tried to convince myself that I wasn't really interested in you, that it was just lust. But this is a first—lustful inklings for a mature woman—and it scares me. Not just because you are someone else's wife but I want another family. I want to start over—babies and all."

"What makes you think I don't? Why do you think these are the dreams only of women in their youth? Is love tied to physical beauty alone?"

"It's not just about firm breasts and tight flesh if that's what you're asking, although that's not my definition of beauty. Young women are so full of life and hope—they never seem depressed, they cheer me up, and they are dependent, not like you. All the ingredients exist in young women to feed my conviction that they would not, could not, disappear."

She was regretting that she had agreed to this excursion. But now she was stuck out in the middle of Guanabara Bay. "So you've made up your mind. You know what you want?" she asked. She was resigned to turning right around on the next ferry and heading back.

"This morning I thought I did. Now I'm not sure."

"If you knew that a wave you were about to ride would either crash on the shore or take you somewhere you had always wanted to go," she said, "would you ride the wave?"

The answer to him seemed obvious. "No. Would you?"

"Yes. I would. I'd take the chance," she said.

"Sandrina, you are a free spirit," he said, with admiration in his voice.

"I wouldn't say that. There is a reason we met. I believe that things happen for a purpose, and rather than fight them, I ride the wave."

They became silent as the motor launch slowly approached Ilha de Paquetá. It looked like a pastel drawing of a sun-baked village from centuries ago, dusty with chalk-box colors. Long before terrorists and mortgage-backed securities.

"Sandrina, do you want to go back? There's a return launch in half an hour."

"Do you?"

He looked at her longingly and shook his head.

"Neither do I then," she said. "We're mature adults. We can handle this."

"I promise you a wonderful experience," he said.

She looked around. "Where are the taxis?" she asked. Warren laughed.

"You're from New York, that's for sure. Cars are prohibited here," he said. "There wouldn't be any access anyway, on the narrow serpentine roads. Only horse-drawn carriages and pedestrians can navigate this maze." He made a sweeping gesture with his arm toward the convolution of cobblestone lanes.

"How did they bring all of this stone here back then?" she asked.

"The cobblestones came from Portugal as ballast for the gold ships; then they were swapped on Paquetá for freshly mined gold ore that, in turn, was shipped back to Lisbon."

"The houses are so low, barely tall enough to stand up in, and they look hundreds of years old. Do people still live here?" Sandrina said.

"Not really, a few squatters maybe. The island was virtually abandoned in the early eighteenth century when new land routes were opened to protect the gold trade from pirates."

The fishermen were closing down their makeshift stalls where they earned a living selling their early-morning catch to tourists and local restaurateurs.

"Are you hungry?" Warren asked. It was shortly after noon.

"Not yet," she said.

"Me neither. Let's explore the island before lunch." Warren paid an old man sitting in a rickety beach chair a few reais to watch their belongings while they took a stroll.

Sandrina was enchanted. Paquetá appeared frozen in time. Nothing, it seemed, had changed much since the Portuguese colonized the island during the sixteenth century. It was lush and tropical, yet European in its quaintness. There were a few cafés, for the tourists, and fishing boats in the bay. As they walked, he started telling her more about himself.

He described his early childhood in England, what he could remember of it anyway. He told her how difficult it had been for his mother when his father died.

"How old were you?"

"Five."

"So young...how did he die?"

Warren didn't answer right away. "It was suicide, Sandrina. A self-inflicted gunshot wound to the heart."

"How awful that must have been for you!"

"It gets worse...I was the one who found him."

"Is that why you left England?" she asked.

"The English are complicated, Sandrina," he said.

Warren confided in her about his failed marriage, and she confirmed what he had suspected, that she had always been faithful to Michael.

"Have you ever been in love?" she asked.

His face contorted. "I thought I had been," he said.

"With your wife?"

"No. Not her. Before...and one since."

"Why didn't they work out?" Sandrina asked.

"They ended badly," was all he would say.

Sandrina could see the slightest shading of perspiration through Warren's shirt, and her shoes were beginning to give her blisters. The bruised toe throbbed. They found a sheltered cove, and Warren suggested that Sandrina wait on the beach while he retrieved the things they had brought with them. While she waited, she took off her shoes and soothed her feet in the cool water. Nothing had ever been so unclear, yet she hadn't felt so safe in years.

Warren returned and slid down beside her on the sand. He opened a bottle of *tinto,* local red wine, a Miolo Reserva Cabernet that had been recommended by a bartender from the hotel. They watched the activity on the water, mainly sailboats and water skiers, for a few minutes.

"What were you thinking about just now? You looked so...happy," he said.

"I was thinking about how safe I feel with you. How certain, even though nothing is secure at all."

"Doesn't your husband take care of you, Sandrina?"

Sandrina shifted uneasily in the sand, leaving his question unanswered. She didn't want to speak much about Michael, out of a kind of primal loyalty and a desire not to spoil the magic by letting her real life intrude.

Three o'clock was the hottest part of the day. The sun and wine made them sleepy and scorched, so they decided to go for a swim before devouring the feast conveniently packed in a thermal carrier with dry ice.

Sandrina wrapped a big hotel towel around her while she slipped out of her dress and into her bikini. Warren gallantly turned around. He wore his bathing trunks under his pants; they were so un-chic—orange with little fish on them—that Sandrina burst out laughing. There wasn't another soul around, but he hid his wallet under some brush where he had intended to watch it out of the corner of his eye while they swam.

She was aware that he ignored his wallet and watched only her. "A forty-something-year-old mind in a twenty-something-year-old body is a formidable combination indeed," he said admiringly.

She blushed. "The icy water feels great."

They were both relaxed and loose from the wine. She watched the water drops glistening on the thick hair on his chest. She thought he looked like Michelangelo's David, and she imagined that his muscular body felt as hard as the marble from which the statue was carved. She wanted to touch him, but she held back, not sure what he wanted from her.

They swam for a while in the clear turquoise water, stopping to rest in water up to their waists.

"We are so alike, we two," Sandrina observed. They faced each other and held their eyes glued in a silent pact. "The tragic fathers, an aching void, some unanswered sensuality."

"Yes we are, but there is a critical difference. I'm afraid of losing something, someone, again." He stated the fear so matter of factly. "And you're afraid of never finding what you think you've always wanted."

Her hair was slicked back from swimming and her nipples were hard from the coldness of the bay. He tried to sweep a stray strand of wet hair from her forehead with his fingers, and then he let his palm rest on her cheek for just a few seconds. That innocent touch was enough to start a brush fire as his hand moved down to her shoulder and the other came up from the water to rest on her waist.

Sandrina tilted her head up to meet his kiss as her hands touched the legs that looked like sculpted marble. He fondled her breasts inside her bikini top. "So perfectly shaped," he said, as he gently extracted one and caressed her nipple softly with his tongue. Hidden by the water, although they were alone in the secluded cove, he slipped his hand into her bikini bottom and deftly found her swollen clitoris, which he massaged until she came.

Afterward, Warren slipped off her suit under the water and encompassed her soft mound with his bold hand while his fingers played and dipped inside her. He teased her tongue with his as she stroked his rock-hard penis with a practiced and expert rhythm. She tried to guide him inside her but she felt his extended member throb in her hand and saw the semen swirl in the water.

It took a few minutes to find the rest of Sandrina's bathing suit. Half-laughing, he looked deeply into her eyes as he held her face in his hands and shook his head from side to side. "Now we're in serious trouble."

By this time it was four o' clock, and they were both famished. Warren opened the thermal sack with their lunch. The hotel had outdone itself—there were cold sliced steak sandwiches, grilled chicken, and imported French cheeses. There were mangoes, persimmons, and, appropriately, passion fruits, as well as local fruit varieties—bacuri and capuacu.

After lunch, and a second bottle of wine, they lay on the beach holding hands. Warren moved closer and licked Sandrina's neck, using as his excuse that some *bacuri* juice had dripped there, and in the process he drove her wild. Then he reached over and rested his arm over her stomach in a territorial claim.

"You are an alpha-female, Sandrina," Warren said.

"I swing both ways," she said exposing her neck for him to bite, but he kissed it instead, driving her crazy again.

Since it was winter in the southern hemisphere, it had started to cool down early. The sun was beginning to set, and they positioned themselves so they could watch the enormous fiery globe get swallowed by the sea. Sandrina pulled the sweater she had brought over her tangled hair and sunburned shoulders. They gathered up the towels and utensils. Tossing everything into the hotel's bag, they shared the job of toting it back to the main road, where Warren hired a horse-drawn carriage to take them back to the ferry dock.

While they waited for the 6:30 launch to arrive, they leaned against a piling. Warren's back was pressed against the wood, and Sandrina leaned into his body. He had his arms around her, and they just stayed there, holding each other, for what seemed like a very long time. She could hear his slow breathing and his heart beating. She felt his penis swelling again against her groin. Her slender body was so relaxed and light, like a feather, that if he pulled his arms away abruptly she knew she would fall.

Sandrina wanted to stay like that forever. She heard the launch arriving behind her and began to feel reluctant about separating in any way. This man intoxicated her. She wanted more of him, and she feared that if she let go he would disappear as fast as he'd entered her life.

On the boat ride they claimed a red plastic row as their own. He rested his head in her lap, closing his eyes.

"Do you remember our conversation about Joseph Conrad?" he asked her.

"Of course." She felt his mood changing.

"You so aptly said his works were dark."

"That's right. I remember."

"I always thought that the fact that my father chose to make the study of Joseph Conrad his life's work should have foretold his state of mind. I've wondered if submerging himself in the labyrinth of Conrad's mind caused him, in some way, to kill himself."

Sandrina felt a sudden chill.

"There are times I'm afraid I'm just like him," he whispered.

"No, that can't be. You're so vital," she said.

"It's all a ruse," he admitted. "I just keep moving to hide it. That's how I try to keep my unhappiness at bay."

"We're all unhappy sometimes," Sandrina said, thinking of her own predicament.

"There are months when I see everything in the world as black," he told her. "The slightest every-day irritations take on larger-than-life significance. At these times I withdraw: I do not want to be touched or reached. I think my employees are conspiring against me. Even the hotel clerk seems to have an agenda."

Was he trying to scare her away? Drawing her into this dark world with him. Fascinated. "So, what do you do to cope?" she asked.

"I wait for these moods to pass. They always do. Seeing my daughters helps but that is so rare these days."

What Sandrina was wondering, but kept to herself, was whether or not his father had had these same mood swings, and if they were passed on through the genes.

"If you want to nip this in the bud now, I wouldn't blame you," he said, as if he could read her mind.

"What you just told me makes me feel closer to you," she said.

They were quite for a long time. His eyes were closed again; his head felt heavier. Warren was asleep.

When Warren opened his eyes it was to a star-lit sky; the Southern hemisphere constellations of Castor & Pollux and Alpha Centauri, as well as the Dog Star Sirius, were clearly visible. The boat jerked its way into the slip. Warren offered his arm for balance. Sandrina leaned on him as they walked up the three wooden steps to the pier. They found and loaded the car.

Despite the wine, Warren was stone sober. As he drove, he asked, "What do you think of our red Jeep?"

"Conspicuous," she replied.

"So then, what kinds of cars do you like?"

"Taxis," she replied, like a true New Yorker.

They were relaxed and enjoying the drive when they passed a makeshift shrine on the side of the road composed of rubble and relics. There were rivulets of fresh blood, as though it were the site of an animal sacrifice.

"Stop!" Sandrina shouted. "What's that?" Warren pulled over. They got out of the car and carefully approached the deliberate arrangement.

"It's a chicken, and a half melted black candle, a bottle of Pinga, popcorn, and bowls of manioc flour," he said.

"Maniac? As in crazy?"

"No, manioc, with an 'o'. It's a local plant. The vegetable itself is ugly, white and tuberous. But potent. Before drying and grinding it into flour, the locals leech the roots because they're loaded with cyanide."

"Is this a shrine of some sort?" she asked.

"These props are sure signs of *macumba*— black magic. Macumba's been around since the African Bantus arrived in Brazil. A sacrifice is part of the ritual performed to seal an evil pact. The food you see is an offering to one of the many gods the Africans worshipped. Even starving wild animals instinctively avoid interfering with this stuff, as if they know it is for a demonic purpose," Warren explained. "Come on, let's go. I'm getting spooked."

Sandrina's curiosity was piqued. On the way back to the hotel she implored, "Tell me more."

"Are you collecting data for your spells, Sandrina? All women are *bruxas*, witches," he teased.

"If I were a bruxa," she threatened, "I would bewitch you."

"You already have, Sandrina, you already have."

"How do you know so much about Brazil? The Portuguese, the witchcraft? You can't tell me it's from a couple of visits to pitch the Gaspar's business," she said.

"No. Of course not. Remember Conrad's *Nostromo*? It takes place in some undisclosed South American country, which I was convinced was Brazil. Spent a year here trying to prove it. Never could. But I became an expert on the culture and fascinated by the mysticism."

"I thought Brazil was a Catholic country. If macumba were some form of voodoo then it would be seen as anti-Christian. How does the Church deal with paganism?"

"Not very well is the answer. The attempt to fuse the pagan Yoruba religion that the African slaves brought with them with Portuguese Catholicism resulted in a type of worship called candomblé. I suppose you want to hear how candomblé got started?"

"What do you think?" she asked.

Warren took his eyes off the road just long enough to look at Sandrina. "Don't you ever get depressed?"

It was then that she almost told him how everything of late had affected her. How world events and her miscarriage had made her lose faith in the future. All of those horrible incidents seemed so far away, though. To speak of them would feel like a crash landing. "Only when people don't finish their stories," she said, laughing.

"Okay, okay," he continued. "When the African slaves were first brought here they were forbidden to practice their own religion. As you so astutely surmised, they were specifically warned against worshipping more than one god. To circumvent the rules, they developed two-faced dolls to substitute for public totems. One side, hidden under a cloth, bore the face of one of their many spirits. The other, more visible side, as well as the clothing the figures wore, resembled a Catholic saint."

"A voodoo doll!"

"Exactly. The dolls were used to cast spells. In the *candomblé* ceremony, the human body is considered a vessel, like the doll. It can be possessed by one of the spirits, which can heal or communicate through the possessed."

"Healing and communicating? That's not the image I have of voodoo dolls."

"No. *Candomblé* is white magic, but there are black magic cults too. Those cults mostly practice macumba—like that shrine we saw earlier on the road. Macumba ceremonies are very secret and are rarely witnessed by outsiders. There are also cults, Indian in origin rather than African, called *batuque*, that practice a form of candomblé called *candomblé do caboclo*. In it, a medicine man invokes a trance to allow possession by one of the Indian spirits, like *matinta pereira*, who is known to confuse and befuddle men."

Sandrina laughed. "You're making that up! That last part—about befuddlement."

"I'm not," he said. "I think that's what I'll call you...matinta pereira."

"It must be a fabulous spectacle."

"Would you like to see it for yourself? I know an old slave's house in the forest just outside of Rio where they perform different kinds of candomblé ceremonies on Saturday nights starting at midnight. You'd have to participate, though. It's the real thing. No gawkers allowed."

"I'd love it," she said. But she would have gone to the moon just to be near him longer.

Warren and Sandrina rolled up to the front entrance of the Copacabana Palace shortly before nine, where they sat for a few moments in the car.

"Look how vast and black the ocean is," he said. "It's hard to see what's ahead."

Sandrina touched his chin to turn his face toward hers. She held his hand and looked into his eyes. No blackness there tonight, just light and expectation.

"What do you see?" she asked.

"A new color," he said. "Half jade, half olive. I think I'll name it Optimism," he said.

Warren made a noise, not a sigh or a groan, but a sound filled with so much emotion it could have been a conversation.

"Listen. You must be tired. Why don't you rest? Freshen up. I'll ring you from the lobby in an hour and we'll get in touch with some spirits."

She leaned toward him, to kiss him, but he sat stone still, with his lips thinly sealed, allowing her only to brush his with hers, full and parted. She looked in his eyes for some explanation, but she had lost him. He was tucked inside himself again.

The white-gloved valet in his pressed uniform opened the door of the car. As Sandrina emerged, several guests lingering outside the hotel entrance turned to look at her. She was sunburned and her hair had dried into a tousled mess of black locks. On the drive she had taken her shoes off, to give her toe a break. Her purse had been leaning against the inside of the car door, and when the door was pulled ajar the contents of her bag spilled onto the pavement.

As the valet scrambled in an effort to help her retrieve her belongings, she watched Warren speed off with her shoes on the floor of the front passenger seat and her gold tube of lipstick rolling after him down the asphalt drive.

Chapter Eight

A small crowd of elegantly dressed carioca, draped in jewels and, to Sandrina's surprise, light-colored furs, had gathered in the hotel lobby. A wedding was taking place in the Salão Nombre ballroom. A cloud of delicate white organza caught the breeze as the bride glided by, accompanied by music wafting down the grand staircase from the ballroom above.

Sandrina made her way, barefoot and bedraggled, to the front desk to retrieve her key and messages before slipping upstairs as discreetly as she could. The fuzzy warmth of the carpet on the tenth-floor hallway yielded softly in contrast to the icy cold marble lobby floor.

She went to the mini-bar and poured herself a tall glass of tonic water before going into the bathroom, where she drew herself a hot bath, testing the water to make sure it was just a few degrees hotter than she could comfortably stand. The bubbles multiplied as she poured a capful of bath foam under the steaming faucet.

As she was soaking in the tub she contemplated all that could happen if she wasn't careful: She could throw her secure life in turmoil, upset her predictable world, her familiar cocoon. She thought of how fragile all these things she once had taken for granted really were — how fragile everything was, how unpredictable.

As she sank deeper into the tub, her mother's voice came back to her. Would her business have been as fulfilling if she hadn't kept her passion in check? She had been afraid to be in love—not so different from Warren when you came right down to it—afraid to lose control, afraid to lose herself.

Sandrina stepped into the enormous glass shower stall to wash the salt out of her hair. She lathered the creamy thyme-scented soap into her neck and breasts and the conditioner into her scalp and the hair between her legs. The cream rinse, Michael told her once, made her hair feel as soft as goose down. She stepped out of the shower, wrapped a fluffy monogrammed towel around her head, smoothed body lotion all over her skin, and dabbed perfume behind her ears, in between her breasts and in the creases where her thighs began.

As was her custom, she applied her makeup skillfully and slowly. Then she blew her hair dry; it was unruly from the moist Brazilian air. Before deciding which outfit to wear, she sank into the oversized pillows on her bed and phoned home.

While listening to the phone ring, Sandrina cringed with shame over the way she'd spent the afternoon.

"Got your e-mail," Michael said, matter of factly. "The lunch with Thomas and Pam is the day after tomorrow, Memorial Day. He says 'time is of the essence' regarding the *Finance Journal*. 'Drina, he's right."

"I'll be exhausted. That's right after I return—"

"I know, but we're running out of time."

"Michael, what if it's too late? What if I fail? This sort of stuff isn't my usual fare. Like I've said, it's Joshua's"

"You won't fail. Aren't you his prize protégé? You'll think of something. You always do."

The pressure was enormous. It was as if Michael was placing all his bets on her. It was like Russian roulette, the cylinder was spinning, he had given her the gun, but she knew how awful the odds were. It was so unfair to place his fate in her hands like that.

"Are you in for the night?" he asked.

"Actually, a group of us are going to a temple. To see a voodoo ceremony. That should be exciting, don't you think?"

"Yes, very," he answered with the slightest bit of disapproval, and resignation, in his voice.

There was a brief silence, then just before hanging up he said, "'Drina, I love you."

"Me too you," she said, and in its way it was true.

For a moment Sandrina contemplated calling the evening off. It would be so simple to cancel. It would be understandable if she were tired, or had a headache, or an attack of common sense. She thought about Michael. And, about the life they had built together.

The telephone in her room buzzed seven times before she decided to answer.

It was Warren, from the lobby, right on schedule. "Were you asleep?"

She paused. A momentary struggle with her conscience. It lost.

"I was on the phone," Sandrina said.

"I've got your shoes."

"I'll be down in a minute."

Rushing to dress, she chose a cappuccino-colored skirt and blouse. She wore black sandals and black silk panties and bra. Thinking of the people she was likely to encounter at a voodoo service, Sandrina selected an amber bead necklace and earrings that were bold and exotic but not very valuable. With her black hair and sunburn, she could have been Brazilian herself.

When Sandrina floated through the lobby ten minutes later, she found Warren with his back propped against the reception desk. He looked her up and down in a predatory way. He was smoking a cigarette, and the ashes had grown very long. A bellman emerged from a hidden doorway with an ashtray in his outstretched hand.

"Let's go," Warren said abruptly. The red car was waiting. He didn't open the door for her as Michael would have done but went around to his side and slid into the driver's seat, leaning over to push open the passenger door from inside. A flustered doorman intervened and held the door for Sandrina as she maneuvered her long legs into a comfortable position.

"Feel like eating?" he asked. He was gruff, not tender, as he'd been earlier that day.

"Not after that lunch." she replied.

"Good, neither do I. We've got until midnight."

Without disclosing their destination, he drove to Mariu's in Leme. It had a small piano bar in the back, with raw plank benches and weathered wooden tables, gray and warped by time. The room had views of the water from windows of sea-sprayed glass. She guessed most of the customers were locals—fishermen, or couples like themselves. They each had a caipirinha and some olives at a corner table, so small and tight that their bodies would have been sandwiched together even if they hadn't wanted it that way.

"I almost didn't come," she said.

His pupils looked completely black in the darkness of the bar. "Me too," he answered. "What made you change your mind?"

"I don't know."

"Yes, I know what you mean."

The piano player was lean and wizened and didn't play a single Brazilian song but launched into an earthy repertoire of Frank Sinatra hits. Sandrina felt enflamed in the places where she and Warren touched. She wanted him to make love to her so badly; she felt constrained by the bar and the plans they had made.

After an hour Warren grew restless and suggested they leave. He drove along the Lagoa Rodrigo de Freitas, where behind them the golden glow from the backlit Christ on Corcovado Mountain illuminated their path.

Halfway around the lake they stopped on the road that led to the Jardim Botanico. The botanical garden had closed at six but Warren parked the car on the side of the road and, taking Sandrina's hand, led her over a guard chain and down a short path to an overgrown pond with an eighteenth-century carved stone fountain at its core.

She felt as though they had walked through a hole in the backdrop of Rio to a tropical rain forest. Thick jungle vines cascaded from the trees along the dirt walkway. The water's surface was overtaken by Victoria Regis water lilies from the Amazon, which looked like giant stuffed mushroom caps. The air was humid and thick with musty smells and aviary noises that sounded more like cats than birds.

"Aren't we trespassing?' Sandrina asked.

"Only if we get caught." Warren turned his face to the sky and closed his eyes as if basking in the sun. "It's a perfect moonlit evening."

Sandrina noticed the full moon too. Man in the moon eyes, eerie and ominous, watching them. She edged closer, sliding her fingers under his shirt to rub his back.

"What do you want? With me." Warren asked. "What happens when you go home?"

"I don't know," she admitted.

He took the hand that had been touching his flesh and held it in his own. "I see a woman who has everything that every woman I have ever known wanted. Beauty, charm, intelligence, a successful career, marriage—but something deep down is missing. What do you want that you don't have?"

"When I step back I see how truly lucky I am, but the one thing you failed to mention is what I want most of all."

"You want to be passionately loved. For the essence of who you are, not for what you appear to be—although you work very hard at those appearances."

The precision of his understanding impressed. "Yes, that. And, I want to love passionately in return."

Silence enveloped them for quite some time. Finally Sandrina asked, "Why are you here?"

He shrugged. "A beautiful woman. A moonlit night. Why not?"

That wasn't the answer she had hoped for, and she didn't want to believe him—his sarcasm, his flippancy. She was trying to capture his attention, and he kept diverting his gaze to avoid being caught.

"Come, matinta pereira. It is time." He took her by the arm and led her back to the car.

On the way to the candomblé ceremony, along the Estrada do Redentor, they drove into the Floresta da Tijuca, where they came upon a small flat clearing completely hidden by leafy fronds. The temple, Igreja de Iansã, was in an old, white house cloaked in peeling paint.

"It looks ancient," she said.

"It probably dates back to the beginning of the nineteenth century, when the number of slaves brought from Africa to Brazil spiked and Brazilian candomblé practice peaked."

"Are there many candomblé temples in Rio?" Sandrina asked.

"A few. But this one is special. Do you see how it's built on an odd ear-shaped piece of land? That's thought to enable better communication with the spirits."

"Warren, I'm confused. If it was built as a slave church, then at one time the slaves must have been allowed to worship freely. Right?"

"In the beginning, before the Portuguese understood their pagan beliefs, slaves were allowed to practice their own religion. But when slave churches were banned, the structures were taken over and the original names retained. When later slaves came from Nigeria they were more independent than their predecessors and embraced candomblé with a vengeance. They thought that through dancing and African ritual they would regain their identity and self-esteem."

"And whites were threatened by the unifying force of the religious community?"

"Isn't binding passion always threatening to those on the outside?" he asked.

The Igreja de Iansã was ablaze with light as they climbed the few rickety steps to a wraparound porch with columns. The gray wood showed through the neglected white paint, giving the veranda a zebra-like appearance. The walls inside the main level of the temple had been removed so that what remained was one large pavilion with faded tiled floors lit by candelabra made from crudely carved wood.

Warren and Sandrina were the only fair-skinned people, and certainly the only Americans, among the two dozen worshippers, who were dancing intensely to the modulated beat of drumming based on the *atabaques* ceremonies of the Nigerian slaves. In the center of the room three drummers were squatting on their haunches pounding out a coordinated rhythm on conical, staved instruments resembling conga drums.

"The beat goes right through me," Sandrina said.

"The drums are thought to be magnets for the spirits," Warren whispered. "They have names: the big one is called *rum*, the middle-sized drum is *rumpi*, and the small one is called *le*."

The candomblé worshippers were poor people, judging by their tattered clothing and lean bodies. Most were chanting while they pitched and rocked. Many were glassy-eyed and wore fevered expressions. The smell of human perspiration was everywhere; Sandrina noticed the sweat shining on the hair and faces of the participants, making the dancers appear to glow when the candlelight reflected off their skin.

"Candomblé temples are called *terreiros*," Warren explained. "Even though this terreiro is headed by a man, most of the powerful leading positions in candomblé belong to women. Men are not thought to have the discipline or patience to communicate with spirits."

Warren nodded his head toward a large, elderly man of African descent swathed in white robes and a multi-colored hat. This *pãi de santo*, father of the spirits, danced frenetically through the room, blowing smoke from his pipe at worshippers of his choosing.

"It smells like marijuana," Sandrina said.

"The smoke comes from burning a hallucinogenic mixture called *ayahuasca*. It's made from a secret combination of jungle plants intended to provoke a trance-like state so that the spirit can enter the body and work its magic," Warren explained.

"Sounds like Brazilian marijuana. Do you know anyone who's done it?

"I did, years ago, in an effort to purge myself of nightmares."

"Did it work?" she asked.

"Not for me," he responded. "The mãe de santo, as the priestess is known, determined that an orixá, or spirit presence, was the cause of my unhappiness. She could cure me, she claimed, but in order for the candomblé magic to work I would have had to dedicate my life to serving the curing spirit. The spirit must have known I'm not the servile type because the ayahuasca made me sick and my nightmares returned the next day."

She stroked his cheek. "Never give up," she said. "Something will eventually banish them."

"I'm not so sure. Seen enough?" he asked.

"Not yet." She tapped her foot on the tile floor. "Warren, do you think they'll try it on me?"

Sandrina saw Warren look at her with a mixed expression of fear and admiration.

"Let's find out," he said.

Warren whispered a few words in Portuguese to the pãi de santo with the pipe and, unbeknownst to Sandrina, he slipped him a few reais.

"What did you say to him?" Sandrina asked.

"I told him to bless your fecundity." She looked up at him inquisitively, not sure if he was joking or not.

The pãi took Sandrina by the hand through a low doorway with a rotting frame, into a *runko*, a small sacred room, where new initiates were prepared to receive the spirits. A senior priestess massaged an herbal infusion into Sandrina's hair while her novice rang a metal bell attached to a long stick over Sandrina's head to invoke the spirit who would enter her through her scalp.

The women draped her in bracelets, armlets, and anklets adorned with small bells to signify her willingness to submit to the spirits. They removed her string of amber beads from around her throat and replaced it with a kele, the sacred necklace of the orixás, made up of 27 turquoise stones, the exact number and color associated with Ezili, the feminine spirit of fertility and protection.

It is said that during the preparation period the children of the orixá flit in and out of the initiate's body. Sandrina couldn't stop giggling. She wasn't sure whether it was the eres, child of Ezili, or the hallucinogenic smoke that caused her giddiness, but she was enjoying the experience immensely. Her levity seemed to irritate the priest and priestess.

The pãi and mãe then took a small white bird and slit its throat, leaving it to drown in its own blood in a clay bowl at Sandrina's feet. Sandrina was frightened, but then she felt a great wind come up from behind and lift her from the chair on which she sat. She started to dance, as if in a dream, where she stood outside herself and watched her own movements. She felt more open than she ever had before.

As Sandrina's dancing quickened, like winds whirling in a storm, the candomblé leaders faded from her view.

During her trance she was transported back to the night she miscarried, the night after she refused the abortion Michael had tried to persuade her to have. In her heart, she blamed him for the miscarriage. She had felt as hapless as the bird dying at her feet.

Michael had taken her to a trendy, whitewashed restaurant that would have the lifespan of a Monarch butterfly. The cramps came so suddenly, and unexpectedly, pulsating into a crescendo, like the drums outside. She remembered sipping the cool Chardonnay, hoping to relax the clenching. The rhythmic throbbing became more and more intense as the evening droned on—not unlike the music she could hear beyond the runko.

When she woke up in their bed later that night in a pool of blood, Michael held her and stroked her hair while she shook with sobs. Trying to comfort her, he had said over and over again: "It's for the best." She had never felt so misunderstood as she had that night, and in the temple she now knew that back then she was like the bird, life draining from her with her own blood.

While Sandrina was dancing and remembering in the seclusion of the *runko*, Warren sought out a tiny old woman sitting on the floor in the corner of the main room. She was in a cross-legged position with her brown feet bare and her long gray hair covered by a lace cloth. On a small mat with its corners curling up from over-use, she had placed a wooden cup that contained 16 cowry shells for her *jogo de buzios*, game of shells.

The *italero*, spiritual reader of the shells, can read into a person by the unique way the shells fall. Through her dilogun, divination with the shells, the italero is presumed to be able to commune with the spirits to cure any sickness or malady.

Warren sat on the floor before her and bowed his head in respect. She touched his forehead with an arthritic finger, shook and scattered her shells, and met his eyes.

"Are you in pain?" she inquired in Portuguese.

"Inside, not out. More anguish," he answered. He gave her a sad half-smile. "I have been haunted for most of my life by the same anguish, and I cannot make it go away."

The italero looked down at the shells and shook her head slowly. For 68 years she had been interpreting the fall of the shells for people of all colors, religions, and ages. She had learned her art from her mother, who had learned it from a great aunt. The skill and, more important, the gift had been passed down through the generations in her matrilineal line. This italero was none other than Mina Nasso, who Warren knew of but had never met. She bore the distinction of being a high priestess in her community of candomblé, and one of only two left in her line of the house of Iya Nasso, known in Brazil as Casa Branca, to whom all authentic candomblé can be traced.

Mina left Warren sitting there while she consulted with her twin sister, the italero Rita Nasso. They spoke quietly, in a dialect of Portuguese.

"Sister, what do you think of the fair stranger?" Mina asked.

"He can be helped. But only if he helps himself," Rita answered. The sisters studied his features, especially his fingers, known barometers for spiritual conductivity.

"So thick and strong," Rita said. "Like a working man."

"Yes, I noticed that too," Mina said. "Look how his hands are rectangular and covered with wiry hairs that dance together chaotically. A sign of conflict?"

"He has a handsome face."

"And a body like an African bull."

"He is sexy," said Rita.

Mina who, like Rita, was 75 years old and granted her high position because she had presumably passed the age of passion, agreed.

"Yes. He is hot, but is he warm?"

"Perhaps," Rita observed. "I think he exudes a type of warmth that belies a loving heart. What you detect, Sister, is heat from an inner fire — maybe anger, or envy."

"Mãe," Warren said impatiently, calling Mina "old mother" in Portuguese. "Toss the shells."

She complied.

"What do you see?" he asked. She concentrated hard.

"Son, you have the rare predicament to be occupied by two spirits, Ogun and Shangô. Ogun represents   love,   strength,   wisdom,   and understanding. He is the messenger of Olodumaré, the spirit of creation. Your counter-spirit is Shangô; he represents anger, energy, forcefulness, and ardor. They are at war."

"War?" he asked. His tone was cynical.

"Do you see the cracked shell with the speckles? There. In the corner of the mat, hidden by the shadow of the curling edge? That is a person from your past who is part of your being. He is the one who let in your counter-spirit, Shangô. Do you know who he is?" Mina asked.

Warren nodded.

"He feeds the spirit and encourages him. Your Anger spirit is very strong. It is overpowering the other spirit, Ogun, suppressing the love that lives within you," she continued.

Warren flinched, ever so subtly.

Rita, who had been watching, whispered in her sister's ear, "You're on the right track."

"I know, but how far will he let me go before he shuts down?" Mina murmured back.

"Who knows? Take the next step," Rita advised.

Pointing to a cluster of six shells, she said, "You have never sustained love for a woman—not your mother, not your wife, not your daughters. You pull them in with your magic. The spirit Ogun, Love, occasionally swims close to the surface, seducing them, and then your counter-spirit Shangô, Anger, builds a wall and keeps them out."

"Mãe—" he tried to interrupt.

"Shh…there is more." She held both hands out toward a dark shell that had settled near the cluster but apart. It lay on its side with the open part facing Mina. The dark, shiny luster of the shell's outer surface was the only part Warren could see. "There is one woman whom you know who is strong enough to break down the wall that Anger has built. Do you know who she is?"

Warren looked around for Sandrina. Dreamy from her trance, she leaned against the far wall near an enormous candelabrum.

"Yes, Mãe, I know who she is."

Mina and Rita exchanged twin looks. Rita signaled toward the black-haired woman.

 "She is your last chance," Mina and Rita said in unison.

Warren held Mina's gaze for a minute or more before bowing his head again and thanking her. He rose from the floor and strode across the room to where Sandrina was standing. It took a few moments for Sandrina to notice him, even though the room was small, because she was dazed and there was a cloud of activity separating them.

The words she had replayed from that awful night with Michael, where she had wanted to scream, were still in her head.

At four in the morning, after they had wakened in the puddle of dark blood, she had called her doctor. He asked her several questions; drawing out responses the way one might extract a splinter, slowly, carefully, and deliberately. Then he said, "I'm sorry."

"Things are meant to stay as they are," Michael said. At that moment she had realized that their life together, as it was, wasn't enough for her.

The drumbeat had intensified to an adarun, a deafening pitch. When Sandrina finally spotted Warren, her face lit up and she smiled at him.

He grinned back. He held her hands for a second, enveloping them in his. Then he linked her arm through his, and led her out the door onto the veranda.

"Do you really think I'm possessed by a spirit?" she asked him.

"You are a spirit yourself," he replied.

Sandrina couldn't yet describe what had happened to her, so she stood on her toes, put her arms around his neck, and kissed him fervently. He put both hands on her tiny waist and pulled away. She looked into his eyes and tried to read his emotions. Was it she or the spirit who initiated the kiss?

"I had an incredible, out-of-body experience in there, Warren," Sandrina said. "I feel lighter. How can I thank you for bringing me here?"

"It's not necessary—" he responded.

"At first it seemed like a game. I didn't take it seriously. All of those poor souls gyrating and grunting. It was funny, in a way. But then the pãi killed a bird at my feet, and the dying bird had me transfixed when a strong gust of energy pushed me up from where I was sitting. I felt as light as one of the bird's feathers. Then I watched myself dance at the same time I felt myself dancing, and in the mirrored wall I saw a blue haze enter my body through my scalp at the same time I felt my head tingle like static electricity. Am I crazy?"

Warren laughed and said, "Yes, a little."

They stopped behind the house. He gently propped her up against the wall. It was near dawn and only a few spent and exhausted devotees remained inside. The drums had stopped. It was silent except for the sounds of tree frogs and crickets. He kissed her throat, her ears, and her closed eyes.

"You look slightly disheveled," he said. "Your hair is a tapestry of dried flowers and herbs. Your blouse is undone. I like you like this—

imperfect." Her smile thanked him for the compliment.

"What did you do...while I was being possessed?"" Sandrina asked.

"I had my shells read by an old woman. The cowry shells are the Tarot cards of candomblé," he explained.

"What did she see in your shells Warren?"

"She saw my inner demon in a cracked shell that is most like the Hangman in Tarot."

"What else?" Sandrina probed.

"She saw you in my future."

He pressed his body against hers and kissed her with so much heat that she felt as though her lips were on fire. His swollen penis pressed against her. She made space between them to allow his hand to wander under her skirt and find her opening inside her black silk panties. He slid his fingers inside, where she wanted him to be. She was wet and hot.

"Let's go," he said, leading her to the car.

He drove about a quarter of a mile, but deeper into the forest not toward the hotel.

"Where are we going?" she asked him trustingly.

"I can't let you go. Not yet," he replied. He parked in a hidden spot behind a slight bluff, where the car was invisible from below but where they could still see the building they just left beneath them.

Warren started to stroke her legs, from ankle to thigh. The drum rhythm was still beating in her imagination as he slipped off her panties and hooked them on the stick shift. He entered her with his thick fingers while he gently massaged her clitoris by moving his thumb in a circular motion.

While his right hand was exploring all the femininity and depth between her legs, Warren's left hand unbuttoned Sandrina's blouse. Her black silk and lace bra fell easily from her breasts as he drew each one out of its cup, alternately fondling and sucking her nipples. Whenever she tried to speak, he either kissed her or took his fingers from her breast and put it to her lips. He was casting his own spell of eroticism on her, and she sensed that he sought her total submission.

His voice got very deep and husky. He kept whispering in her ear that he wanted her to come. He kept kissing her neck, which ignited her passion. She had never told him that her neck was the most erogenous part of her body, but he knew, instinctively, everything about her sexuality, as if they had been lovers in another life. He treated her breasts as if they were perfectly shaped planets, circling his fingertips around the nipples as if they were moons drawn there by centrifugal force.

All of a sudden he planted both hands on the insides of her thighs and drew her legs apart. He leaned over and used his mouth in such a skilled and practiced way that he brought her to a level of ecstasy that she had never known before. As she was engulfed in orgasm after orgasm, barely able to catch her breath, she reached over and felt his penis, so engorged that his pants would have split open if she hadn't unzipped them at exactly that moment. He groaned as her long fingers stroked his hardness. She could feel how urgently he wanted to be inside her, so she maneuvered her body over his and guided his strong hard maleness inside her, so deep she thought he had penetrated her womb.

Warren hit the electric switch on the panel that made the driver's seat lie flat. She pulled her skirt over her head and slid her unhooked bra off her shoulders. Completely naked now, with the sun rising, the sky the color of bruises, purple and pink with traces of yellow, she straddled and rode him, pausing every now and then to keep him from coming too soon. He was watching her body, slick with sweat, her firm breasts and hard nipples, the muscles in her stomach contracting as she slid up and down his wood-hard shaft. Her body stiffened, and her softness that encompassed him throbbed every time she came.

Just when she thought he would go mad, Warren locked both hands behind Sandrina's head, burying his fingers in her black hair and kissing her so deeply that with his final thrust inside her she thought she would split in two. When he finally shot his seed, it was with so much force that he asked if he had hurt her. She gasped, "No, no," and secretly hoped that he never would.

Just then a bird called, and Sandrina imagined that she saw Ezili's blue haze flying around their joined genitalia.

A warning?

A blessing?

She couldn't be sure.

Chapter Nine

Hours later, Sandrina opened her eyes and realized she could hardly move. Her hips and back ached from dancing, and her knees were killing her from pressing against the stiff leather seat of the Jeep during her amorous predawn adventure.

She rolled over and phoned room service for a café com leite, then called back and asked for the operator.

"Mr. Waterhouse, please."

"He has checked out, Senhora."

"Really, when?"

"An hour ago."

"Thank you. May I have the front desk, please?"

"Boa tarde." Good afternoon.

"Yes, hello. It's Mrs. Morgan. Do I have any messages?"

"Four phone messages from last night. A letter. And a book—from the gentleman."

The gentleman, not *a* gentleman. As if there were only one in the whole universe. "Send them up, please," she commanded.

She wobbled into the bathroom, hardly able to walk. She peeled off her clothes from last night — what was left of them anyway — and assessed herself, naked, in front of the full-length mirror. Her hair was matted; her mascara had run down her face. She had bruises on her neck where Warren had kissed her, hard, and her knees were black and blue.

She brushed her teeth and started to pull tend to her bruises when she heard the doorbell chime.   As she was signing for her coffee, the bellman arrived with her mail: two messages from Michael from last night, one from Christoff and John asking her to dinner, another from Harvey saying goodbye, and an envelope that she ripped open impatiently, expecting it to be from Warren.   It wasn't.   It was from the beautiful woman from Oberoi Hotels telling her how much she enjoyed Sandrina's impromptu module at the conference and suggesting that perhaps they could do business together.

And, there was the book: *The Screwtape Letters* by C.S. Lewis.   She knew it was from Warren because she remembered him referring to it in the bar on that first night.   It had a hand-written inscription in Portuguese:

O homem é um Diabo, não ha mulher que o negue, mas toda mulher deseja que um diabo a carregue.

Unsigned.

Sandrina gulped down her coffee and stepped into the steaming shower. The water felt wonderful. Her mind wandered back to the hours passed. Had a spirit really possessed her? Or had herself, her true self, finally emerged?

Sandrina dressed in a lavender cotton pants suit with a sleeveless white ruffled blouse underneath. Her shoes were patent leather flats with tiny bows and square toes, like gift boxes. She stuffed her outfit from last night, with all its incriminating evidence, in the bottom of her bag. She phoned her friends, Christoff and John to decline dinner, and her clients, the Gaspars, to say thanks and farewell.

A bluster of commotion ensued as the bellman and Afonso descended upon her simultaneously. It was like the changing of the guard at Buckingham Palace as the bellman handed her ten-year-old Louis Vuitton suitcases, the ones she and Michael bought in Cannes, to Afonso. Afonso looked rested and fit from his day off.

By the time they had covered a short distance toward the airport, the weather had turned colder and it had started to rain. Sandrina put her jacket over her shoulders and began to rearrange her belongings. She pulled out the book.

"Afonso, may I ask you a question?"

"I hope I have the answer," he said.

"What do these words mean?" she asked, phonetically reading the enigmatic scribbling from the face page of the book:

'*O homem é um Diabo, não ha mulher que o negue, mas toda mulher deseja que um diabo a carregue*'?"

The driver glanced at her in the rear view mirror. "It is a Brazilian proverb. It means 'A man is a devil that no woman can deny, and every woman wishes to be taken away by him.'"

As Sandrina Morgan settled into Seat 2B, to begin the trip that would return her to her husband and life, the events of the last 48 hours seemed surreal to her.

Weary from lack of sleep, Sandrina looked forward to nine hours of solitude. When the flight attendant approached with a tray, she requested her champagne with orange juice, to dilute the alcohol and its aftereffects. As she was just about to take a sip of her mimosa, a large, squarish woman of indeterminate age, built bulky like a man, squeezed by her and collapsed into Seat 2A.

"Good evening," said the newcomer shyly and in a very slow and plodding tongue. Her accent was neither Portuguese nor American; she was hard to place.

"Hello," Sandrina replied.

The flight attendant returned. She brought straight champagne for Sandrina's companion and placed a small bowl filled with salted nuts equidistant from each of their elbows. Sandrina's neighbor scooped up half the bowl in one handful and, pressing the open palm to her mouth, vacuumed up the contents except for one fugitive nut that rolled down her dress and onto the floor, stopping an inch from where the stewardess stood.

"Are you American or Brazilian?" the woman asked.

"I am American. I live in New York."

"That is good," she didn't explain why. "I am Swiss." She harrumphed to signal that the conversation had come to an end as far as she was concerned, and she began flipping through the duty-free catalogue.

Sandrina recognized the characteristic intonation of Schwyzerdeutsch. It was the woman's singsong lilt, more than her rather neutral accent, that confirmed her nationality. She had an aristocratic air, and her only piece of jewelry was an ornate cross on an antique woven gold chain.

To distract herself, Sandrina began reading the book Warren had left for her.

All of a sudden, her seatmate shuddered.

"Are you ill?" Sandrina asked her.

"Goodness, no. It is that book you are reading."

"This one? I haven't started it yet. What is it about?"

"Oh *Gott im Himmel*! It is a series of essays about the corruptibility of human nature. Screwtape, the title character, is the undersecretary to Satan." Another shudder. "He writes letters to his nephew, Wormwood, who is a young Devil in training."

At this point in the conversation she started to hyperventilate. She gasped and sputtered like an engine about to die. Sandrina was scared.

"Please," Sandrina said. "No more. It's just a book."

"It's not just a book," she warned. "It's the Devil's calling card."

Sandrina opened the book again. As she read, she saw that Warren had provided a road map to understanding him. Clue number one, the reasoning behind his views on love and marriage:

"A curious, and usually short-lived, experience which they call 'being in love' is the only respectable ground for marriage." [The Bible] describes "a married couple as 'one flesh.' [It does] not say 'a happily married couple' or 'a couple who married because they were in love.' Mere copulation…makes 'one flesh.' You can thus get the humans to accept as rhetorical eulogies of 'being in love' what were in fact plain descriptions of the real significance of sexual intercourse."

She remembered that he had said she was in the book too; she saw herself in many places, although she wondered which one he had meant. She related to the amphibious nature of humans, 'half spirit and half animal,' especially after last night.

After some time she drifted into slumber with the book open on her chest. She must have been sleep-talking because her neighbor was shaking her and looked disturbed.

"Miss, wake up. *Mein Gott*. Wake up. You are having a nightmare."

Sandrina felt dazed. For an instant, she didn't know where she was. Her hair was plastered to her forehead. *The Screwtape Letters* had fallen to the floor.

The lady next to her was sympathetically shaking her head. "I told you so," she said. "The Devil's calling card."

Another shudder. This time it was Sandrina.

Chapter Ten

Despite the early hour, the first thing Sandrina did when she stepped off the plane was call her husband's cell phone. She would beg Michael to release her from the visit to his brother's house.

"Are you here, Sandrina? At the airport?" Michael asked. "There's a car meeting you at the baggage claim. "I'm already in the Hamptons.

When Sandrina arrived at Thomas and Pamela's house in Southampton, she dropped her bags on the front lawn and circled around to the beach side before going in; she needed to muster her strength. The "herself" they'd be expecting was reluctant to reemerge.

The house was a many chimneyed, shingled mansion, with dark green shutters on the windows of its 28 rooms. The deep porch stretched from the house to the dunes, with an unobstructed view of the Atlantic Ocean and its mountainous waves. On the patio by the pool was a round table set for lunch. The tablecloth was covered in an innocent floral pattern, like a baby's sheet. There were red zinnias in a pot and four white garden chairs, indicating that they would be the only two couples at lunch.

The house had been built in 1867 and, based on the old pictures Pamela had shown her, she knew that at one time there had been a hundred feet of lawn between the house and the beach. In another sixty years, the sea would most likely swallow up the house itself, but Thomas said he couldn't care less since he and Pamela were childless and he himself expected to be dead by then.

Sandrina tiptoed into the living room through a screen door from the porch. The vast living room was all white, with overstuffed sectional sofas set in wicker frames and pine tables scattered about. Pamela collected 'tramp art,' so there were birdhouses and sculptures on the table surfaces made from cigar boxes and fruit crates. The only other objects were oversized seashells and dried starfishes, purchased by a decorator rather than found by the owner, as one was led to expect.

Sandrina had a clear view from the back door through the house to the front, where she could see the trimmed privet hedges, butterball bushes of hydrangea, and bowing weeping beeches through the glass panels that flanked the front door. She opened it and retrieved her bags.

"Michael? Pamela?" she called. No answer.

She followed the sisal carpeting, with its neoclassical trim, up the stairs to the guest room. Again she called for Michael but heard nothing in response, so she figured everyone had gone to the beach or to the Meadow Club for a game of tennis.

She decided to rest and freshen up before they returned for lunch.

The guest room in Thomas and Pamela's house had always been her favorite. Because Thomas instructed Pamela to spend the least on the guests, it was the only room not overdone. Its color scheme of sand white and aquamarine was soothing. Instead of contrived expressions of tramp artists, there were antique botanical prints propped on chairs and ledges, not calculatedly spaced and hung up on the walls.

Rufus, the gardener, had brought Ruby, the maid, the loveliest flowers from the cutting garden, which Ruby had arranged in brightly colored earthenware pitchers throughout the room. The multicolored sprays posed a sharp contrast to the pristine orchids that had graced Sandrina's room in Brazil. And the brief comparison between flowers momentarily placed her back in Brazil, forgetting where, and even whom, she was.

The guest bath abutted the master bathroom, but rather than redoing it in marble and brass, as she had theirs, Pamela renovated the guest bathroom using inexpensive white tile.

Sandrina assumed she was alone in the house, but then she heard Thomas's voice through the bathroom wall. She felt like a burglar, and froze. She stayed still because she then heard quick footsteps on the stairs and shouting going on below.

"Ruby!" Thomas yelled from the bathroom. "There's no damn toilet paper."

"I'm coming," Ruby answered. Sandrina heard her scurrying until she finally found the stash of spares in the linen closet outside the guest room door. The antique walls were so thin that she could hear Ruby open the master bathroom door and toss a roll of tissue across the marble floor in the general direction of Thomas's voice.

"Damn it, Walter," Sandrina heard Thomas say. She wondered who Walter was, and what he was doing in the bathroom with Thomas, but quickly realized that Thomas was talking on the phone.

"I told you to shred the fucking documents and delete the e-mails. If you don't, I'll fire your ass and that whole uptight, white shoe accounting firm of yours."

There was a pause while she assumed Walter was responding. There was a loud flush.

"What noise?" Thomas asked. He flushed again.

Silence.

"I told you. This time it's the Feds, not just that moron reporter."

Pause.

"Don't tell me it's illegal. If you don't do it, Walter, I'm telling the Feds we followed your advice."

Suddenly, behind her, she heard Michael's voice.

"'Drina? What are you doing? Eavesdropping?"

"Shhh," she said, finger to her lips. "I just got here."

"I expected you to call —"

"You won't believe what I just overheard."

"You'll have to tell me later," Michael said. "I just saw Ruby on the stairs and she told me lunch will be served in five minutes."

Michael was wearing tennis whites, as was Pamela, while Thomas came to lunch in his bathrobe and his scrunched down brown socks, looking as though he had just woken up. Unshaven, with bags under his eyes, he looked sixty, although he was only four years older than Michael. He loathed physical activity of any kind, so his belly protruded as though he'd swallowed a basketball, although his arms and legs were quite slim. His hair was dark like Michael's, but his had started to thin, leaving a bald pate on top of his head.

Long-suffering Pamela had never been gainfully employed. Thomas had never permitted it. Even so, Sandrina thought Pamela worked harder than she did running TravelSmart because Thomas gave his wife tasks and orders as he would an army of paid employees.

Pam was perfectly coiffed, with colored ash-blond hair that she wore in a pageboy style. She was skinny, in a dissipated way, and must have been pretty once, long before she came into Sandrina's life. She wore white jeans, that had been ironed, with high heels, and a matching t-shirt with the double C logo emblazoned across her flat chest.

Over drinks one evening long ago, Pamela had confided in Sandrina that the pre-nuptial agreement Thomas had insisted that she sign required her to exercise four times a week or he could divorce her for free. Even worse, it stipulated that if they had a child he would get it; if they had had two, he would get first choice. Sandrina always suspected that the stipulation was why poor Pamela never conceived; it certainly would have deterred her if she'd been in Pamela's shoes.

Ruby had prepared a lunch of tuna salad with fresh pineapple. Rufus helped her serve and brought a small silver tray to the table with at least a dozen pills for Thomas and a miniature Long flower pot full of bran flakes for Pamela, which she sprinkled over her lettuce leaves. They ate quickly. Thomas, Michael, and Sandrina drank iced tea while Pamela managed to consume the carafe of Chablis all by herself.

"So, world traveler," Thomas said. "How was Brazil?" The fact that Sandrina and Michael's marriage had lasted so long, disproving Thomas's predictions, made him more curious about her goings-on with each passing year.

"It was very interesting," Sandrina replied. With Thomas, she gave as little information as possible. She never knew what his motive for asking could be.

"Do they have museums there?" Pamela asked.

"I'm sure they do," Sandrina replied. "But I didn't have time to visit any."

Every molecule of her being wanted to be in Brazil. She ached for the island of Paquetá, for the sweet salt taste of caipirinha, for the scent of wood shavings and hyacinth. The ocean breezes from the beach kept blowing her thoughts back to Brazil.

"Well, let's get to the point," Thomas said, breaking her reverie. Sandrina looked at Michael. He was studying a pineapple chunk intently. "We're not very happy with your handling of the *Finance Journal* investigation of Morgan Paper," he said.

"What?! I—" She kicked her husband under the table. Is this what she had been summoned for? She knew Thomas was lashing out at her because she was a convenient target — by the time she had gotten involved, the serious damage had been done.

"Now Thomas, as I told you earlier, Sandrina never wanted to touch it," Michael said, caution in his voice.

"I warned you that this kind of thing is not my forte; I specialize in building brands and markets, not crisis PR. If you recall, I suggested you hire an expert, like Joshua Baum," she said.

"That old coot! Never," Thomas said.

Michael tried to defend her. He really did. "What did you expect Sandrina to do, Thomas? You'd never listen to her advice anyway."

"Seeing as we're family," Thomas continued, calmer after his initial attack. "I wanted to tell you in person that you need to step up your involvement, meet with the reporter, find out his sources, and how much the paper knows. If you love my brother, you'll do whatever it takes. If you can't do at least that, then you're officially out."

"Are you threatening to fire me, Thomas? I don't remember ever sending you a bill for my time." Sandrina said coolly. She was furious at being treated like the hired help.

"Isn't there anything you can do, darling?" Michael asked.

The pleading sound in his voice tugged at her. They had no idea what they were asking her to do—snuff out a lit fuse with her bare hands.

"I'll try, for you Michael, but I have no idea how committed to this they are. Ken Larkin came to the *Finance Journal* from the *Wall Street Journal* last year; he's smart and a straight shooter but tough, and he has a name to make for himself," Sandrina said, thinking out loud.

"So you know him?" Michael asked, his face brightening with hope.

"Not personally—but he's a friend of Joshua's," she said, as she turned to face her brother-in-law, making sure he heard.

"What can I do to help?" Thomas asked.

"Don't lie to the reporter—he's bound to find out," Sandrina said. "And no more bribes!"

"I wouldn't think of it," Thomas replied, in his reptilian way.

Pamela rang her little silver bell, the one with the billy goat on top, signaling for Ruby to appear, which she did instantly. "We seem to be out of wine, Ruby."

"It's such a glorious day," Sandrina said. "And I'm stiff from the long flight. Do you and Thomas mind if Michael and I take a beach walk?"

Pamela looked at Thomas for permission to speak. He nodded once in her direction.

"Of course not, dear," Pamela said in her tiny voice, almost like a whisper.

"Thanks!" said Sandrina. She kicked off her shoes and took Michael by the hand.

After she was sure she had put enough distance between herself and her brother-in-law she asked, "Who's Walter?"

"Walter Schneider? He's the senior auditor on our account. Why?"

She told him what she had overheard. "Thomas is ordering your auditors to shred documents. Hasn't he ever heard of Enron?"

"I can't believe that—" Michael said when she was finished.

"I swear it's true. Do you know what this means? Michael, you could go to jail. This is criminal stuff. You should walk away. Resign on ethical grounds."

"Do you know what my stock will be worth in a few years when I'm fifty? If I leave now, it reverts to the other stockholder, Thomas. It's illiquid, 'Drina; we're a privately held company."

"It's only money, Michael—the easiest thing in the world to replace."

He was shaking his head. "Let's go back."

Sandrina stood facing him. She planted both feet in the sand and took his hands in hers. "If you won't do it for yourself, Michael, do it for me."

They stood so close she could see the white moons in his eyes. "Help me think of another idea, Sandrina. If you show me an alternative, it'll be easier to jump."

"I'd better think fast. I don't think we have much time. And to be completely honest, if the *Finance Journal* has two sources willing to confirm the facts, there's not a damn thing I can do to kill the story—I'd only make it worse for you if I tried."

When they returned to the house, Thomas was napping and Pamela was drunk. Michael and Sandrina tiptoed out to go back to the City without saying goodbye.

Family life is distinguished by patterns and routines, private nuances and dependable habits. It felt good to be home. As Sandrina recounted the details of her candomblé adventure, the abridged version, the whole episode started to seem like a distant dream.

Sandrina settled into her study to read the mail, pay the bills, and organize her thoughts for the next day. Sandrina turned on the communal desktop computer and logged on. And there it was, an e-mail from Warren:

"When will I see you again?"

The world stopped dead. With her finger on the delete key, her shoulders and neck cramped with indecision, she remembered what Thomas and Michael wanted her to do. Without concern for the consequences, she typed: "Send me your phone number. I'll call you tomorrow."

Delete. Delete. Delete.

Michael poked his head through the door. "How about a glass of wine?" he asked.

"Sounds good."

They sat side by side on the living room sofa. The perfect room, clad in its original wood paneling, each table laden with personal treasures and well-loved books, each candle resting comfortably in its sconce, was a stage set. Her eyes beheld the profusion of color and texture and inviting places to sit that she had so successfully designed.

They sipped their wine and stared into the fireplace, cold and empty this time of year.

"Michael. Tell me a secret."

"Like what?"

"Something. Anything. Just as long as you've never told it to me before."

He thought for several minutes. He considered her composedly, and then said, "Remember the guy Thomas and I bought the Oregon tree farm from? We had dinner with him once. He has completely deteriorated. Thomas told me he was arrested for driving drunk with his children in the car. A week later the police responded to a 911 call. He had wandered naked into the living room of his house with a hypodermic needle hanging from his arm. His eleven-year-old son made the call."

Sandrina forced a sad smile. That wasn't what she had meant. Where had their intimacy gone?

Later that evening, Sandrina and Michael lay side by side in bed, he reading *A Conspiracy of Paper* and she restless and on edge.

The sheets had been freshly laundered, expensive linens from Frette; they smelled sweet and felt satiny on her legs. Michael was wearing black pajamas with thin red stripes. He was still lean, although he had given up running for swimming. Warren, she remembered, was bulky and muscular. So different in so many ways.

"How's the book, Michael?"

"Hmmm? Did you say something?"

Placing her reading glasses on her nose, she surveyed the pile of books and magazines on the night table by her bed. She picked up *Vanity Fair* and then put it down. She looked at the ceiling, and then at the walls. Finally she took off her glasses and closed her eyes. Michael leaned over and kissed her hair. She felt Warren's lips instead.

With her eyes closed and the lights off, Sandrina felt for her husband under the covers. She started to play with him and felt him become erect in her hand. He reached over to find her wet and welcoming. He rolled over and entered her, as he had hundreds of times before, and moved gently inside her while stroking her with his fingers until she came. A few thrusts and grunts and he came too. It had been years since they'd kissed, or spoke, or completely removed their nightclothes. In the few minutes it took them to complete the act, Sandrina's mind flip-flopped back and forth between Michael and Warren, Warren and Michael. When she came, it was Warren's turn.

"Glad you're back, 'Drina," Michael said.

"Michael?" He was already snoring.

Sandrina couldn't sleep. She had started to see the cracks in the dam, the hairline weaknesses in her marriage. How hard she had worked, as she did on her make-up, to paint a pretty picture and to convince herself that her world was perfect. One choice would be to spackle over the faults, sand them smooth again, and try to hold the wall up so the dam wouldn't burst. Or she could let nature take its course. There was a big body of water out there that she could not see—a wave—trying to surge forward. It had momentum; Sandrina didn't think she could hold it back if she tried.

Chapter Eleven

It was a real conspiracy of paper that Sandrina returned to at the office on Tuesday morning. Beth had left her a fistful of phone messages to return and a stack of memos and letters. She saw her schedule for the day. It would be a busy one: a creative meeting at ten; lunch with her client, Gary Brent, at 12:30; a debrief with the Gaspar Hotels team at 3:00; a meeting about the Brenner's Park pitch at 4:00; a short recap on time sheets with the CFO at 4:45; and, cocktails at 5:30 at Joshua Baum's house on Sutton Place.

She booted up her computer. The phone number was there.

How could seven little numbers, innocently sitting there after a benign journey through cyberspace, cause a grown woman to flush from head to toe? Keeping the relationship encased in Brazil gave it a frame; if it continued in New York there was no telling where it could go or how it would end. Sandrina stood on a cliff overlooking a vast ocean of unknowns. She decided to take the plunge.

"If you're free," she e-mailed, "we could meet at the Kings Arms Bar on West 44th Street on Thursday at six."

Sandrina was so hypnotized by Warren's e-mail that she jumped when she heard a voice behind her.

"Sandrina, welcome back." It was Beth. "You look tanned."

"The weather was beautiful. Really hot."

"It was quiet here on Thursday and Friday. Holiday weekend and all." Beth studied Sandrina. "You look different. You're glowing."

"It's just the sunburn, Beth. And, maybe my makeup."

"Well, anyway, it's good to have you back."

As Beth left, Robert, one of the two men who worked at TravelSmart, came in to say hello. He was fashion-model handsome, and Sandrina suspected he spent his entire salary on clothes.

"Hi, Robert. Oops, one blue and one black," she teased.

"I knew you would notice. This morning when I put on my last two socks in the drawer, one blue and one black, I said to myself, 'Who'd notice, anyway?' Sandrina would, that's who."

"Don't worry. Your secret's safe with me. Leave a little early today so you can do your laundry," she said.

The office was buzzing like a hive. Phones were ringing, people were laughing, work was getting done, and fun was being had.

Isabel Riley popped her head in to welcome Sandrina back. "Good trip?" she asked.

"Great," Sandrina replied.

"Nice outfit," Isabel said.

"Thanks. By the way, did Jason cool down?"

"Nothing to worry about. The report is on your desk," Isabel said. They both regarded the four-inch pile.

Beth observed the exchange from the hallway. As Sandrina joined her, so that they could walk down the hall to the conference room together, Beth whispered, "I don't like her."

"Isabel? Since when?"

"There are things you don't see, Sandrina. When you're out of town she's in here looking at your photographs. No one else does that."

"Well, maybe she wants a family."

"She studies you too. The way you walk, talk, act, dress—"

Sandrina remembered Betty Halbreich, and secretly admired Isabel for aspiring to be pick up clues . "I don't know, Beth. Maybe she's just trying to learn. She's very pretty, and smart too, don't you think?"

"Ambitious is more the word I would use," Beth said.

"Tough life, Beth. Parents divorced. Grew up in several countries. Maybe she just wants to better herself?"

"Maybe. Lately she's been in early every morning," Beth said. "Before me."

So that was it. Beth was threatened.

"I listen. She's always talking to Jason or Max. Sucking up. She doesn't even work on that account," Beth said.

"She does now — I just haven't had a chance to tell you. I'm bringing her in, not only to SH but on other accounts as well."

"I never questioned your judgment before, Sandrina, but do you really think that's wise?"

"I need a number two, Beth. The travel is getting to me," Sandrina said. "Don't worry. She'll never replace you as my confidant."

Beth walked on, shaking her head.

Everyone was assembled in the conference room as Sandrina and Beth came in. "So, gang, what's first on the agenda?"

Lucy spoke up. "We've got this pitch next week at the Brenner's Park in Baden-Baden. We need an original approach. It will be a tough place to run press junkets because, well, the Black Forest is not exactly a sexy destination."

Victoria said, "What's special about the hotel and the town?"

"It's a beautiful hotel, at least from the brochures. And it's set in a park. The swimming pool is world-class; they built it inside a glass pavilion on the edge of the park. Apparently, in winter, guests can swim and watch the snow fall all around them," Lucy said.

"The town is really cool," Maria chimed in. "There's a casino, like the one in Monte Carlo, all-elegant, where ladies wear evening gowns and men sport tuxedos. Not tacky like Las Vegas or anything. There are these awesome old buildings with public baths, whirlpools, and massages. The Stephanie les Bains is a private clinic practically next door to the hotel where rich people go to lose weight. In late May and early June and then again in late August through September every year, the town hosts two famous horse races at its track—Spring Meet and Grand Week—and during the summer there are classical music festivals conducted in the open air."

"Focus on the marketing problem," Sandrina interrupted. "Ask yourselves: Why do they need us? What can we do for them? How can we show them a return on their investment if they hire us? They're in business to make profits. Remember that."

Maria said, "Well, Lucy's right. The destination is part of the problem. But also the long-term clientele's average age is about ninety-nine years old. The customers are dying off."

"Sounds like the Tides," Jenny said.

Sandrina caught Isabel out of the corner of her eye. She was taking in the discussion, but her mind was elsewhere.

"Isabel," Sandrina said. "What do you think?"

"About what?"

"About the new pitch."

Isabel smiled a winning smile, her even white teeth set in an ingenuous expression. Lately she had begun wearing her strawberry-blond hair in a style similar to Sandrina's. "I'm sorry. I'm so preoccupied with—" Isabel said.

"'Scuse me." It was Marguerite, the bookkeeper, sitting in the corner raising her hand like a schoolgirl.

"Marguerite, do you want to say something?" Sandrina asked. Ideas from unexpected sources were often the freshest.

"When I have my hair cut I sometimes read *Vogue* and *Harper's Bazaar* while I wait. Almost every travel article is about this spa or that. None of them are in glamorous locations. They're in places like San Diego or Phoenix or Tecate, Mexico. Why don't we play down the location and play up the all-inclusive spa angle."

"Now you're talking. We can target special spa packages to ladies of leisure. Who wants to walk around Bali or Cap d'Antibes with massage oil in your hair or goop on your face anyway?" Sandrina asked.

"Okay, I'm getting it," Maria and Lucy said in unison. They looked at each other and giggled.

"Get to work, guys, on a sampling of spa packages. Be creative. Maybe we can throw in Botox injections. Or private previews of the prêt a porté. Let's reconvene this afternoon at four to see what you've come up with," Sandrina concluded.

She updated everyone else on the Copacabana Palace and the tourism conference. Arnelle needed some additional contacts for an invitation list for Sharf and Rothstein's new hotel, the Millennium Universal.

"Arnelle, put your heart and soul in this one. Jason and Max have a lot riding on it. I'd hate to disappoint them."

Sandrina grabbed Isabel's elbow as she was about to slip out of the meeting. "So, Isabel, what happened at SH once I left the meeting?"

"Everything's fine. It's all in my report."

"Give me the bottom line," Sandrina demanded.

"The bottom line is...they're opening a hotel in Hawaii. They've hired a pre-opening General Manager, Kevin Clark, and a local PR person, Daisy Hana. As soon as the Millennium Universal opens they want one of us out there—"

"Hawaii?" Another trip halfway around the globe.

When everyone else had left the conference room, Sandrina casually asked, "Oh, Beth, speaking of spas, can you call Bliss and book me a facial and waxing with Natasha tomorrow after work?"

"No prob—" Beth replied

When Sandrina got back to her desk there was a message…from him: "I'll be there."

The intercom buzzed. It was Beth. "Sandrina. Your mother is on the phone."

"Sandy, I'm calling to see if we can have lunch this week." Only her mother called her Sandy. She hated it.

"I can't, Mom. I'm booked solid… I've got an idea, though. I'm going to Bliss tomorrow night. Why don't you join me? We can dish while our toes soak. Meet me there at six. I'll have Beth book you the usual."

"Splendid!" Sandrina's mother, Diana, replied.

Lunch with Gary Brent was scheduled at The China Grill, an enormous facility that looked more like a space station than a restaurant, with fan-like parasols suspended from the 30-foot ceiling to diffuse the glare from the overhead lighting. The food was exotic Eurasian, with dishes like Chinese rice noodles with calamari and veal spare ribs in orange sauce.

Gary Brent owned a vineyard on the West Coast, with the Alexander Valley Luxury Inn and Spa attached. He looked like a 1920s gangster with slicked back hair and a wiry mustache and goatee. He was short, quick, and used to getting his way. What he lacked in formal education he had learned in the competitive world of wine—a business that was not at all effete, as outsiders thought, but scrappy and underhanded, like any other.

He held a hundred dollar bill in the air to catch the eye of a passing waiter. "Bust this up for me, buddy, will 'ya," he said. Sandrina cringed.

"So, Gary, what's the problem?" she asked.

"I'm payin' your exorbitant fee on the first of every month or you shut me down. But you don't finish delivering services until the thirtieth," he said.

She could see his logic, but she knew from experience that if a client wanted to stiff her after delivery she couldn't exactly repossess the merchandise. When service hours were gone, they were gone.

"Gary, we bill monthly in advance because our services are contracted on an annual retainer basis," Sandrina explained.

"But you haven't delivered the month's services by the first," he argued.

"Gary, it is pro rata: one twelfth paid monthly of the agreed annual amount. We do not bill for actual hours expended on your behalf. If we did," she said with a spark in her eye, "your fee would be six times what it is. Retainer billing in advance is for cash-flow control. And it's standard in our industry."

"So you're not backing down?" he asked.

"'Fraid not," she said. With clients like Gary she had to stick to her guns.

"You're a tough cookie, Sandrina," Gary said.

"I know, Gary. So are you."

"Just want you to know that I'm really happy with the final press list for the junket next month," Gary said.

"Jenny did a good job. But of course the spa is always a draw, and a luxury for wine writers. Usually they stay in modest Bed & Breakfasts while reviewing a winery," Sandrina said.

"*Miami Herald, Los Angeles Times, Elle, Wine Spectator, W,*" Gary said, reciting from the list of acceptances. "It reads like a Who's Who."

Sandrina gleamed. "Well, hat's off to you, Gary. Love the new spa services—Merlot Massage, Chardonnay Cuticle Wrap, Pinot Noir Pedicure."

"They were your ideas," Gary said.

"I know. But ideas are a dime a dozen; it's the execution that counts." She gave the waiter her Platinum American Express card.

"Thanks for lunch, Sandrina."

"My pleasure."

Back in the office, she delighted in the first cut of the Baden-Baden spa packages her team had developed. Especially Baden-Baden Botox-ication.

"Great creative thinking," she told Lucy and Maria, who had assembled in her office. "I especially like the tie-ins with the casino and racing weeks, although the hotel is probably full during that time period. Can you call my friend Christoff Peipers? Tell him that you work for me. He handles PR for the town, and I just saw him in Rio. He can fact-check the dates and details."

"Do you know anyone else who can help?" Maria asked.

"Well…not sure if he's willing, but Michael's school friend's family owns the hotel."

"No kidding," Maria said.

"Sandrina knows everyone," Lucy said, beaming.

"One last thing. If you don't mind my saying, I think the tie-in with Italy called 'Spa-ghetti Week' is a bit over the top," Sandrina said.

On the way home, Sandrina stopped by Joshua Baum's house on Sutton Place. It was a wonderful early summer evening, just as it had been the first time she had seen it nearly two decades before. The ivy, thicker now than it had been then, was bright green with fresh leaves. All the doors and windows facing the East River were open, and a bar was set up in the garden. You could hear the chamber music playing as soon as you entered the front hall.

The Beechmans were there, and so were several other couples that Sandrina knew. There was an attractive music industry executive, around her age, with dark hair and blue eyes, who Joshua made a point of introducing her to while she paused in the hall to admire the Klimt.

"Robert Andrews, meet Sandrina Morgan," he said.

"Beautiful drawing, isn't it?" Robert Andrews asked.

"It's my favorite," she said, smiling.

"Are you a friend of Joshua's?" he asked.

"Forever. I've know him for nearly twenty years," Sandrina replied.

"Really? Was he attending your birth?" Another charmer. "I have only just met him myself," Robert continued. "I was just transferred here to be CEO of TransEuropa Records."

"Really? Are you happy with New York so far?"

"Well, I certainly prefer the sunny weather to London's infernal rain. The school thing is rather preposterous, though, don't you think? It's driving my wife dotty."

"How many children do you have?" Sandrina asked.

"Three. Noisy little buggers they are too. Bloody nuisances."

It was a British thing, to disparage one's own children, as opposed to Americans who exalted theirs.

"But I'd rather talk about you, Sandrina," he said.

"Me? What would you like to know?"

"Let's see...where were you on New Year's Eve?" Robert asked her.

"Are you asking me that because the waiter just refilled your champagne glass?"

"No. I am doing a private poll. I ask all beautiful women that question."

"Did you ask your wife?"

"No, I know where she was. Filling out school applications. Bloody, hell... "So where were you?" he said.

"Over the holidays I went skiing in Aspen. There is a restaurant nearby, in Snowmass. Well, a restaurant and a husky breeding farm—"

"Krabloonik's?"

"You've been there?"

"Yes." He laughed in a way that sounded like a fit of coughing. "I was bonding with my lead dog when he urinated all over my pants leg. I had to endure a two-hour sled ride with soaking wet trousers," Robert said.

"Sandrina," Joshua called.

"Excuse me," she said to Robert.

"Are you coming to the Avi Goldstein lunch on Friday? It should be great fun. It's to celebrate the success of his new book."

"Yes. I know. People even heard of it in Brazil—"

"That doesn't surprise me. It's an international bestseller," he said.

"Something tells me that you've had a hand in that," Sandrina said.

"As usual, dear, you're right," Joshua answered. "But remember...we are in the background, so no one must know."

"Yes, Professor," she said. "Anything else?"

"Yes, bring Michael, dear. I'm a man short. Remember what I taught you about balance."

She pulled him aside, under the stairwell, by the wall with the collection of nineteenth-century drawings.

"Joshua, I need to ask you something personal."

"Anything, dear. You know that."

"You've been married a long time— "

"Sixty years. I didn't get married, Sandrina. I got grafted."

"Joshua. Have you ever, you know, met someone else?"

"Does this mean you have?" Joshua squinted in a way that accentuated the crows' feet.

"I've met someone."

"How far has it gone?" he asked. But when she didn't answer immediately, he said: "Be careful, Sandrina. You had better let me meet him, and as soon as possible."

When Sandrina got home that night, Michael was in the kitchen eating leftovers. She asked him if he could come to Joshua's luncheon on Friday, but she knew he would have some excuse, because he had told her before that he considered Joshua's Balzac-esque salons to be frivolous.

"I'm not in the mood for chit-chat," he said.

Chapter Twelve

"Feel like chatting?" Sandrina asked Warren when she called him the next morning.

"With you, anytime," he said. "But I've had quite a morning. Clients complaining—"

"What do they complain about?" she asked. Sandrina believed in being customer-focused, listening to what they had to say.

"Usually fees. It's hard to differentiate our services in my business. My competitors are undercutting my prices—primarily Inns and Wins, a new upstart founded by two ex-Chaucer employees, and your friend John D'Angelo's Hotel Association of America. Let me ask you a question. Do you think a public relations campaign would help?"

She thought about it for a moment. "Sure," she said. "It could both increase bookings for your client hotels, as well as enhance Chaucer's image in the industry, attracting more members and increasing visibility. It would be a question of the cost and the potential return on investment, I suppose. It's more expensive than people think."

"How much?" he asked.

"At least a couple of hundred thousand." She heard him whistle.

"If I tagged a thousand dollars a year onto the marketing fees per property," he was calculating as he spoke, "I could create a budget of a couple of hundred thousand."

"Good luck. I can give you some names if you like."

"Thanks. Anyway, see you tomorrow…"

The Bliss Salon reminded Sandrina of the beauty factory in The Wizard of Oz. She felt as she imagined Dorothy must have when she finally left the dusty yellow brick road behind and had an army of clippers and buffers give her a makeover for her appointment with the great Oz himself. It was a respite from the pressures of her job, and the grittiness of the city that seemed to coat her skin with a fine film of soot every day.

Sandrina and her mother sat side by side soaking their feet, two working women after a long day. They sipped on their lemon water.

"I hate water, don't you?" Sandrina asked.

"I'd certainly rather have a glass of wine," Diana said.

"Shhh," Sandrina said, finger to lips. "That's a dirty word here. It dries the skin."

"So how was Brazil?"

"Pretty interesting. The hotel was gorgeous, the food was great, I went to a voodoo ceremony, and someone was shot on the grounds of my hotel—"

Sandrina saw that look on her mother's face. "What else?" Diana asked

"Isn't that enough for four days?"

"For a normal person, sure. Hmmm, what are you not telling me?"

"What makes you think — ?"

"Sandy, since you were a little girl I could always tell when you were withholding something. Remember when you didn't want to go to school and would hold the thermometer to the lightbulb?"

"You knew?"

"Um-hum. And that you flushed my cigarettes down the toilet — "

"To stop you from killing yourself!"

They were both laughing. The Park Avenue socialites on the bench across the way were appalled at such an overt display of emotion. Sandrina motioned for her mother to move closer. When she was within inches, Sandrina whispered: "I met someone."

"I knew it!"

"How? How could you know?"

"You look so beautiful. A woman in love always looks beautiful."

"Aren't you going to spank me? Tell me I'm awful. Remind me of my responsibilities, my husband?"

"Obviously I don't need to."

"The second I saw him, I knew."

"Are you in love?"

"Or maybe in lust."

"Well, which one is it?"

Sandrina thought about the things she and Warren had talked about, so easily. She had never felt so instantly close to someone in her whole life.

"It's love...I think."

"Well, congratulations. It's about time."

"A fine mother figure you've turned out to be."

"Oh, I'm not saying you should leave Michael. Being in love and having a successful relationship, a functioning marriage, is not necessarily the same thing. Hell, look at me."

"You were in love with him, weren't you?"

"You know what, Sandrina. I still am. We just couldn't live together."

"Why not?"

"I was the lover, he was the lovee—you're always one or the other, you know. I would have done anything for him. In the end I had to make a choice. Him or me. Him or...you, really."

"Couldn't he change? Stop the gambling, the drinking?"

"People never change, Sandy. Remember that. They are who they are. Anyway, my story is old news. Where does he live? Brazil?"

"He lives here."

"Uh-oh—that's a purse of a different color. Are you going to see him again?"

"Tomorrow. Do you think I should cancel?"

Diana yelped as the pedicurist cut her toenail too short.

"That's a tough one, Sandy. You have no scarcity of love in your life—a husband, friends, me. On the other hand—" She stopped.

"What?"

"I would love to see you find your soul mate in life."

"I thought you liked Michael."

"I do. He's good for you. That's not the same thing as love."

Sandrina picked up a bottle of red nail polish, the same hue as the Jeep in Brazil. "This one," she said to the lady working on her toes.

"I've watched you and Michael for fifteen years. He's stable, he's reliable. He doesn't drink, he doesn't smoke, he doesn't gamble, and I don't think he plays around, but I can't be sure—after all, he is a man. But my point is, instead of spending your life saving him, as most of us women do, you have built a business and a life. Sandy, you have been the rocket and Michael your launching pad."

"Do you think I couldn't have done it without him?"

"No. If you had been married to the other type you would have left. I don't think any man could have held you down."

Sandrina and her mother waddled over to the drying section. Two young women massaged their shoulders while they waited.

"Mom, don't you think it's possible to both be the lover and the lovee, to switch back and forth?"

"I've never seen it. Someone always seems to dominate," Diana said.

"What about Joshua and Esther Baum? They're in their eighties and they still hold hands."

"Age is a great equalizer, Sandy. Who knows who was in charge during the first fifty years of their marriage."

Sandrina thought about Joshua and Esther. She had always assumed they were happy. But other than them, she had to admit, her mother was right. She couldn't think of a single other couple she had known intimately who were equal.

"Just don't have sex with this man, Sandy. Sex is the power women hold over men. Once you go there, he's in charge."

She wondered if her mother noticed that her face matched her toes. "Oh, Mom, sometimes you're so old-fashioned."

Chapter Thirteen

On Thursday morning Sandrina carefully selected a classic-cut beige raw silk suit and a green cotton blouse that brought out the jade rings around her irises. She kept her jewelry simple and professional. Her legs were freshly waxed and her skin fully exfoliated so she wore little makeup and no pantyhose. Her Jeep-red toes posed a jarring contrast to the otherwise conservative package. She wore the tiniest black thong panties she owned and a matching bra with a small pad built in to give her just the right amount of lift to make her breasts look thirty instead of forty-one.

"So what's on your agenda for today?" Michael asked, looking her up and down.

"The usual. Meetings, phone calls—starting with the *Finance Journal* in just a few minutes. I may be home late. I'm meeting a prospective new client at six. Don't know how long it will take. I'll call."

Ken Larkin's secretary had instructed Sandrina to phone his office at seven sharp. He was a no-nonsense editor who agreed to speak with her only as a favor to Joshua, whom he had known during his 20-year tenure at the *Wall Street Journal*. Despite repeated requests for him to call her by her first name, Ken Larkin persisted in addressing her as Ms. Morgan. He politely but firmly informed her that he had nothing to say to her regarding the piece the *Finance Journal* was developing on Morgan Paper and that unless she had some new revealing information to share, she shouldn't bother calling him again.

"I'm not sure that I have anything new to tell you, although I might be able to make sense of the information you already have."

"No good, Ms. Morgan; that would entail my disclosing to you the depth of our knowledge."

Darn. "How about the source? How reliable is your source?"

"Sourc-*es*, Ms. Morgan. They are quite credible."

Double darn. "Can I at least take you to lunch? There may be some information we can swap—" She couldn't believe she just said that, or that she would put her reputation at risk.

"Are you suggesting—?"

"Yes. A trade. Morgan Paper is a sardine compared to some of the big fish I know."

"Do I hear you right? Are you trying to bribe me?

Bribe was not the word she would have used. Her whole professional life had been based on sharing information. But Ken Larkin was right, in this case, and he made her feel dirty.

"No, of course not. Just trying to be helpful…quid pro quo, tit for tat."

"Oh, is that what you call it? I'm not interested."

"And, my husband…can I convince you to at least listen to his side of the story?"

"Tell him to call me the day he resigns. Then I may believe what he has to say about Old MacDonald and the family farm." Ken Larkin hung up the phone.

The rest of the day dragged on. There were surprisingly few phone calls, probably because Memorial Day marked the official beginning of summer, with its vacations and general business malaise. It gave her more time to brood over Michael's situation and how impossible it had become.

Isabel came in to tell her about the meeting she had scheduled with Jason and Max.

"I hope you don't mind?" Isabel asked her.

"Not at all. It was a good idea."

"I have great news. They approved the proposal yesterday. I'm really excited. When can you read it?"

"When did you give them a proposal?"

"While you were in Brazil."

"Without my having seen it?"

"Sandrina, I thought that's what you wanted me to do. Move fast. Cover for you. Make the client happy. It was all in my report."

The one Sandrina still had not had time to read. "Of course," she said. "You're right. Let me read the proposal."

After Sandrina read Isabel's plan she wished she had been available to intervene. It was competent and well organized, but there wasn't an original thought in the entire 30 pages. And she knew that if SH had any hope of succeeding in an entirely new market segment, they would need serious differentiation. Otherwise, not only would the project fail, but also they could undermine their existing stellar reputation, which they had all worked so hard to establish over the past 19 years.

When they arrived she told them so.

"Interesting point of view," Max said. "What do you suggest we do?"

"I've done a little research. It seems the Aloha and the Halekulani hotels are the leaders in that market. I propose we study them, discover what they are doing wrong, and position the new property against their gaps," Sandrina said.

"Do you have any specific ideas?" Jason asked. She could tell he was eager to move fast.

"Not yet. But I just know that we've got to find a niche, something the other resorts have missed."

"Excellent!" Jason said. "Right after the Millennium Universal opens we'll get you on a plane to — "

Sandrina slumped. Her enthusiasm seemed to have gotten her into another trip. Without thinking she offered: "My travel schedule for the next few weeks is a killer. Maybe Isabel could go? I could stay in touch by phone—"

"No, Sandrina," Jason said. "You."

Max said, "We like your Isabel, don't misunderstand—"

"But if we wanted Isabel, we would have hired Isabel," Jason said. He raised his voice. "It has to be you."

The Kings Arms Hotel on West 44th Street between Fifth and Sixth Avenues used to be a welfare residence owned and operated by the City of New York. The Times Square area had become increasingly seedy over the years and Max Sharf and Jason Rothstein picked the hotel up for a song. They sunk in $62 million of investors' money to renovate it, substituting style in the place of luxury, just as the neighborhood began to gentrify.

Unlike the Pierre or the Park Lane, which had installed semi-precious materials in their guest rooms, the SH development budget favored sheet rock and glue. What differentiated their hotels from more opulent competitors was a unique and trendy signature, like stainless steel basins in the bathrooms, apple holders in every suite and all-white bedding. And they had Sandrina.

From the outside, the Kings Arms was a rather nondescript gray stone edifice. It was hard to distinguish from the other similarly dated buildings on the block, including The Harvard and Century Clubs. But once inside these gathering places the experiences were completely different. The serious established private clubs were all dark wood and red leather; the upstart Kings Arms was friendly, light, and welcoming.

Sharf and Rothstein's architect worked with the designer Jean-Yves Rotundo to turn a long, narrow lobby into a personal living room, with overstuffed seating arrangements conducive to conversation. The space had been opened up by making the ceiling double-height and by adding mirrors to one wall, which ran from the entrance to the Pesce restaurant, leased to a young chef trained by Jean-Georges Vongerichten.

The people populating the lobby of the Kings Arms were young and fashionable, in jarring contrast to the stuffy businessmen reading their *Finance Journals* in the clubs across the street. Here iPhones were whizzing every other second, while in the lobbies of the neighboring clubs cell phone usage was strictly not allowed. It was a fine example of new New York versus old New York.

Everybody knew Sandrina at the Kings Arms, and it occurred to her when she walked in at five minutes to six that a hotel owned by one of her clients might not have been the best meeting place for a tryst. The equation of convenience plus denial seemed to result in indiscretion.

"Hi, Sandrina," said Oscar the doorman. "You look great. Should I call Mr. Sharf? He's in his office. Is he expecting you?"

"No, Oscar. I'm off-duty. I'm having a drink with a friend."

She chose a cozy corner near the bar and settled into a goosedown armchair upholstered in white duck. Mary, the bartender, sent over a Cosmopolitan, without having to be asked. Sandrina instructed Jerry, the waiter, to bring a Grey Goose vodka martini, with a twist, for her guest, who would, she explained, be arriving soon.

Sandrina saw an old colleague from *Journey* sitting at the bar. They waved. It looked as though he was interviewing someone for his *Seen in New York* column. It's good that he's here, she thought. Good publicity for the hotel.

Sandrina saw Oscar identify her location for Warren. Like the point of a compass, she stayed focused directly on him, held there by magnetic attraction, as he approached her. He was wearing a casual shirt that sashayed around his body as he walked, the easy gait underscoring his undiluted self-confidence. He noticed the martini, and smiled as he sat down and took a sip.

"You think of everything," he said.

"I only wish I could," she responded, coquettishly.

He laughed. A lion's roar. She felt her edges soften, like the blurry outlines on a watercolor painting.

"Listen, Sandrina. I have an idea of how to put your talents to use." She wondered which talents he had in mind. "I want to hire your company to do public relations for Chaucer Suites."

"Really?" She was hoping he wouldn't go there. "What do you hope to accomplish by that?"

"Does that mean you're not interested?"

"I'm always interested in new business. Thinking conflict of interest, that's all."

"The idea for a public relations campaign for Chaucer has been lurking for a while, but until I met you I couldn't work out how to implement it—it's not the idea but the execution that counts." He sounded just like her.

"We seem to think alike," she said wryly.

"As I told you, my business is a parity product. Several new competitors—not just Inns and Wins—are springing up offering the same things—central reservations, brochure production, trade show representation, advertising, et cetera. My idea was original ten years ago, but now lower-priced competitors are moving in on what was previously exclusive territory." He paused to drain his glass and signal for another martini.

"It's the classic B-school case. As soon as the first-mover builds the market and his rewards increase, competitors enter the market. It's called ceteris paribus in economics parlance," Sandrina explained.

"Literally, 'others alike' in Latin," he said.

"I didn't know that," Sandrina said.

"Well, I didn't know about ceteris paribus, so we're even." His eyes were so alive, his smile charming. "What happens afterwards?"

"If the first-mover doesn't do something to defend his position or differentiate his product, or if the demand doesn't increase in proportion to the supply of new firms, then the price keeps dropping. Eventually, price and cost meet and nobody is making any money. In micro-economics they call it 'perfect competition,'" she said.

He looked impressed. "They should call it 'stupid competition.'"

"Obviously the market can't stay like that. Some firms drop out; others try to form cartels; yet others rely on the high cost of entry to maintain a low-profit margin among a limited number of competitors. That's how commodities operate, like steel, soybeans, and *paper*..." Her voice trailed off.

"You're proving my point. Let's get back to Chaucer for a minute. First, I'd like to help solidify our position with existing clients," he continued, hardly missing a beat. "Then, I've always wanted to expand into new markets beyond the U.K.; Brazil for instance, if you remember…" She remembered vividly. "…So I need help establishing a presence in other geographies. And, third, I want to upgrade the image of what we do. Underscore the value of our services to our customers. *De*-commoditize."

A man with a plan, she noted. She wanted to ask "what about us" but decided to play it cool. "All of that is a tall order. But, I'm game. I need to know more about your company, your clients. I'm kind of brain dead after six p.m. When can we talk further about this?"

"How about Monday?" he asked.

"I can't. I'm leaving Sunday night for Baden-Baden."

"What a coincidence! I'm Europe bound too, due in London on Thursday. Why don't I meet you in Germany before?" He moved closer when he said it.

Discreetly pressing the mute button on her Blackberry, she said, "Yes, I think that could work."

"Good," he said. "It's settled." He ordered another round—her second, his third—and relaxed into the sofa on her right. She watched his expression soften and his eyes rove her face, hair, and neck. She remembered how she had responded when he kissed her neck. Her muscles turned to jelly.

"Warren—"

"Yes—"

"Is this just a business meeting? I mean, what do you want?"

Her question changed his mood. He got very quiet, almost withdrawn. "I wish I knew, Sandrina, I wish I knew. When I'm with you I want one thing; then I come to my senses and know better. The only thing I know that I want right now is food. Are you free for dinner?"

"Maybe. Wait here. I need to make a call."

When she returned from the ladies' room, with fresh lipstick and a blush of guilt across her cheeks for leaving Michael a message that her meeting was running late, she said, "Where to?"

"I hear the food here is great. I booked us a table while you were visiting the WC."

Sandrina swallowed hard, but she followed Warren down the stairs to the restaurant. The three house-like rooms had low-beamed ceilings and distressed wooden floors with hand-hewn plugs and uneven planks. Some of the walls were still composed of the original exposed gray stone from the underbelly of New York, spiffed up and regrouted to look like some chic new tile design. The aureate lighting gave off a cozy glow.

"Dinner or cocktails?" the maitre d' asked Sandrina.

"A little bit of both. But we'd like to sit at the bar," Warren answered.

The host looked surprised and glanced at Sandrina for approval, but he finally led them up a couple of steps to a room with five or six tables and a long bar made of solid oak. The bartender looked like a moonlighting accountant, with boyish blond hair and spectacles, so different from the usual unemployed actor type Jason and Max tended to hire.

"One vodka martini, Grey Goose, very cold with a twist, and a Cosmopolitan for the lady," Warren said.

"I forgot to thank you for the book, the one you left with the concierge," Sandrina said.

"Did you like it?"

"I loved it. But, I was wondering, was there a hidden message I was meant to decipher?"

"I thought of it when we first met. How ripe you were to being seduced, corrupted. I was right, wasn't I?"

"Is that what you think this is about?"

"Not completely. But I'm not sure. I have asked myself, 'Is she a free spirit? Or an unhappy wife? If it wasn't me, would it have been somebody else?'"

"Did you take advantage of me? Are you a seducer, as you say, Screwtape and the City? —"

"Absolutely. But I'm also a little in love with you. Anyway, as I recall, you did the seducing."

She felt her cheeks get hot. "I'm starving, let's order," she said, changing the subject. She plucked the lemon peel out of his glass and chewed.

Warren lifted the menu off the bar and ordered a feast of Sandrina's favorite foods: focaccia with olive oil and mushrooms, arugula salad, and gnocchi with a creamy sauce. How could he have known? He had never asked her. He could only have read her mind, she concluded.

"Bartender, a bottle of Gavi di Gavi, please," he said.

A drop of olive oil from the focaccia started to roll down her chin but before she could catch it with her tongue Warren wiped it off with his fingertip.

"What was it like to go home, after Brazil," he asked. "What did you feel?"

She studied him, trying to decide if she should tell him or not. "At first I was nervous, to see my husband again, after what happened between us. Then I was surprised at how easily I fell back into the familiar rhythms. I love him too. That's the odd thing. And, I know he loves me," she replied. Warren wasn't really listening. He was dreamy. Watching her.

"What are you thinking about?" she asked.

"I am thinking what beautiful hair you have, and what your ears would look like if you pulled it back. And what it would feel like to touch them, your ears, with my tongue," he said. "I just have to know that what I feel for you isn't only lust. This kind of sexual heat makes men think all kinds of things, makes them make mistakes. You are matinta pereira, remember? I don't want to be wrong. There are too many things at stake. Too many times—"

Suddenly, Sandrina was afraid that if she allowed him to go down a trail of negativity she would lose him.

"I have a friend, Joshua Baum," she interrupted. "He's having a lunch tomorrow. Would you like to come with me?"

"Is Joshua in love with you too, Sandrina?"

"God, no. In fact he always tells me he's at the age where he can't take 'yes' for an answer. And he's been using that line for nearly twenty years!"

He roared. "If he's that funny, and if I can spend another couple of hours with you, I'd love to come." As he spoke he slid his hand up her skirt and stroked her thighs. She tightened them reflexively, terrified that Max or Jason might walk in.

"Strong," he said.

A party of four sitting at one of the bar room tables very close to them was staring. Sandrina smiled at them, embarrassed by her and Warren's open display. One of the men blurted out an apology.

"It is almost impossible to look in your direction and not stare," he said.

"Isn't she gorgeous," Warren said.

"Breathtaking," said the other.

"Thank you," said Sandrina. "Are you from out of town?"

"We work in the garment center."

"Same thing," Warren whispered.

There was one woman at the table. She stated, "You're not married. To each other. Are you?"

Warren was highly charged when he asked, "How do you know? How do you know we're not married to each other?"

The woman shook her head. Her entire facial expression changed, as if she had just swallowed a bad oyster and knew it would make her sick but it was too late to do anything about it. When the foursome got up to leave, the men shook hands with Sandrina and Warren but the woman disapprovingly glared.

Alone again, Warren and Sandrina's conversation escalated to a new level of intimacy.

"Where does this duality come from? You are so powerful and so vulnerable at the same time," he said.

"You are one of the few to detect the vulnerable part."

"Why would you want to hide it?"

"Powerful is less vulnerable than vulnerable is powerful," she replied.

The hours passed quickly then they were finally ready to leave when he left her, momentarily, by the door while he went back to the bar to retrieve something he had forgotten. When he returned, he came up behind her and put his arms around her waist from the back and pressed his body up against her. She could feel him hard against her buttocks through the thin fabric of her skirt. He kissed her neck, in front of everyone.

"I've never come this close," he said. "To loving someone. I'm terrified."

"Of what?" she asked. She turned and met his lips.

"Of losing control. Of losing..."

As soon as Sandrina walked into the apartment she could see that Michael was upset. He was standing there, in his racing stripe pajamas, in the hall; he had come downstairs when he heard her fumbling with her key in the front door.

"Where have you been?" he demanded.

"I left a message on your voice mail. Didn't you get it?"

"Yes, you said you had a meeting. But it's late and you've been drinking."

"And, I'm very tired. I told you I had to see a new client. Can we discuss this in the morning?"

"Why didn't you answer your cell phone?"

"I didn't hear it ring."

"Who were you with?"

"It was a new business thing. Really, Michael, I need to go to bed—"

He was visibly shaken. "Sandrina, you look drunk—"

"Michael, you'll be much more interested in this: I spoke with Ken Larkin this morning—Joshua arranged it. The *Finance Journal*'s got more than one source, but I couldn't get Larkin to reveal what information they've compiled—"

Michael shook his head. "When it rains, it pours."

Sandrina fell into bed with the alcohol mixing up her thoughts like a spiked fruit salad. Startled by her husband's acuity and obsessed by her attraction to Warren, soon she'd have to sort things out.

Was it too late? She felt her world spinning out of control, gathering speed as everything merged toward the vortex of sleep, where she had dark dreams too alarming to remember.

Chapter Fourteen

If only Michael had embraced the idea of a child. Would she be in love with Warren then? If she'd had a baby, would she have even been interested in him to begin with?

She stumbled out of bed into the bathroom. Bleary, bloodshot eyes stared back at her from the mirror.

The television in the background considerately informed her that it would be a hot day. Today was Joshua's lunch. She had to remind herself to call and tell him that she would be bringing Warren, not Michael, as he would expect.

Sandrina selected a pink dress with aqua trim, made of a stretchy material that clung in all the right places. She had shoes and a purse, just the same hue as the aqua in her dress, and her earrings were the color that would have resulted if computer paint matching software had perfectly blended her eyes with her pocketbook. She atomized herself with Calvin Klein's *Contradiction* and let out a sigh wrought with conflict.

"Another meeting?" Michael asked her, sarcastically, when he passed her in the kitchen.

"Not tonight, Michael. Not tonight. I'll be home for dinner. I promise."

* * *

The office was unusually quiet. A couple of people were traveling for clients and others took Friday off so that they could enjoy their Hamptons or Fire Island summer shares. She waved to this one and that, casting her warm smile, making them feel part of a family rather than just a company.

She picked up the phone and dialed. While it was ringing Beth walked in with an array of roses in a vase. They were from Michael. The card simply said, "I love you. Thanks for trying to save Morgan Paper."

Someone picked up on the other end, but she was so diverted by the flowers and Michael's message that she forgot whom she had called.

"Baum residence, may I help you?" Stewart's clipped English accent.

"Hi, Stewart. It's Mrs. Morgan. Is Mr. Baum at home?"

"Yes, Madam. He's in the study. Hold the line please."

The study was Sandrina's favorite room in Joshua's house. It was a small, square room off the foyer just to the left of the front hall. It had a wood-burning fireplace and beautiful, original dentil moldings painted a tobacco faux bois finish. The walls were covered in red damask. The room smelled like a blend of old cedar and eucalyptus, from an always replenished bowl of shavings on

Joshua's desk, angled so that Joshua could see exactly who entered his domain before being seen.

"Sandrina, good morning! How did it go with Larkin?" Joshua asked.

"Not well; he was curt and intransient on the subject of Morgan Paper," she replied. "And I slipped, Josh. I offered to trade him information."

"What kind of information?"

Lowering her voice, she said: "Bad stuff about other people if he'd just let Michael go."

"What have I always told you about integrity?" he chastised. "And of all people—Ken Larkin. When I called him he expressed doubt about the motives and veracity of any member of the Morgan family. Don't forget, his people have uncovered some pretty dirty dealings—"

"But Michael's innocent, Joshua. He wouldn't hurt a fly."

"That may be, but if Larkin smells blood he'll behave more like a mosquito than a fly. Remember, that's the nature of the beast."

"Do you think if I can convince Michael to resign Larkin will spare his reputation?"

"Why would you think that?"

"That's what Ken Larkin implied."

"If you read him right, I suppose it's possible. After all, if Michael's willing to walk away from ill-gotten gains, it'll be easier to convince Larkin and others that he had no part in the ill-getting."

"Then I'll start working on that right away."

"Good. I'll be sure to follow up with Larkin myself shortly. You're still coming to the party, aren't you?

"Are you expecting a lot of people?"

"Well, let's see. There's the official guest of honor, Dr. Avi Goldstein, and his wife, Barbara. Felicia Taylor, you remember her, don't you? Pretty, used to be on CNBC with Maria. Peter Rogers from Goldman Sachs, Florence Fabricant from the *New York Times*, two couples whom you don't know and you, our unofficial guest of honor, and Michael—"

"Um, actually, Joshua, that's the real reason for my call. Michael couldn't make it today, so I took the liberty of inviting another friend to round out your table."

"Oh, really. Who is he, my dear?"

"His name is Warren Waterhouse. I met him recently through business."

Silence.

"Is he the one, Sandrina?"

"Which one, Joshua?"

"The one, Sandrina. The one you mentioned the other evening."

More silence. Eighty-two and sharp as a tack, she thought.

"Yes."

As soon as Sandrina entered the foyer of the Baum house before the party, she heard voices coming from the landing at the top of the stairs. She smiled as she listened to Joshua and Esther Baum exchange a kiss as Josh's wife of 60 years passed him traveling up the center stairs on her electric seat while he carefully walked down, one step at a time.

"Stewart tells me we are entertaining again, dear," Esther said.

"Stewart is accurate as usual," Joshua replied. Sandrina peeked around the banister and saw a playful smile lift the ends of his dove-gray handlebar mustache.

"Third time this week if my ancient memory serves me well," she said.

"You miss nothing, as always."

"Anyone I like coming this time?" Esther asked.

"Sandrina will be here. I'll send her up to your sitting room if she arrives early enough. I know how fond of her you are," he said. At this, Sandrina could not suppress a grin.

"Oh, yes. Quite. Well, have a nice luncheon party, Josh."

"Thank you, dear. I am sure we will."

Joshua Baum's wife was eighty-two, like him. She had long ago given up on hosting and attending Joshua's endless parties. Her interests gravitated more toward watching the History Channel with her motley collection of seven cats, all of which she found in various states of suspended survival on or near Sutton Place. She and Sandrina got on very well, actually, largely because Sandrina had a passion for animals of all sorts. Every Valentine's Day, Sandrina sent a catnip mouse to each of Esther's cats, which made her quite popular with Joshua's wife indeed.

Esther's abhorrence of human socializing, however, often led to Sandrina playing hostess at Joshua's soirées, a role she relished and was quite adept at. Anticipating Joshua's expectation that she should be there to cast her charms over his guests as they arrived, she came precisely 30 minutes early. She briefly paid her respects to Esther and her feline entourage—Catherine, Golda, Thatcher, Josephine, Elizabeth I, Elizabeth II, and Mata Hari.

"You are the original admirer of powerful women," Sandrina said, as she scratched Josephine behind the ears.

"That's why I like you, dear," Esther said. Then Sandrina went back downstairs to confer with Stewart about the seating chart. She interviewed him about the couples who were coming whom she did not know and learned that the Sperlings lived in Palm Beach but kept a pied à terre at The Carlyle and that the Ransoms lived in Greenwich but had an apartment at Trump Tower.

"Pardon, Madam," Stewart asked while reviewing the guest list. "And who exactly is Mr. Waterhouse?"

It was a normal question for him to ask under the circumstances, but Sandrina realized she could not really give him an apt reply.

"He is a new friend of mine, Stewart."

"Next to whom shall we seat him?"

"Next to me. And on the other side ..." she thought for a moment "...next to the most unattractive woman we expect, Stewart."

Stewart raised a haughty eyebrow. The door chimes sang again, and Joshua magically appeared with a glass of champagne for her and another for himself. He linked arms with his protégé, and they received the first guests, Martin and Charlotte Sperling, together.

"Welcome!" Joshua said. "We have ordered Florida weather in New York in your honor."

"So it seems. I actually think it's cooler in Palm Beach today than it is here," Charlotte said, mock-fanning herself with her hand.

"Ah, perhaps. But I'm sure you will find the company here more engaging," Joshua said.

"Is this your lovely wife?" Martin asked. A 40-year age difference did nothing to deter Martin Sperling's presumption that they could be married.

"Oh heavens, no," Joshua said. "Allow me to introduce my charming friend, Sandrina Morgan."

"A pleasure," Sandrina said.

While Sandrina was sizing up the Sperlings—Charlotte an attractive bleached blonde in her late forties with a tight, boyish body and Martin a pear-shaped but very bright and funny shopping center developer—Florence Fabricant arrived and, right behind her, as if on the same gust of wind, Warren Waterhouse.

"Hello, Sandrina. You look marvelous. It's been years," Florence said.

"It's wonderful to see you again. Florence, meet Warren Waterhouse. Warren represents quite a few hotels in the U.K. Warren, Florence, as you know I'm sure, is a famous food writer. And, a divine cook, I might add," Sandrina said.

Warren said hello to Florence; then he couldn't help but look around. The Baum residence was like a small museum. "This place is amazing," he said.

Sandrina took his hand. "Come. Let me show you something. It's a drawing by Gustav Klimt." They stood before *Woman in Profile* in awe.

"What is she hiding, I wonder," he said, staring at the blue figure.

Sandrina looked at the drawing. "Hiding? I think her expression is quite open."

"She lets you see only half of who she is, Sandrina," Warren said. "That half is beautiful, I agree. But the side we don't see is more intriguing."

While Sandrina was trying to figure out Warren's meaning, Stewart arrived with a silver tray laden with four champagne glasses, one each for the Sperlings, Warren and Florence. Warren turned to join the group.

Joshua joined them to report that the wonderful smell coming from the kitchen was lunch cooking.

Warren leaned over toward Sandrina and whispered into her ear. "Matinta pereira." She felt his torrid words on her neck, lingering in her hair, like seeds blown from a dandelion looking to take root. Sandrina looked up at him, into his eyes. The gold flecks were teasing her. She felt her panties get moist. Just as she was trying to think of a snappy comeback, Charlotte slinked over to be near Warren. Warren turned his attention to her.

Peter Rogers and Dale and John Ransom arrived just a few moments before the famous Dr. Avi Goldstein and his wife, Barbara. Stewart made sure everyone had a filled glass and continued to keep them full to the brim with Taittinger Comptes de Champagne rosé. As the surrogate hostess, Sandrina greeted the Ransoms and introduced all of the guests to one another. Joshua purloined the Goldsteins and took them on a private guided tour of the house.

Sandrina had known Peter Rogers for nearly 20 years, and he had been infatuated with her, from afar, for most of them. Six foot five, dark and swarthy, Peter came from a wealthy New York family and married into an even wealthier one. When Sandrina first met him, at one of Thomas and Pamela's summer parties in the Hamptons, he was already married.

But for at least the whole first year of their acquaintance, Sandrina saw him only with his mistress, Renée, who wore fishnet stockings with seams in the back and had a raspy voice and Mona Lisa smile. It came as quite a surprise, later, when Sandrina met Judy, Peter's wife. Beautiful, poised, and a natural redhead, with a petite but perfect figure, she outclassed the mistress by a mile. Go figure.

"Sandrina, when are you leaving Michael and running away with me?"

"You wouldn't want me, Peter. My IQ is too high."

"We wouldn't have to have conversations."

"Peter, have you met Dale Ransom?"

Dale was an extremely tall brunette with a regal air. Her Amazon-like appearance belied an extraordinarily gentle and magnanimous nature that she managed to convey in her carriage. She exuded warmth and acceptance, contentment surrounding her like a halo.

"Hello, Peter. Nice to see you. A beautiful house, isn't it? I'm always amazed to find a real home in Manhattan," Dale said.

Sandrina left Dale with Peter, spotted John chatting with Florence and the Sperlings, and felt Joshua take her elbow and guide her to the study, where Warren, Dr. Goldstein, and Dr. Goldstein's highly verbal wife were talking.

"Avi, Barbara, you have not yet properly met our other guest of honor, Sandrina Morgan," Joshua said.

"And, Joshua, you have not yet been introduced to my new friend, Warren Waterhouse," Sandrina said.

Joshua studied Warren intently. Sandrina saw him register every detail, from the cracked button on Warren's cuff to the stockiness of his physique. She could tell that Warren's easy manner and air of self-confidence disarmed Joshua, whom she knew usually associated those qualities with a more polished persona. He had a quizzical expression on his brow as he was trying to place the accent, American with a twinge of Brit.

"Warren has just been telling us about your voodoo adventure in Brazil," Avi said. Joshua gave her a look at once disapproving and curious.

"Very Jungian, dear. I believe we all need to go back to our primal beginnings to achieve true psychological enlightenment," Barbara said.

Sandrina caught Joshua's eye.

"Barbara, allow me to introduce you around," Joshua said. Sandrina and Warren exchanged a touch of fingers that lasted a fraction of a second but communicated a world of mutual relief.

"Did Warren also tell you that your book was being discussed in Rio?" Sandrina asked.

Avi looked at Warren. "I would have if I had known," Warren said. He shrugged, reminding Sandrina that he had been absent from that conversation. Her memory of Brazil, after the fact, was that he had been everywhere, that he was everything, the true lasting experience.

"Tell us, Avi, what do we need to know about relationships. Are men from Mars and women from Venus?" Sandrina asked.

"Not really. Well, most are. But mature people of both sexes have the same deep emotional needs. We all need to be loved and understood."

"I haven't had a chance yet to read your book. I guess I'm waiting for an autographed copy. But in Brazil I remember that one of your devotees was discussing something about grooves in a record," Sandrina said.

Avi was wiry and intense, with a thick mane of silver hair that crested like an ocean wave.

"Let me try to explain. I see from your ring that you are married," Avi said.

"Yes —"

"For how long, may I ask?" Avi asked.

"Fifteen years," Sandrina replied. She was beginning to regret having started this conversation.

"And you?" Avi asked Warren.

"Divorced," Warren said.

"And I ask you both, why did you choose your spouses?"

"For breeding," Warren said.

"Good question. Security ... safety maybe?" Sandrina replied.

"Well, I ask you, Warren, now that you know what you do, would you marry a second time for breeding? And, Sandrina, does the woman you are today need to be protected like the girl who married for safety?"

"I don't know," Sandrina said.

"If I may be so bold, but I do have a lot of experience in this area, the grooves in your record have been filled."

"Like a CD?" Sandrina asked.

"Yes, like a CD. I predict you would now marry someone just like you — passionate, fearless, and strong."

"You can tell that just by talking to her for five minutes?" Warren asked.

"Yes, can't you?"

"Luncheon is served," Stewart interrupted.

"I'll send you the book," Avi said.

The lunch was magnificent. Eight tiny mouth-watering courses beginning with asperges verts avec émulsion de truffe noire, followed by foie gras de canard des Landes, bar de ligne a la diable, volaille de Bresse en chapelure, agneau de lait des Pyrénées a la Florentine, fromages et poires and two desserts, a composition forte en chocolat and a clémentine de Corse en coupe refraîche. Each portion was little more than a mouthful.

"It's delicious, every taste is as satisfying as a feast," John said.

"Have you ever seen such tiny lamb chops?" Dale asked.

"The size of a finger, really," Peter replied. "And the cheeses—did he smuggle them in?" "Shhh, he probably did," Florence added. "Most cheeses sold in America have the flavor pasteurized and homogenized out."

"That's why they taste nuked," Martin said.

"And what do you do?" John asked Barbara to be polite. He had not realized that he was opening a floodgate that would enable her to rattle on endlessly about her own theories on the psychology of artists.

"I'm an art dealer. But I'm especially interested in what motivates the artists," she said.

"Motivates?" Charlotte asked.

"You know, inspires. For example, I figured out why Georg Baselitz paints upside down—" Barbara said.

"He paints drunk?" Warren guessed. Maybe he was wondering if he had a future in art.

"No." She clearly did not like being interrupted now that she had the floor. "His mother, who became pregnant again immediately after he was born, nursed him with his legs over her head so he wouldn't weigh on her stomach," Barbara explained smugly.

Warren rolled his eyes, and Martin laughed out loud.

"It's true," Barbara said. "I heard it from a very reliable source, who heard it from Baselitz himself."

"Do you have any thoughts on why Edvard Munch's screamer screams," Dale asked to show support.

"Because he had to listen to Barbara for an hour," Warren leaned over and whispered in Sandrina's ear.

Martin Sperling told off-color jokes but so brilliantly that they were funny and not offensive. Charlotte, somewhat inebriated, confided in her that Martin had been unfaithful frequently in the past but that after a while she had gotten used to it.

"How long have you been married?" Sandrina asked Charlotte.

"Twenty-five years," she replied.

"That's quite an accomplishment," Sandrina said.

"I suppose...turn the other cheek and all that."

"Does he still make love to you?" Sandrina asked, tipsy too.

"Yes," she said. "If you can call it that. It isn't really love-making, more like duty I would say."

"And you," Charlotte said, gesturing toward Warren with her eyes. "How long have you two been married?"

"Oh, we're not married," Sandrina said, stifling a hiccup. "Well, I am, but he's not." Charlotte looked confused.

Florence tested Warren by challenging him to identify ingredients in every dish, but, unbeknownst to Sandrina, Warren was a master chef himself and rose magnificently to the occasion. And Joshua, seated at the head of the table with Sandrina to his right, presided while Dr. Avi Goldstein analyzed.

It was a great party.

Warren lingered while the other guests drifted out. Sandrina spotted him in the garden with Joshua, deep in conversation.

When Joshua walked Warren and Sandrina to the door, the last two guests to depart, he looked a bit peaked. The party had worn on him. Sushi

Fukasawa, Joshua's shiatsu masseuse, poked her head out of the galley door to signal that she had arrived.

"Are you all right?" Sandrina asked quietly.

"A bit tired, dear. That's all. Nothing that Sushi can't fix," he replied.

"Thank you. It was an outstanding party," Warren said to Joshua, extending his hand. Distracted, or deliberately, Sandrina couldn't tell which, Joshua neglected to take it. Instead, he kissed Sandrina lightly on the cheek, standing on his toes to reach, and turned away, preoccupied by his own private thoughts.

Warren and Sandrina left together and began walking west on 57th Street.

"That was terrific. Thanks for inviting me," Warren said.

"Now what?" she asked.

"Let's stroll for a while," Warren suggested.

Sandrina glanced at her watch. It was only 4:00. She could surely take a short detour through Central Park and make it home in time for dinner.

They entered the park at 60th Street and Fifth Avenue and walked north toward the Metropolitan Museum. She felt a sharp pang of guilt when they reached the zoo, where he grasped her hand as they lingered in front of the sea lions. If her husband had been home and known what to look for, he could have seen her from the vast picture windows of their apartment across the way.

Near the boat pond, they sat on a bench. Sandrina's other life kept intruding. It was 5:00 and she felt time running out. Several office workers walked briskly by, carving out for themselves the only exercise time they probably got, overlapped with the commute, an efficient New York thing to do.

"You know, being possessed by a man she loves only increases a woman's affection, her desire to be in constant proximity," Sandrina said.

"Yes, I know. And, it is exactly that characteristic that has, in the past, propelled me to seek variety. I find it suffocating." He threw his broken twig in the water. "I doubt I could ever be monogamous," he added.

Yet another face she had not seen before. But she looked at his profile and felt her smooth, manicured hand enveloped by his large, strong square one and thought that at least at that moment she didn't care. Her needs, for the first time ever, were nonexistent, a speck of inconsequential dust that sailed away on the boat pond. She had become the lover to Warren's lovee.

"Since Brazil, whenever I think about loving you, I see walls. Your husband, your business, and your independence—" he said, surprising her that he now added her business and independence as obstacles.

"Is it possible that you erect these walls to hide behind? How can you lose someone you never form an attachment to?"

"Of course, I've thought of these things. Especially since I met you. Come on, let's walk," he said, restless.

When they reached 79th Street, Sandrina glanced at her watch. Five thirty. She looked south, knowing she should go home. She looked north, where Warren had turned, leading her in a direction away from where she knew she should go.

"Where are we going?" she asked.

"I need a drink," he said.

She looked at her watch again. "Just a quick one."

They went to the bar at the Stanhope Hotel, across from the Metropolitan Museum. It was surprisingly empty. She had a Cosmopolitan and he a martini. After all the champagne at lunch, Sandrina got woozy fast; she draped her arms over his and felt him pull back just a bit, the slightest recoiling.

"What were you and Joshua discussing for so long?"

"He asked me a lot of questions about myself. Silly things. Where I lived before. How long I've owned Chaucer. What I used to do. He was overly curious, and he made notes in a little pad he had in his breast pocket," Warren said.

"How weird. Did you talk about anything else?"

"You. He asked how we met."

"What did you say?"

"At a conference. That I'm thinking of hiring you to do PR for my company. Then he launched into his own public relations campaign about you. He thinks you're the smartest 'woman' — his qualifier, not mine — he's ever known. Then he went on for twenty minutes about your business acumen and charm. He made a point of telling me how happily married you are."

Sounded like Joshua. Always promoting. "On the surface we are. Michael and I. Happily married, that is."

"Maybe beneath the surface is a well. Look carefully and you may see more depth there than you suspected."

Before she could begin to fathom his philosophy, she realized that the room was spinning. It was already 6:00 p.m. She had promised Michael that she would be home. "I have to go," she said.

"Would you like me to walk you home?"

"No, I'd better take a taxi." She had expected him to gallantly escort her into a cab and drop her off in front of her apartment building.

"Okay. Goodbye then." He turned away from her with an audible snort and ordered another martini. The last thing she heard him say was "Make sure it's Grey Goose."

Feeling dismissed, Sandrina stumbled to the hotel entrance and slipped the doorman five dollars. He hailed her a cab.

The wonderful afternoon ended on a flat, if not sour, note.

Sandrina walked into her apartment at 6:20 p.m. A headache was brewing and she felt depressed. Michael was talking loudly on the telephone down the hall in his study, and she jumped when she heard him sneeze. Michael had the loudest sneeze she had ever heard, and she remembered how it would wake her when they were first married.

"Where the hell have you been?" Michael said, emerging from his office. "I tried your office, your cell phone. No one knew where you were. Josh said you left at four. I was about to call the police."

"I'm sorry."

He scowled at her. "You smell like cigarettes."

"I had a drink with a client. I didn't hear the phone ring. I lost track of time."

"I think you need a new cell phone, Sandrina. This one seems to be broken—"

Sandrina walked past him and went upstairs to get some Advil. She did not like the person she saw in the bathroom mirror. If only one could stop time, flash-freeze a happy moment, a time before all the irritations and hurts intruded.

"Are we eating dinner?" Michael yelled from downstairs.

Sandrina went to the kitchen, where she set two places for dinner. The kitchen smelled like rosemary and lemon from the chicken their housekeeper had cooked and left in the oven. While Sandrina was putting the food on a serving platter, she heard Michael's footsteps approaching down the hall. As he walked into the kitchen, Michael still held the portable phone in his hand. She saw the green light go off. Michael was upset.

She lit two tapers for them and poured Michael a glass of wine. Then she prepared two plates of food and set them down.

Michael tipped his glass in her direction. "Thank you."

She started to massage his shoulders and was about to sit down when she asked, "Michael, who were you talking to?"

"It was Walter Schneider. He's been subpoenaed, by the FBI—served right in the lobby of his office building in Rockefeller Plaza. He's scared, 'Drina. Really scared."

"What do you think he'll do?"

"I'm not sure if he's more afraid of Thomas or of the Feds," Michael said.

"Did you tell him that Thomas is a coward? That he should tell the truth, that Thomas sanctioned the kickbacks and will use him to hide behind? That you will back him up?"

"No. I—"

"For God's sake, Michael. Call him back."

"Before I do, he also received a call from <u>The Finance Journal</u>—"

"Tell him Ken Larkin would consider the only noble thing for innocent men to do is resign and disassociate from the guilty."

"What about rats deserting a sinking ship?"

"If the ship's coffers are lined with gold, then the true rats would stay. Larkin cryptically mentioned Old McDonald—"

"The Farmer?" Michael asked.

"Yes. What do you think he meant by that?"

"The cheese stands alone…in Thomas's case, the stinky cheese."

All of this was too much. Sandrina felt dizzy and excused herself to lie down. Exhausted, she fell asleep fully clothed with her makeup still on and her teeth unbrushed. Michael found her there and loitered in the darkened doorway like a shadow. He left her there, covering her with a cashmere throw folded at the foot of the bed, and shut off the light.

Sandrina woke up shortly after midnight soaked in sweat. Her heart was beating so fast and hard she wondered if she were having a stroke. Alcohol affected her like that, especially on an empty stomach. She did not immediately know where she was, what hotel room in which country, and she started to panic. As the pounding in her chest and head subsided, she realized that she'd had a dreadful nightmare.

In her dream, Michael was dead and Warren had killed him.

It was impossible to fall back asleep. She washed in the bathroom attached to her study and rested her face in her hands.

Saturday morning Michael had an announcement to make at breakfast.

"I've decided to take you to Paris next weekend, Sandrina. I'll meet you there after your Germany trip. A romantic weekend is just what we both need."

Sandrina's mother Diana lived a few blocks away in a building filled with divorced and widowed women with moderate or dwindling fortunes. It had the panache of a Park Avenue co-op, and the requisite prestigious address so that it was socially acceptable, but its location on the through street to the Queensboro Bridge made the apartments noisy and dark. Diana had decorated in fruit basket colors to cheer the place up, but she still had to have all the lights on in the lemon yellow living room during the middle of a sunny summer afternoon.

"What's wrong?" Diana asked as soon as she opened the door and took one look at her daughter. In her hand she held a dog-eared paperback copy of *Hard Times* by Charles Dickens.

"Don't I get coffee first?"

"Of course! It's freshly made. And I even have those gooey black and white cookies from Dumas that you used to love as a child."

"If only a cookie and a Band-Aid could still solve my problems," Sandrina sighed.

"Is it man trouble, Sandy? That one from Brazil? I knew he meant trouble as soon as you told me about him. I could tell by the look in your eyes," she said.

"I just don't know what to do. I don't want to break up my marriage. I love Michael. And he needs me more than he ever has. He has business troubles you wouldn't believe. Yet I feel this may be my last chance at...passion, being in love, having children, oh, I don't know. After all, I'm forty-one."

"Forty-shmorty, love can come at any age. I happen to think you're more beautiful and interesting now than you ever were before," Diana said.

"You're my mother."

"Well, Warren isn't, and he seems to think so too. Doesn't he make you feel that way?"

"He makes me feel alive."

"Do you and Michael still make love?" Diana asked as she poured coffee into oversized mugs.

Sandrina hesitated. "Yes, but...the passion is petering out, to put it mildly."

"You can get it back, you know. Life intrudes. Take a trip—"

"Have you been talking to Michael?"

"Not about this! Why do you ask?"

"Because he's taking me to Paris—to 'inject a little romance' into the relationship, "Sandrina said.

"I think it's good that you and Michael are going to Paris."

"I'm not sure that will help. I think it's more complicated than that. Michael is clear and easy, like the surface of a pond on a windless day. But that's all he let's me see. I know that Warren is troubled, but he's deep. He's a stormy sea to Michael's placid pond. And now that I've met him I feel like I'm missing something with Michael."

"Why?"

"I think I've denied what's lacking for a long time." She reached over to take a cookie. "It's part of the public relations persona that I've perfected. Put on a happy face, and it will be a happy world. Michael tries to please me, but it's all so superficial. He's never touched that nerve. Not the way Warren has."

"What is it that you want, Sandy?"

"To be known, really known —"

"Have you ever felt known by any man?" Diana wanted to know.

"No, not really. Warren is the only one. When he loves me I feel complete. When he hurts me it reminds me of —"

"Of what?"

"Oh, never mind."

"Were you going to say of your father?"

"Yes, of Daddy."

Sandrina remembered how, after her parent's divorce, her father would unexpectedly appear in her life, for a day, and fill her world with his large presence. Everywhere he took her, people were drawn to him. Children, men. And women, always women.

Then he would disappear as quickly and dramatically as he had come. Her father left a gaping hole in her that until she met Warren only he had been able to fill. They were magicians in a way, her father and Warren; in addition to disappearing acts they hinted at the promise of the unattainable, beautiful birds from mundane scarves, love out of emptiness.

"I don't know how to advise you," Diana said. "But if you want the truth, I don't think he's right for you."

The doorbell rang. It was one of Diana's jewelry clients. "I'd better go," Sandrina said. "I'll slip out the service door."

"Honey, I can tell Mrs. Ulmann to come back later…"

"It's okay, Mom. I've got plans with Michael—he's waiting."

Diana escorted Sandrina to the door, pressing another cookie wrapped in a flowered napkin into her hand. She kissed her daughter on the cheek and said, "Don't worry about anything, Sandy. It'll all work out for the best."

That afternoon Michael and Sandrina went to Central Park, retracing the route Sandrina and Warren had taken only the day before. As they left the Park on East 79th Street they ate Good Humor ice creams that they bought from a cart. They walked east to Third Avenue and down to 59th Street, where they were able to just catch a five o'clock show. The city was empty on a beautiful Saturday afternoon in June, and getting tickets had been a breeze. After the film they lingered, discussing the high jinx and special effects of the film.

To all onlookers they appeared to be the perfect, happy couple. Sandrina's mind flitted between her husband and her lover. She felt so confused.

"'Drina, what's wrong?" Michael asked.

"Nothing. Why?"

"You are far away. Since Brazil. What happened there?" he probed.

"What do you think—" she snapped.

"I think—" He looked at her and refrained from continuing what he had started to say.

Michael fell asleep that night on the sofa in his study shortly after they returned. Suddenly Sandrina felt overwhelmed by the confusion of her own emotions, and she lay down on the bed, overcome, and fell asleep.

She woke up to Michael's familiar voice and his hand on her shoulder. He sat near her on the bed, put his arms around her and kissed her.

"You never sleep until eleven." He looked worried.

"I know. The night before last I woke up in the middle of the night and couldn't go back to sleep," she said. He was nodding his head, understanding, before she even finished her thought.

"And last night I couldn't get to sleep until late," she added. "And now I have to go to Germany and Paris, soon Hawaii…. oh, Michael, I'm exhausted."

"It will be okay, 'Drina."

He patted her hand.

Chapter Fifteen

The entrance to the Brenner's Park Hotel in Baden-Baden was on a quiet residential street. The luxurious establishment, one of the most famous in Europe, was so understated that it could have been easily mistaken for a mansion belonging to a wealthy family in London or Rome. Maria and Lucy were amazed as they entered the smooth marble jewel box of a lobby. After Sandrina checked them in, they were ushered up to individual suites that were more like chambers in a palace than rooms in a hotel.

Stiff ecru silk draperies puddled on crew-cut carpeting just one shade of beige darker. Antique mirrors and furnishings, with inlaid checkerboard parquetry and fabrics imported from France, completed the regal setting. Within an hour of checking in, Maria and Lucy had unpacked and were in the spa downstairs, enjoying the steam bath and whirlpool tubs.

Sandrina retired to her suite, which was larger than the other two. On the desk, under an oil painting of the Lichtentaler Allee, she found a stack of faxes and messages. It was only Monday morning, so the plethora of correspondence surprised her. Nothing from the office. Nothing from Warren.

"Sandrina, I spoke to Claudius late last night when he returned from the country. He is aware you are coming. He'll do what he can. Michael."

Christoff Peipers had called, asking that she phone him as soon as she arrived.

There was a message on thick, engraved stationery:

> *"Welcome to Baden-Baden, Frau Morgan,*
>
> *Your presentation is scheduled for Tuesday at 10:00 AM in my office on the mezzanine level. In the meantime, enjoy the complimentary bottle of champagne and explore our facility.*
>
> *I enclose passes to our Roman Baths, Friedrichsbad. Let the concierge know when we should schedule your private visit.*
>
> *Helmut Mangold, General Manager."*

Sandrina unpacked and set up her laptop on the antique desk, plugging an adapter into the back of her computer.

After ordering tea and toast from room service, she took a soothing bath while she waited for breakfast to arrive. She dressed in a pair of khakis. a striped cotton sweater and a raincoat before venturing out for a walk.

She strolled along the Lichtentaler Allee promenade until she came to the Gonnerlanlage, a pocket of a park, with pergolas skirting a rose garden. She sat in the middle of a cornucopia of color, with a mist of dew-like rain encompassing her, and reminisced. Sandrina and Michael had visited Baden-Baden several times before, but not for many years. The last time they were here she had been a young woman of thirty.

They had visited the Iffezheim racetrack, where the women had worn fanciful hats and drank *eiscafe*, so much richer than the iced coffees back home. The tall glass mugs had overflowed with vanilla ice cream and *sahne*, leaving white mustaches on women. She had taught Michael how to handicap at the track on that trip, one of the few useful things she'd learned from her gambler father, and something she'd doubted the other woman there knew how to do.

Sandrina remembered the gold ball gown she had worn to the last Grand Prix Ball she had attended. She and Michael were a golden couple— that was enough for her then.

Restlessly, Sandrina left the park and continued walking toward the main shopping street near the Markplatz. She passed the spot in the Kurgarten, a speck of a square in front of the Corinthian columns of the Kurhaus, where she had captured Michael in a photograph that sat on their piano back home. She looked longingly at her watch. If only she could set it back ten years. Instead, she saw that it was time to go.

Back at the Brenner's she found Lucy and Maria sipping coffee, *Nachmittagskaffee*, in the lobby.

"What have you been up to this afternoon?" Sandrina asked Lucy and Maria.

"Oh, Sandrina. It's marvelous here!" Lucy exclaimed. "We've had facials and back rubs and salt treatments."

"I feel like the roast my mother used to make on Christmas Day. I've been salt-rubbed and baked. The only thing missing is the pepper," Maria added. "Where have you been? You look wet."

I've been down memory lane, she thought. What she said was: "Around. Taking in the sights. Listen, girls, I'll be down in half an hour. I need to check messages and change for dinner. Okay?"

"Sure. We'll be here," they chimed.

There was another message from Christoff Peipers. She called him back immediately.

"Christoff, thanks for helping my team out," Sandrina said.

"Are you joking? I am praying you get the account. They have money; I do not. I know if you are promoting the Brenner's, Baden-Baden will benefit. I put a call into Mangold to give you the recommendation of the Tourism Bureau," he said.

"You are a true friend."

She quickly logged on. Several messages forwarded from Beth. Nothing from Warren.

There was an alarming one from Jason wanting to know 'Where the hell' she was, to which she replied, with a copy to Isabel: "So sorry. I'll be out of town for a week. I have left Isabel in charge. Can you all get together and keep things moving?"

From her mother: Sandy — While you're in Baden-Baden get me some Caracalla cream. Fountain-of-youth in a bottle. Love, Mom.

She dined with her staff and went to bed early.

The next morning, Sandrina wore a charcoal pinstriped suit for the pitch. The few words that she knew that weren't *schlafzimmer Deutsch*, bedroom German, she used to try to charm Herren Mangold and Junger and Frau Clayton.

"*Guten morgen!*" she opened the presentation. "*Danke fur die einladung. Das hotel ist fabelhaft. Wir haben viele ideen.*"

"We all speak English here, Mrs. Morgan," Mangold assured her in a stern tone. His associates, Herr Junger and Frau Clayton, were energetically bobbing their heads.

"Of course," Sandrina said. "And I've just exhausted my German vocabulary anyway."

The Germans stared.

"Our presentation today is the result of serious thinking about your marketing challenges.

There are so many hotels and destinations competing with the Brenner's Park that we have tried to focus on your unique points of difference and build around those so that we can make your hotel a destination unto itself, with Baden-Baden the glorious backdrop rather than the other way around," Sandrina continued.

At this point, and much to everyone's surprise, Michael's friend Claudius, and the hotel's owner, entered the room. Herr Mangold corrected his slouch. Claudius's wavy golden hair and aquiline nose, athletic body and easy manner, would have placed him as a movie star any day — except for his sliced off ear, a result of a kidnapping he suffered at the hand of the Red Army faction when he was just a child.

Claudius smiled warmly at Sandrina and begged her to go on.

"What we have developed for you are a series of spa packages," said Sandrina, as Lucy woke up her laptop and launched enthusiastically into a description of the creative spa packages the team had assembled.

"'Faces and Races' combines five days of morning facials — Oxygen, Herbal, Glycolic, Collagen, and Vitamin C — with afternoons at the track, a pass to the International Club, and a private consultation with Baden-Baden's famous milliner Frau Katzen. 'Body Beautiful' bundles daily massages with European body treatments, including Body Polish, Aroma Body Glow, Seaweed Wrap, Paraffin, and Bronzing. In conjunction with the Stephanie les Bains medical staff, we have created 'Fountain of Youth,' which includes optional Botox injections and liposuction," Lucy explained.

Sandrina observed Frau Clayton looking at herself in the wall mirror.

"We want to position Baden-Baden and the Brenner's Park as the world's premier destination for beauty weeks. We would like to subtly de-emphasize the 'curative' waters because we think this is contributing to the image of the resort as a haven for the old and budget-conscious. We've built in price discrimination strategies so that the merely rich can enjoy 'Faces and Races' for 3,250 euros for five days, while the even richer can opt for the 'Fountain of Youth' packages, which range from 5,300 to 7,700 euros depending on the treatments selected," Maria added.

"How many of these packages do you think we can sell?" Mangold asked.

"We're projecting that if we sell a thousand seven-night packages we can add at least seven thousand room nights per year," Sandrina added. "At rack rate."

"Hmmm. Junger, do you have a calculator?" Mangold asked his associate.

Junger hadn't really been paying attention and was taken by surprise by being addressed directly. He shrugged his shoulders, indicating that he did not.

"Doesn't matter. At 274 euros per night, that's about 1,918,000 euros in incremental revenue. If you and your team can do that, Ms. Morgan, I would be very impressed," Mangold said.

"Bundling seems the right way to go, but you can get most of these things individually in Baden-Baden already. Any more exotic ideas?" Claudius asked.

"If you're willing to import a specialist — that would add to the cost structure, of course — the adventuresome could enjoy a week of Ayurvedic Treatments, such as Stone Massage, Ear Candling, Rain Drop Therapy, and Shirodhara in the comfort of your spa rather than in a dreary cinderblock clinic in the Catskills," Lucy added.

"And, finally, in conjunction with the Kurhaus, Pilates, and the Brenner's swimming pool, we propose to offer 'Slimming and Swimming,' a diet and exercise program that includes a daily sports massage. We believe the exercise regime will attract a younger, more vigorous clientele," Maria said.

"Throw in some touring, German lessons, a private jewelry exhibition, Escada and Jil Sander trunk shows, opera, and the casino and not a woman in her right mind would choose any other vacation," Lucy concluded.

Sandrina thanked the Brenner's management team and asked if there were any other questions.

"What's 'ear candling'?" asked Claudius, always curious about anything having to do with ears.

"It's a centuries-old science developed in India to remove ear wax and noxious toxins," Maria said. "It's very in."

"And, how do you intend to promote these packages?" Herr Mangold asked.

"The originality alone makes them newsworthy. But we also thought we would hire a spokeswoman with the title of Vice President of International Beauty. She might be a world-class model or perhaps a German actress. Her business card would place her office here, at the Brenner's Park Hotel, in the newly created Brenner's Park Center for International Beauty," Sandrina said.

"How else would the Brenner's benefit?" asked Frau Clayton.

"Your hotel would be built into every package. It would be the only place to stay included in the bundles, and the spa offerings would be mostly scheduled October through April to fill your off-seasons," Sandrina replied.

"Well done, ladies," Herr Mangold stated.

"Good job," Herr Junger echoed. Now that the lunch break was looming, he woke up. He hadn't said another word during the whole session.

"We will be in touch," Mangold closed.

Mangold and Clayton filed out with Junger trailing behind; Claudius remained behind, eyes gleaming.

"I commend you on your originality and spunk!" he declared. He pulled Sandrina aside. "How long are you in town for?" he asked her.

"I'm staying tonight to attend the Grand Prix Ball," Sandrina replied.

"What a coincidence! I am also going. May I escort you this evening? he asked.

"It would be an honor," she responded.

Sandrina said goodbye to Lucy and Maria before they left for the airport with not a moment to spare. Claudius arranged to pick Sandrina up at seven o' clock. She booked a facial, massage, and manicure with the spa for the afternoon and requested her private appointment at the Friedrichsbad for Wednesday at two. If Warren didn't show, she figured she could always go alone.

After her Spa Glow facial, with Dead Sea salts and essential oils, and her Reiki massage by a strong, blind Moroccan boy with intoxicating fingers, Sandrina slept for four hours on the massage table. She dreamed that she was in Warren's arms. The spa attendants tried to rouse her, but she wouldn't move. So they left her in the warm, dimly lit room with a tape of nature sounds playing softly in the background.

When she woke up she was refreshed but ravenous. She took the spa elevator to her suite, ordered a club sandwich and tea, and logged on. Nothing from him. It was eleven in New York. She called Michael at his office.

"Hey, 'Drina! How did it go?" he asked.

"I think we were a hit. Claudius came."

"That's a good sign—"

"He's taking me to the ball tonight," she said.

"Good old Claudius. Watch out. I think he's always had a thing for you."

"Don't worry. He's a perfect gentleman. Michael, how are things?"

"Same old, same old. Every time I talk to the lawyers, some new wrinkle emerges—"

"Did you call Walter Schneider back as I suggested?"

"I did. And, as usual, it was a good idea. He believes me that I had no part in the kickbacks. He told me that Thomas threatened to fire the whole accounting firm if they didn't comply with his orders, confirming what you overheard, despite their repeated pleas to be completely honest. Of course, Thomas destroyed the evidence on our side, but Walter was smart. He made copies of the wire transfer instructions and kept them on file with his general counsel. Apparently, he's got two documents that exonerate me as well. They're letters from Thomas warning them not to let me know what he instructed them to do, that the wires were confidential."

"Where are those letters now? Did he send you copies?"

"Unfortunately not. His firm is holding the letters and other documentation hostage until the first *Finance Journal* piece breaks and they see what the fallout will be. He doesn't want any copies to get into the wrong hands—such as Ken Larkin's or the FBI's—unless they become evidence."

"Michael, you've got to get those letters."

"I know. I just don't know how."

"What's he like, Michael? Does he have any passions? Golf? Coins? Cars?"

Michael laughed. "He works all the time. Wrinkled suits, tortoise shell glasses, nerdy really. The only thing I've ever seen him do to relax is read *People* magazine. Apparently he's nuts about celebrities. Must be the glamour."

"What are you going to do next?"

"I'm not sure. I'm taking it a day at a time. Meanwhile, I'm liquidating assets, trying to raise cash, and expecting the worst—"

"I'll try to think of something."

She inhaled her sandwich and thought hard about the potential fallout from an investigative exposé on Morgan Paper such as the one she suspected the *Finance Journal* had planned. The media deluge alone could destroy the company, even without a criminal investigation. She knew she couldn't kill the piece, and after her conversation with Ken Larkin the other morning she doubted that she could even soften it. There seemed no other solution for Michael than to get his hands on those letters and get out while he still could.

Sandrina knew Michael would never switch industries at this point in his career. He was trapped by his legacy; he had never done anything but work for his father, and then his brother, so paper was all he knew.

Paper. Paper. The answer for Michael would be found in the paper industry somewhere. How could such a common commodity as paper be turned into something new?

Despite having eaten, she felt an aching in the pit of her stomach. Depressed but determined, she dressed in an apple-green sleeveless shantung dress to the floor with an asymmetrical neckline and matching shawl. Her Manolo Blahnik mules were the exact same shade as the dress, which, when she found them, she thought was nothing short of a miracle. She wore the diamond earrings and necklace that Michael had bought her for her fortieth birthday.

Claudius was waiting in the lobby when she emerged from the elevator. He looked like an ad from the *New York Times* magazine supplement on men's fashion in his elegant custom-made tuxedo that fit him like glove, adorned with gold rhinoceros cufflinks and studs, their bright ruby eyes fierce. He wore white gloves.

"What color is that—McIntosh or Delicious?" he asked.

"I'm afraid it's Granny Smith," she replied.

They kissed platonically three times on the cheeks, then he placed her arm through his as they wafted through the salon's French doors out onto the terrace and across the Lichtentaler Allee to the limestone mansion that houses The International Club of Baden-Baden.

It was right smack in the middle of Spring Meet. The atmosphere was charged. Horse people from all over the world, many from Dubai, where the sheik himself owned over four thousand racehorses, had gathered in Baden-Baden to mingle and compete. The Grand Prix Ball threw them all together for a farewell fête.

The magic of the evening took her mind off everything else.

Claudius and Sandrina were among the last to leave and they seemed to sway, feet and hearts light, out the door and through the Park. In front of the Trinkhalle on the Kaiserallee he tried to kiss her, but she turned her head and demurred.

"We'd better go back," she said.

Rebuffed, he walked in silence at a quicker pace. Sandrina did her best to keep up. When they got back to the hotel, Claudius sat her down at the bar at the Brenner's.

"*Eine Flasche* Taittinger Compte de Champagne, rosé," he ordered.

"That's my favorite," she said.

"I remember."

"But that was ten years ago—"

"I know. Sandrina—"

"Claudius, please don't. My life is complicated enough. You have no idea."

Back upstairs, she called home. Michael was out. The housekeeper answered the phone.

"A mister Warren called," she said. "He will meet you for breakfast tomorrow."

A chill coursed through Sandrina's body.

The wake-up call came, as ordered, at 8:30. She didn't look too bad, considering how much she'd had to drink and how poorly she had slept. She showered carefully and invoked her artistic talents to paint herself a face that would make heads turn. She wore a casual but sexy dress, in oyster white and royal blue, and she deliberately left her shoulders and legs bare because it must have gotten much hotter overnight. Or so she thought by the way she felt.

When Sandrina walked into the breakfast room of the Steigenberger Europäischer Hof, Warren was already there. He was sitting at a table facing her, with a *Kännchen*, pot of coffee, and two cups. He was reading the *International Herald Tribune*. As she approached, he shifted his eyes from the paper to her.

He did not stand up to hold her chair, or kiss her hello. But he was genuinely happy to see her, she knew, not a shadow of sadness in his eyes.

"Hey," he said. "You made it."

"That's my line," she said.

"How'd your pitch go yesterday?"

"Well, I think. Never know for sure until the contract is signed."

"Yeah. And, then the problems really begin."

"Have you eaten?"

"No. I waited for you."

"Breakfasts here turn me off. Cold meat, cold cheese, marmalade on bread —"

"I should have predicted that you wouldn't like things German. Like Fire and Ice — most Germans I've met are cold fish."

She remembered Claudius's advances from the night before. "That's not really true."

"Well, maybe not. What do I know? Must be my early years in England. The English hate the Germans, you know. The war—"

"Why didn't you respond to my e-mails?" She blurted it out.

"I thought I did," he answered defensively.

"A call, to my home yet."

"I've been busy."

"Well, me too. But—" She stopped; she sounded pathetic, pleading. "Anyway, that's water under the bridge. We're here to discuss business, aren't we?"

"That's part of it, yes."

"Then go ahead. What's on your mind?" She was angry—at him and at herself.

"One of the things that I've been busy with this week has been garnering support for the PR effort," he said, hands flat on the table, eyes on her.

"So were you successful? Do you have a budget for this?"

"I think I can drum up about two hundred thousand."

"Now we're talking," she said.

"The account is yours if you want it."

"No competition? No beauty pageant?"

"None."

The more she tried to sound tough and business-like, the more she was crumbling inside.

"So you want me to publicize the properties, run press junkets, and drive business to your members, right?" Her hands were trembling.

"And, make me famous as a spokesperson for the industry, so I get the calls before the other rep company presidents," he said, calming her hands with his.

"Great." She tried to convince herself that she could handle any relationship he dished out. "As soon as we're back in New York, we can get started."

His knee was touching hers under the table. Neither could deny the attraction. The question was what to do with it.

"I know you can't be on the account day to day," he said.

"Under the circumstances, I don't think it would be wise, do you?"

"Maybe night to night?"

"Very funny. No, we'll have to keep it business-like...and maybe eventually we can be friends." She was adamant.

"Do you know whom you'll put on the account?" he asked.

"I have to think about it." She scanned the faces of her staff in her mind. "Maybe a young woman named Isabel Riley." If she kept Isabel busy with Chaucer, then she could wean her off Max and Jason's account. Chaucer was more straightforward

PR...Max and Jason needed a seasoned pro. "Smart, dedicated. She's a bit...rambunctious, but if I'm supervising, it should be okay. I know she lived in Ireland and in England for a while. She would have a good feel for Chaucer's properties and destinations."

"Sounds like the right choice then." The words rang with disappointment.

"I'll e-mail my secretary to schedule a kick-off meeting for next Thursday morning, if that works for you. That will give us each a couple of days to catch up."

He looked at his Blackberry. "That works for me."

"Good," she said. "That's settled — now what?"

When Sandrina had made the reservations at the Friedrichsbad, before she had decided that they should just be friends, she had instructed the concierge to book the private Therma room with the gilded domed ceiling and Roman arches, to ensure they would be alone. Sandrina and Warren lolled in the 158° waters for an hour, trying to deny the sexual tension as it continued to mount. Then he kissed her tenderly and longingly, pausing only to lick beads of moisture from her ears and brow. Rivulets of her water-sodden black hair stuck to his neck like tentacles. They did not touch, except with lips and teeth and tongue, and nowhere below the V that formed beneath their throats.

Wrapped in towels, they exited through separate doors, their bodies heavy and hard to move from the heat. Each had a hot mineral oil massage in the segregation of the treatment rooms. A paste made from crushed alpenrose petals and hibiscus was added to the oil to eradicate the sulfur smell from the thermal waters. They showered and then reconvened in a private resting room, a stark chamber with a hard cot and scratchy blanket. It resembled a prison cell.

The fire lurking since Brazil, and stoked by the heat of the bath and the coarse rubbing of the masseurs, resulted in frantic lovemaking. Sandrina's pent-up passions exploded upon seeing him again, fueled by her anger and conflict. She scratched him and bit him, leaving long red threads down his back and bite marks on his muscular shoulders. She wrapped her long legs around his, locking him into place to keep him from escaping her assault.

His only recourse was to thrust into her with reciprocated force, contracting and flexing the muscles in his thighs and buttocks to channel his power. The legs of the creaky cot almost collapsed from the nearly violent siege and as the rhythmic lunging gave way to a slower, steadier rocking, they noticed that the cot had moved clear across the room, leaving scratch marks on the floor in its wake.

They fell asleep in each other's arms, with him still inside her. A loud banging on the door by the matron woke them up.

"We are closing. You must leave."

Sandrina's lips were sore and tasted like blood and cherry lollipops. She managed a few hoarse words, "I want to stay like this forever."

He pulled away and cleared his throat. Without looking at her, he hastily dressed, and then sat on the edge of the cot staring at the wall.

"We have to hurry before they send in the police," he said coldly, matter-of-fact. "Sandrina, why don't you go back to your hotel and freshen up? Let's have a think. I'll call you later."

If she could have chained herself to him she would have. "But..."

Warren looked at her. "I never know what's coming next."

They left the Friedrichsbad together but walked in opposite directions back to their respective hotels. No sooner had Sandrina entered the Brenner's Park-Hotel lobby than her iPhone rang. After fumbling around for in her purse she answered, in an exasperated tone: "Hello?"

It was Beth. "Sandrina, can you talk? You've had a few urgent calls today."

"Actually, Beth, I'm in the hotel lobby. Can it wait?"

"I've been trying to reach you all day," she said.

"Go ahead, what's up?"

"Jason instructed me to book you to Hawaii, right after the Millennium Universal opening."

A whirlwind of Warren and Michael and Jason and Claudius clouded her judgment. "Beth, I know I promised, but find some way to postpone it."

"I'll try."

"That's fine. Really, I've got to go—"

"One more thing—"

"What?"

"Joshua Baum called. He said it was urgent. Said it can't wait until you get back."

"Did he say anything else?"

"Nope."

"Okay. Thanks, I'll call him tomorrow."

When Sandrina got up to her room, she noticed an e-mail from Warren on her iPhone.

S: That was the most erotic experience of my life. I'm water logged and confused. I need to think. W

Her shoulders sagged. Everything else could wait until tomorrow.

Chapter Sixteen

Michael was standing at the gate at the airport in Paris, radiant in expectation, holding a large bouquet of flowers.

He looked at her suspiciously, admiringly, responding to the sensuality that had been reawakened by someone else. The lips that he perceived to be so luscious were fuller, yes, because they were swollen and bruised by the coarseness of Warren's beard. Her green eyes were wild, not with passion for Michael but with a thesaurus of emotions ranging from terror to confusion. The follicles of her skin and hair were charged, but the source of the current was not her husband.

Michael smiled and took her bag, filled with soiled underwear and rumpled dresses. They were both nervous as they stepped into a taxi.

"Satisfied?" he asked.

She jumped. "What do you mean?"

"Did you get the account?" She thought he was trying to read her face.

"Oh. I think so. Let's hope. How about you? Any news?"

"Nothing you don't know. Frankly, I want to relax and focus on you. Everything else will—unfortunately—still be there when we get back."

She turned her eyes toward him as the car snailed along in traffic on the Avenue Foch. The taxi entered the traffic circle that rounds the Arc de Triomphe.

"There," Michael said pointing. "Those names inscribed on the façade, they were Napoleon's six hundred generals. The underlined names are of the ones who died."

"What about the wives and mistresses they left behind? They were felled too, by the wars, weren't they? Where are their names? And Josephine, poor Josephine. Dumped for a younger princess, more fertile than she. Oh god, wasn't Josephine exactly my age when Napoleon left her?" she asked.

Michael looked at her, bafflement in his blue eyes. "Are you afraid I might leave you, Sandrina? I would never leave you."

The door to the car opened in front of a pair of large double wooden doors that were originally built to accommodate horse-drawn carriages. Sandrina and Michael entered a dark stone passageway that led into a cobblestone courtyard. On the far side stood the former seventeenth-century *hôtel particulier* that had recently been remodeled as the Hotel de Vichy. They had spent their honeymoon at the Hotel de Crillon on the Place de la Concorde.

"Was the Crillon full?" she asked.

"No 'Drina. Just thought we would try something new."

She thought he might think she was disappointed, which she wasn't, just surprised.

"It's charming," she said. Although small, like a dollhouse replica of Versailles, it was vibrant and unique. The concierge, Patrice, exuded enthusiasm and made her feel as though they were his personal guests. A trompe l'oeil of Parisian rooftops graced the elevator doors, and the staff was young and eager, unlike the seasoned but jaded pros at the Crillon.

The decorator Renzo Mongiardino, whose clients included Rudolf Nureyev and Baron Guy de Rothschild, had designed the interiors. The bedroom walls were covered in cashmere, and the draperies and bedcovers were made of matching velvet, all in rich shades of brown, ranging from chestnut to roan. On the bed stand was a box of sweets from Sandrina's favorite chocolate shop in Paris, Debauve & Gallais, spanning the same spectrum of hues as the decor.

The first thing Sandrina did when she entered the suite was bathe. She excused herself from her husband's company and closed the door to the bathroom, undressing inside like a shy bride. She filled the enormous white porcelain tub with steaming water and bath salts that were supplied by the hotel. Chaud et froid, froid et chaud. That was how she too was running. She removed her makeup and underwear, tossing the latter into the corner, and stepped into the basin in the hopes of a spiritual cleansing.

Had she used Lava soap and a scouring brush she could not have washed away the presence of Warren. He had infiltrated every pore. He was under her skin, in her ears, her throat, her hair. She was replaying conversations with Warren in her mind when Michael entered the bathroom to apprise her of his plans. That evening, he told her, they would dine out after seeing the exhibit at the Pompidou and then take in the evening show at the Moulin Rouge.

The evening passed as if it were a dream. Immersed in the activities, but not really there, she had to pretend to be enjoying herself for Michael's sake. When the evening ended and they went to bed, Sandrina was relieved that she could stop working so hard to act like the person her husband wanted to see.

They slept late the next morning and walked along the Seine in the afternoon, browsing the bookstalls and antique shops on the Left Bank. Friday evening Michael took her to a modern production of Puccini's *Tosca* at the Opera Bastille.

Tosca, the opera's tragic heroine, loses her artist lover, Cavaradossi, to a firing squad by order of the corrupt police chief, Scarpia, who wants Tosca for himself. Tosca was in love with one man and another was in love with her. The sets were austere and depressing, contributing to the edginess Sandrina felt as the evening wore on.

"Pardonnez-moi," said an attractive French woman seated next to Michael during the first intermission. *"Êtes-vous Americains?"*

"Yes, we are both American," Michael replied.

"Oh, my husband is also American," she said, pointing to her husband and switching to English. "We live half of the time in Nassau."

"Lyford Cay?" Sandrina probed.

"Yes," the husband smiled.

"How do you like it? The opera," Michael asked.

"So far, it's not great," the American husband said. "Her lover is not convincing."

"Not at all," agreed his wife. "Why would she risk so much for a man who loves her so little?"

At a brasserie, also on the Place de la Bastille, the same couple appeared again. They asked Sandrina and Michael to join them, but Michael declined, explaining to them that he was eager to be alone with his wife. The restaurant was filled with chic Parisians, laughing and smoking and dining late. The design was very modern, with chairs upholstered like court jester costumes and the walls adorned with photographs of odd people doing commonplace things. A family was gathered nearby for a birthday celebration, with sparklers brightening up the festivities as presents were passed across a long table.

Michael ordered a tray of oysters, lobster, langoustines, and crab, arranged on curls of shaved ice. They drank champagne and wiped tears from their eyes caused by the cigarette smoke that surrounded them. Through most of the dinner they ate in silence.

The hour-long walk back to the hotel, through winding streets filled with young people and charming storefronts, was filled with laughing and talking. It was so much like their honeymoon 15 years before. The memory helped ease some of the recent estrangements, transporting them back to a happier time.

They weaved in and out of side alleys, where the streets smelled like sawdust from the furniture-making shops. At No. 3 Cour de Mai they found an ancient timber house with a seventeenth-century staircase. Peering through the windows, they could imagine an obscure specialist or two, like a gold and silver metal plater, or a lithographer, struggling to hang on to their traditional ways amidst technological innovation.

"Look!" Sandrina said. "I remember the rue du Faubourg Saint-Antoine from *A Tale of Two Cities* by Charles Dickens. It was the street on which the French Revolution began—a hotbed of social unrest."

Michael didn't answer.

"Is anything wrong?" Sandrina asked.

"Speaking of plots and rebellion reminds me of Thomas," Michael said. "There's another dinner at his place next Saturday; he wants an update on the *Finance Journal* story from you and to discuss 'a business idea' with me." The depth of Michael's concern showed on his face; it became dark and lined. She noticed that he changed from looking relaxed and joyous to haggard and unhappy at the mere thought of his brother.

"Can't we forget about everything else just for this weekend?"

"In addition to the public humiliation and shame, there's a lot of money involved. Everything I have is tied up in the company, even though Thomas is the majority shareholder and CEO."

"Look, I make enough money—"

"I couldn't, wouldn't use yours. How can I keep a woman like you with just a pack on my back? You wouldn't respect me. You would leave me."

How little he knew about her. She might leave him, but not because of money.

"Michael, I don't care about the money. As you've cut your feelings off to be able to deal with your family, you've withdrawn from me too. And, you're always so preoccupied," she said. Then, thinking of the baby she lost: "So…selfish."

"I know; I know I've neglected you. That's why—"

"Then do something about it. Resign."

"I can't, not yet."

"That's what I don't respect," she said, raising her voice.

"I'll be in a stronger position if I wait until the investigation runs its course."

"I see it as exactly the opposite. You can put it in writing that you are leaving on ethical grounds—because you want no part of it," she shouted. "If you're there when the dam bursts, you are guilty by complicity. Those letters Walter has will become more and more important if this goes beyond bad publicity into a federal investigation."

"That eventuality looks inevitable," Michael admitted. "The other day the lawyers told me that the government is thinking of invoking the Foreign Corrupt Practices Act—it prohibits corrupt payments to foreign officials for the purpose of obtaining or keeping business. All of my clients for currency paper were foreign government officials. The Department of Justice is the enforcement agency, and the lawyers tell me they're out for blood," he explained.

"Oh, Michael," she said shaking her head. "That's not you. You're not a criminal."

"No, just a patsy. 'Drina, I didn't want any part of it, ever. In retrospect, I should have seen what was going on; I was in denial. The law specifically states that individuals with knowledge of the act can be penalized as conspirators, even if they did not personally order, authorize, or assist someone else to violate the anti-bribery provisions. If made to testify, I don't know what I knew and didn't know any more."

"Is there anything in writing, any proof, that you suspected?"

"No. I don't think so. But with the U.S. government you are guilty until proven innocent."

"Isn't there anyone you know who could influence Walter into giving you those letters?"

"Not unless you know Jennifer Aniston or Cameron Diaz or Halle Barry. Walter'd probably hand over state secrets to them."

"Without those letters it's just your word against Thomas's. Walk away, Michael. You must walk away."

"To what, Sandrina? Nothing? I can't," he said. Then he looked deeply into her eyes and said, "Thank God I have you."

When they returned to the hotel they made love, kissing and touching in places they had neglected for years. Sandrina detached herself emotionally from the infidelities she had committed and thirsted for the familiar, secure embrace of the man she had married.

As in almost all the nights since they had met, they fell asleep in each other's arms. Michael slept peacefully, but Sandrina woke up several times aching for Warren and not understanding why. Love is, she thought, so unfair.

The next day they walked to the Rodin Museum and all along the Left Bank in the rain. The sculptures of Auguste Rodin were so daring and energetic. Like the large figure of the writer Balzac, cape flying away, standing naked for all to see, the body brazen but the soul still elusive. The statue reminded her of Warren.

"Joshua has a Rodin drawing in his collection. *Nude with Serpent.* The snake lurks in water beneath the figure, where her genitalia would be visible if not obscured by a green wash of watercolor," she said to Michael.

"I'll have to check it out next time we go to the Baums'."

"Damn, Joshua called me and I forgot to call him back," Sandrina remembered.

"I'm sure it can wait."

They sauntered along the rue du Bac, stopping to admire clever window dressings along the way, and then went to rue des Canettes, where they joined a client of Michael's for lunch at an Italian restaurant called Santa Lucia.

The Santa Lucia had a dark wood façade that blended in with the restaurants on either side of it, making it hard to find. One had to duck to avoid head contact with the doorframe. Behind a silver-and-glass cart abundant with antipasti was a narrow spiral staircase leading to a loft-like room where Pierre and Odile were waiting.

Michael had told her that he did not know whom to expect: Pierre's wife, Chantal, or his new girlfriend, Odile. After half an hour, and the first bottle of coarse red wine, they learned that the marriage was over and that the new couple was happily cohabiting. The men started talking in French, a language Michael knew well, although everyone was fluent in English, about people they used to know and business matters that they had in common.

"Odile," Sandrina asked in a hushed tone and with greater personal interest than Odile could deign. "How did it happen?"

"You mean Pierre and me?"

"Yes."

"I was unhappy in my marriage for a long time," she replied.

"Did you know why?"

"First, Frederic, my ex-husband, started to criticize. You know, he'd say, 'You've put on a few kilos' or 'I remember when your breasts were firm.' Then, for the past five years, we stopped making love."

"So you started looking?" Sandrina asked. The women were whispering now.

"Yes, I started looking. And I found Pierre. I just wanted to feel...desirable. Yes, that's it. I needed to be wanted, as a woman, not just...a partner."

"I understand—"

"Do you? How? It is so obvious your husband adores you." Odile said this as a compliment, not a challenge.

"Thank you. But, there are many kinds of intimacy that a woman yearns for," Sandrina said.

Odile looked perplexed. "Ah, be grateful for what you have."

After the bill was paid, the two couples darted into the pouring rain, taking leave in opposite directions. Michael and Sandrina were soaking wet when they finally returned to the hotel. They ordered hot tea from room service and dressed for a much-anticipated dinner at the Plaza Athenée.

After the dinner, the incessant rain started to take its toll, and Sandrina felt her throat getting scratchy. She said nothing to Michael, so as not to spoil his romantic weekend. But within minutes of returning to the suite she lay down and fell into a feverish slumber. Michael kissed her hot forehead and pulled the blankets over her bare shoulders. He quickly fell asleep as well.

Sandrina had wild dreams during the night. In her nightmare, she and Warren were back in the rain forest. She was naked, in a clearing, surrounded by partially clothed candomblé worshipers in tribal costumes. They were chanting to the beat of the drums; their images obscured by hazy smoke. Warren emerged through the circle of masked and painted men. He was naked too. And while four men held her down and watched, he raped her repeatedly.

At eleven the next morning, a knock on the door woke Michael. The room service waiter rolled in a cart covered with a white starched linen tablecloth. Domes sheltered their plates of shirred eggs, which were accompanied by a basket of flaky croissants. Freshly made peach, strawberry, and blueberry preserves rested in little pots near jars of blossom honey. In lieu of flowers, an African violet graced the center of the inviting display.

Michael wrapped the plush bathrobe provided by the hotel around himself and poured a cup of tea while Sandrina slept, her hair spread out on the pillow like tributaries, a veil of perspiration on her lip. Reading the *International Herald Tribune,* he saw the headline:

Joshua Baum, Public Relations Pioneer, Dead at 82

NEW YORK, N.Y. June 11 (AP). Joshua Baum, credited with having invented the modern public relations business, died on June 10 in New York City. He was 82.

Mr. Baum, a German immigrant, became an invaluable and trusted resource for America's most influential CEOs. In addition to his role as corporate advisor, he was active in Democratic politics, having served as *ex officio* counsel to Presidents Clinton and Obama.

Mr. Baum collected art for more than four decades, notably 19th century drawings as well as works by the French Impressionists. In 2005, the Columbia University Art Gallery had a major exhibition entitled "19th Century Masterpieces on Paper from the Collection of Joshua Baum."

At his death, he was a member of the chairman's council of the Metropolitan Museum of Art. He had been a trustee of The NYC Ballet, The Municipal Arts Society, and The Union League Club. At the 2006 graduation ceremony, Joshua Baum was presented with the Columbia Journalism School Medal for "extraordinary service" to the communications industry.

He is survived by his wife, Esther; two sons, Benjamin of Greenwich and Gerald of Short Hills; a daughter, Rachel, of Boca Raton; seven grandchildren, and two great-grandchildren."

"'Drina, wake up," Michael said, shaking her gently. "Something's happened."

She heard his words through sleep-dulled ears but still knew something was wrong from the tone. "What? Are you all right?"

"I'm fine. It's Joshua," he said.

"Joshua?"

"Yes. He's dead."

"Oh no. It can't be—"

"I know it's hard, darling, but he was eighty-two. It was bound to happen sooner rather than later." He poured her a cup of coffee.

"Oh, God, he just called me. Beth said it was urgent."

"About what?"

"I don't know. Remember? I told you, I never called him back."

"'Drina, why don't you call Esther? She must be distraught."

Sandrina was shattered. "It's only six in the morning there. I wouldn't know what to say to her."

"Think about it. In the meantime, I'll try to get us back to New York," he said.

There were two non-stop flights to New York, each with one seat available. Michael booked himself on the American Airlines flight, which left an hour earlier than the Air France one, both to appease her anxiety about American carriers and so that he could meet her at the gate when she arrived an hour later in New York. He then dialed the Baums and, on the third ring, handed her the phone.

Stewart answered in his most supercilious tone. "Stewart, it's me. Mrs. Morgan."

"Oh, Madam. I am sorry if I appeared rude just now. It's—"

"I can imagine. Don't worry. It's all right. Is Mrs. Baum awake yet?"

"She's in the kitchen having tea. But she hasn't been taking calls. Since it happened—"

"What exactly did happen, Stewart?"

"I was already changed, ready to leave for my Saturday afternoon off. I heard a loud noise from the main floor. I thought it might be a burglar, so I went upstairs and saw him lying there by the desk."

She heard him choke back tears. "If this is too painful to recount—" she said sympathetically, her eyes stinging too.

"No, of course not, Madam." He composed himself, stiff upper lip and all. "I called 911. It took the ambulance forty-seven minutes and twelve seconds to arrive. By then he was gone," Stewart continued.

"That's an awfully long time," Sandrina said, crying.

"Traffic from the parade, they said. Hold the line a moment, please, Madam. Mrs. Baum may take the call if she knows it is you."

Sandrina covered the mouthpiece with her hand so Esther wouldn't hear her sobs. She repeated the conversation to Michael, most of which he had already gleaned by eavesdropping. She took a deep breath to compose herself.

A tiny voice came on the line and said, "Sandrina, is that you?"

"Esther. Dear, dear Esther. It's me. I am so sorry—"

"I know, dear. We all are. Josh was loved by many."

"Are you okay?"

"I am now. My daughter flew in late last night from Florida."

"Are you able to discuss the arrangements? Do you need any help? Michael and I are in Paris but Michael has just rebooked our flights. We should be home tonight."

"That will be just fine, dear. The funeral will be tomorrow morning, at ten, at Parkside on Central Park West," Esther said.

"This must be an enormous hardship for you, Esther," Sandrina said.

"Not really, Sandrina. Ralph Aiken, Josh's attorney, made all the arrangements. He has been a godsend. But I am a bit tired now. Do you mind calling him for the details? Stewart can give you the number."

"Of course. Take it easy. I'll see you tomorrow."

Sandrina covered the mouthpiece. "Michael, I need a pen."

Stewart came back on the line with Ralph Aiken's home and office numbers, which she scribbled on a hotel de Vichy notepad. She stuffed the pad and pen in her purse.

"Michael, I'm so sad."

"I can imagine. Let's go for a walk. The rain has stopped. Some fresh air will do you good."

They only had a couple of hours until they had to leave Paris for Charles de Gaulle airport. They decided to take a stroll along the Champs Elysées, past the former courtesan's mansions, the Lido nightclub, fast-food shops and office buildings, and, at the corner of rue de Bassano, an ornate Art

Nouveau building that was once the l'Elysée Palace, where the spy Mata Hari, namesake for one of Esther's cats, was arrested in 1917. They had lunch at Le Fouquet's, where Sandrina ignored her food.

Michael and Sandrina sat suffocating from the cigarette smoke at the Paris airport for two hours until Michael's American Airlines flight departed, on time, at 5:55 p.m. Sandrina boarded her Air France flight, and sat sweltering on the runway for four hours while the mechanics tried to fix an ambiguous electrical problem. She felt her flu-like symptoms worsen, aggravated by her grief, the late hour without food or drink, and the heat in the cabin. When the airline finally canceled the flight after midnight, she could barely stand.

The passengers, angry and exhausted, filed out. The lines through passport control, and to rebook new flights for the next day, were overwhelming. Sandrina fainted at the feet of an Italian businessman, who picked her up in his arms and took her to customer service, where they revived her with cognac and smelling salts.

The only direct flight wouldn't get her home until Monday afternoon; long after the funeral would be over. Defeated, sick, and thinking things couldn't get any worse, Sandrina boarded the bus for the cinder-block airport hotel where Air France had decided to put them up for the night.

Yet another line awaited her, and this one took even longer than those in the airport, as the unsuspecting hotel had one desk clerk on duty to check in the unexpected guests. Her fever was raging as she finally unlocked the door to her cell-like room. She called to order room service, only to discover that there are hotels with neither room service nor, as she learned later when she tried to take a shower, soap.

She watched a cockroach scurry across the floor. Then she went to sleep.

Chapter Seventeen

The first person Sandrina called on Tuesday morning when she returned to the office was Ralph Aiken at Sherwood & Long. It was a link to Josh, and she used as her excuse that she wanted to find out Esther's state of mind before calling to explain why she had missed the funeral.

"I have been expecting your call. Are you calling about the Klimt or Mr. Larkin?"

Now Sandrina was really confused. "Excuse me, Mr. Aiken. I was calling to find out where Esther Baum is and how she is doing. I missed the funeral due to an airline snafu. I want to apologize, that's all."

"Forgive me for jumping the gun. I thought—"

"But now that you've mentioned them, what should I know about Misters Klimt and Larkin that I don't?"

"Well, the Klimt is good news. Joshua left it to you in his will."

"The drawing?"

"Yes, *Woman in Profile.*"

Sandrina was overwhelmed. "And, Mr. Larkin?"

"When I left Joshua on Thursday he said he was going to call you immediately, to tell you—"

"I was in Paris. We never spoke."

"Are you free today at four?" Aiken asked.

Sandrina glanced at her calendar. She had promised to stop by to see her mother at four. "How about tomorrow?"

"I'll buy you lunch at the Four Seasons. It's quiet there so we can talk. If you're still feeling up to it, we can walk over to Sutton Place and pay a call on Esther. She'll be at home."

What did he mean by 'feeling up to it'? "I'll be there," she assured him.

While Sandrina was pondering her conversation with Ralph Aiken, Beth plopped herself down in the corner chair of her office with the day's agenda and a list of phone calls Sandrina needed to return. Warren was not on the list. She realized that she had not heard a word from Warren since she had seen him in Baden-Baden, not sure if she felt relieved or a fool.

Joshua's death, the closeness to Michael, Baden-Baden—Death, Love, Betrayal—how like an opera her life had become! But it wasn't *Tosca*, where a curtain came down and the singers went home. It was real, and she became acutely aware that with every act of hers, real people were being hurt.

Snapping two fingers to get her attention, Beth reminded Sandrina of the Sharf and Rothstein hotel opening, the upcoming trip to Hawaii, some HR problems, a few billing questions, and other priorities that she needed to focus on. Randall Lamar from the *New York Post* called to get an advance copy of the celebrity list for the Millennium Universal opening, and Sandrina told Beth to order a few extra security guards to fend off the mob of paparazzi that she knew would be there. "Tell Isabel to come in here," she said. "To go over a few things."

"I'm sorry about Joshua Baum, Sandrina. I know you two were close," Beth said.

"Thanks, Mil. It's like losing a father."

"Why don't you take a few days off?" Beth asked.

"I think I will stay in Hawaii for the weekend after July fourth. I could use the rest, Michael will be away on business, and then I can pass through San Francisco on Monday to meet with Gary Brent and check in on the press junket at the spa," she said, reviewing her calendar. "It will be more therapeutic for me to stay busy."

When Beth had left, Sandrina checked her e-mail. She sighed. Not a word. Well, maybe he was doing her a favor—a crashed wave diverted.

There was, however, an e-mail from Herr Mangold at the Brenner's requesting a conference call.

And another from Claudius, spilling the beans. "Good news! You are getting the account. Act surprised."

Finally, one from her mother, "Sandy, can't wait to see you. Are you still coming at 4 pm? Love, Mom."

She forwarded Mangold's message to Beth to set up the call and answered the rest. She lost the tug of war with her better judgment and gave in, e-mailing Warren, wishing she hadn't as soon as she pressed send. "W - Did you arrive back safely? Love, Sandrina."

Then she saw Isabel's reflection in the glare of her computer screen.

"I understand you met with Max and Jason while I was gone," Sandrina said, turning around.

"Yes, a couple of times. I want to put your mind at ease about Jason. He's perfectly happy now. In fact, I'll be going to Hawaii the day after the opening—"

"Really? That's a surprise," Sandrina said. "Jason seemed so determined that I should be the one to go."

Isabel was different. Cocky, arrogant. Sandrina could see it through the sugar-coated veneer. "Well, I convinced him otherwise," she said.

"It may not be possible for you to go to Hawaii, Isabel. I am putting you on a new account." Sandrina briefly considered the wisdom of this decision but decided that she trusted Warren more than she trusted Jason.

Isabel's face became impassive. "Oh. Who are they?"

"Chaucer Suites. It is a hotel representation company with 212 properties throughout the U.K. The principal is a man named Warren—"

"Waterhouse!" Isabel blurted out, craning her neck to get a better view of Sandrina's computer screen. Sandrina thought Isabel looked as though she might shout "Eureka" at any moment.

"Do you know Warren Waterhouse?" Sandrina asked.

Isabel regained her composure. "Only by reputation."

"Well, you will meet him in person on Thursday. He's coming here." At least she thought he was still coming. "And, Isabel. Call Jason and tell him that you can't make it. Tell him you have conflicting business. Tell him that I am going instead, right after the fourth of July holiday."

"But Sandrina—"

"No buts about it. Do as I say."

Isabel reluctantly deferred. "I'll keep you posted," she said.

"You do that."

At 3:30 p.m. Sandrina announced that she was leaving and not coming back to the office. Staff members clamored for her attention, three of them escorting her down the elevator, throwing questions at her like tennis balls from an automatic pitching machine.

At four sharp, Sandrina arrived at Diana's door. In her hand she held a shopping bag filled with jars of Caracalla cream.

"You're here!" Diana exclaimed.

"Did you expect me not to be?" Sandrina asked.

"Well, with Joshua's passing so unexpectedly like that. I thought you might be in shock—" she replied.

"I am depressed about Joshua. Other than you, he was the greatest friend I had. His death makes life seem so urgent."

"That's not all that's bothering you though, is it?"

"No, there's something else too," she continued.

"Go ahead—"

"I'm so confused," she admitted. "I love Michael, but I'm in love with someone else."

"The one from Brazil?"

"Yes."

"Sandy, think of the consequences."

"I am."

"Is he pressuring you to leave Michael?"

"No."

"Is he in love with you too?"

"He's noncommittal."

"He knows you have more to lose than he does and he doesn't let you know where he stands?"

"The relationship is so new. Maybe he's just not sure."

"But you are?"

"Yes. I think so. Oh, I don't know. Why can't I just be content with what I have—a loving husband, a successful career?"

"Only cows are content, darling."

"Well, you and Dad divorced."

"Do you know why we divorced?"

"He was a gambler."

"And a cheat," Diana added.

They stared at each other. "You never told me that before."

"There wasn't any need to. Is Michael also—"

"No, at least I don't think so. He doesn't gamble either, or smoke, or drink. In fact, there's nothing really wrong with Michael."

"So what's the problem with your marriage, Sandy?"

Sandrina thought about the roles she and Michael played; how she was the strong one, having to take all the risks and make most of the decisions. How she wanted Michael to do more, but what she couldn't really say. And there always seemed to be something in the way—Thomas, business, life. But none of those reasons alone would be enough to cause her to stray.

"I was pregnant again, Mom. Last year."

"You never told me that!"

"There was no need to. I miscarried —"

"That's no cause for alarm, happens every day. You and Michael could have tried again."

"That's just it. He thinks things are fine the way they are. Before I miscarried, he was insisting on an abortion."

"Look at it this way, Sandy. Marriage is compromise. Two people may want or need different things at any given moment in time. Give a little, get a little. Over many years it all evens out."

"What about being 'in love'? Passion?" Sandrina asked.

"Love is a nearly infinite spectrum of emotions, and at different times everyone yearns to be in a place on the continuum other than the one she finds herself on. But after investing in a relationship for as long as you have, I think you should consider surrendering to where you are and be happy there, rather than searching for something not necessarily better, just...new," Diana said. "Have you ever read *The History of Rasselas*?"

"By Samuel Johnson? Yes, you gave it to me when I was fourteen."

"Well, read it again. Sometimes nirvana is right under our noses. We're just so used to the scent that we don't recognize it any more." Diana smiled.

In other parts of the world, noon may be the hottest time of the day. Not so in New York City. The tall glass buildings magnify and trap the heat so that as the day wears on it gets more and more uncomfortable. When Sandrina emerged from her mother's co-op building at five o'clock, it was downright steamy.

Ambling west along 57th Street, she stopped to admire the store windows along the way. In Burberry's she bought an umbrella for Michael, on impulse, then she entered Central Park at 60th Street and immersed herself in the innocence and oblivion of children playing late on a summer afternoon.

When she got home, Michael was already there.

"A present?" Michael said, kissing Sandrina on the cheek and eyeing the Burberry's bag.

"Yes. For you," Sandrina said handing him the long package.

"Gee, I can't imagine what this could be. A new shirt? An extra-long tie?"

"Very funny," Sandrina said.

"Just curious, 'Drina. What made you get me an umbrella?"

"I dunno…into every life a little rain must fall, I guess."

"How about dinner at Sant' Ambrose?"

"When?"

"In an hour or so? I have a little work to do."

"Sure. I'll change, watch the news."

It was dark downstairs when Sandrina went looking for Michael. She approached the study casually. When she knocked, there was no answer. She opened the door and peered in. He wasn't there. She combed the house, thinking perhaps he went to get a beer out of the fridge or a book from the library. Then she went back to her bedroom and tried the page on the intercom. No answer.

Michael was gone. Sandrina tried to reassure herself that he must have just run out for something. He didn't want to disturb her, so he hadn't told her he was leaving. When two hours had passed, she began to worry. Something was wrong. She felt it. She called downstairs and Angel, the night doorman, confirmed that he had seen Michael storm out just after the night shift had started.

Sandrina waited up, listening for the clicking of the key in the lock.

After two a.m., Michael came back. As soon as Sandrina heard the rumbling of the elevator stop at their floor she ran to the door and held her breath as she peered through the peephole. She saw Michael step off the elevator into the vestibule; with its trompe l'oeil murals and scented candle, burning there all the time, it made her think of the flame in

Arlington Cemetery. The brass knob twisted. Sandrina stood there looking at Michael and she at him.

"Michael—" Sandrina said. "What's happened? I was so worried."

He just looked at her. "I went for a walk."

Her first thought was that Thomas had been arrested, but she guessed that if that had been it Michael would have told her immediately.

Michael walked down the hall the other way. Sandrina heard him stomp up the stairs.

After some minutes, wondering what she should do, Sandrina turned the knob to the master bedroom and entered. Michael was lying on the bed, fully dressed, including his shoes, unshaven, rumpled, and sweaty. He had his arms folded across his chest and his fingers intertwined like a complex step in the game Cat's Cradle. Sandrina stood at the door, unsure if she should intrude or not.

Finally, she entered and sat on the bed in silence. Michael had dark shadows under his eyes, and his curly hair was matted like a pad of steel wool that had just scrubbed a pot.

"Michael, are you going to talk to me or not?" Sandrina asked.

She saw her husband's face register a multitude of feelings, from anger to pain to grief and, finally, as his eyes shifted to her, to love.

Sandrina sat on her marital bed, wringing her long fingers between her knees, willing herself not to cry. She stood up and hesitatingly moved toward him, to kiss him, to touch his shoulder, but he flinched and returned to his muted state of isolation. She recoiled, hurt, like a struck dog, and returned to her sentry position on the bed. She couldn't suppress the tears any longer.

All of a sudden Michael swung his legs to the floor with such force that the magazines blew off the night table. He walked away from her, to the other side of the room.

"I was sitting in the study, thinking about everything. These should be the best years of our lives. I feel so betrayed."

She felt the heat rush up from her chest to her face like a tidal wave of fire. *How does he know? He can't know.*

"Michael, I don't know what you're talking about. Help me to understand."

He slammed his fist on her vanity, shattering the glass top. "There was an e mail from Fernanda Calleja—she works in Accounts Payable. Fernanda resigned today, but apparently this evening she went home and sent me an e-mail from her personal address to tell me that not only did Thomas authorize those illegal payments but he also told her to use my signature stamp on them as well. My own brother."

Poor Michael, betrayed by the people closest to him.

Michael grabbed her by the shoulders and stared deep into her eyes. She felt accused.

"We need a plan—" As his arm fell to his side it hit her dressing table, sending the picture frames and shattered glass to the floor.

She covered her face with her hands, trying to hide her shame. What she should have done was embrace him, comfort him. But she was so overwhelmed by a feeling of relief that he hadn't found out about her—that she had betrayed him too—a feeling that was quickly replaced by guilt over ever having felt relief in the first place. When she let her hand fall to her sides he was gone again, as if the whole episode hadn't happened at all. Sandrina tiptoed down the hall and, seeing light coming from under the guestroom door, she knocked softly.

No answer. But she understood that he needed to be alone with his pain, just as she had when she'd lost the baby. At that moment, she knew she had failed him, as he had her. "Michael, I love you."

"I can wake myself," Michael said through the door.

In the morning, he had to be coaxed into joining Sandrina and her mother for breakfast at the

Carlyle. He sat stonily still throughout the meal, barely touching his eggs. Afterwards, on Madison Avenue, Michael turned on his heels and grabbed the first cab that passed by, leaving both women on the curb without so much as a goodbye.

"What's with him?" Diana asked.

Sandrina shrugged her shoulders, "He's so.... disappointed. And, angry too..."

"About what?"

"It's a long story..."

Diana thought for a few minutes. "Sandy, do you think he knows? They always do."

Sandrina knew what her mother meant. "I don't see how."

"A woman in love looks...different. If he didn't notice, it would be because he didn't want to know."

She remembered how he had looked deep into her eyes the night before. Had he been looking for answers, or the truth? "Do you think he'd leave me if he knew?"

"No. I think he'd forgive you." It started to drizzle. "Are you going to the office?"

"I'm too upset, Mom. I think I'll go home,"

"Want company?"

"You're always there for me, aren't you? Better not. I need to think. I promise to call you when I figure things out."

"Lie down and put cucumbers slices on your eyes, honey. Gets rid of the swelling from crying. Love you," Diana said, as she watched Sandrina move away.

"Me too you."

When Sandrina got home she sat on her bed for quite a while. She heard the phone ring several times but chose to disregard it, choosing to go downstairs instead, to the kitchen, to brew a pot of coffee. While it was dripping, she played back the messages on the answering machine.

Beth had called twice, saying it was urgent, as well as Michael, from his cell phone. Michael's message said that he would be in meetings for the rest of the day, and couldn't be reached, but that he would call her later.

She called Beth back. Her voice was weak.

"Sandrina, are you okay?" Beth asked.

"We've had a bit of a trauma here today, Mil."

"Your Mom okay? Michael?"

"Yes, everybody's fine now." She wondered if that was true. "I'm not coming in today."

"Sure. No problem."

"Anything important?"

"Arnelle is hysterical. She's got to talk to you about the opening."

"Ask Lucy to step in and help her out. I'll call Arnelle later. Around three."

"Betty from Mr. Aiken's office called, to confirm lunch today."

"Oh darn, I forgot."

"What should I do?"

"Tell her I'm out ill. Reschedule for next week."

"Max Sharf called. He and Jason want to see you."

"Tell him something personal came up. That I'll call him later. Set up a meeting with them and the team at two tomorrow to go over the details for the opening."

"A Mr. Waterhouse called. He wouldn't tell me what it was about."

"Did he leave a number?"

"He said you have it."

"Anything else?"

"You have that conference call in five minutes with Mr. Mangold from the Brenner's Park. Should I reschedule?"

Sandrina looked at the clock. It was five minutes to twelve. "No, what's the number?"

Steaming coffee mug in hand, she went down the hall to the study. There seemed a time lag between what she told her body to do and its delayed reaction. She wanted to turn off all the lights and hide under the covers, drift into a dreamless sleep, and wake up two months ago. While going through the motions of what she knew she should do, she battled with what her heart wanted her to do.

She dialed.

"*Guten abend.* Brenner's Park Hotel."

"*Sprechen sie Englisch, bitte.*" She did not have the strength to converse in German.

"Naturally," the operator said.

"Mr. Mangold, please."

He answered his own phone, which surprised her, until she realized that it was six p.m. in Baden-Baden.

"Hello. It's Sandrina Morgan. How are you?" She tried to muster up as much enthusiasm as possible. She had to be professional. She had to go on.

"Ah, good. Thank you for calling," he said. "Our presentations are complete. I have a couple of questions."

"Of course. I'm happy to answer them if I can."

"We were very impressed by your company's creativity and energy."

"Thank you."

"Your staff seems very competent."

"They are."

"How much of your time will we get?"

She took a deep breath, thinking that that question deserved a drumroll. "I am always available to you, whenever you need me. We don't charge by the hour—we're in a service business, Mr. Mangold. And I do tend to spend extra time with clients during the first year, to make sure things get off smoothly." Although she meant it, after she said it she realized she would have to stop promising herself to everyone who asked.

"Could you come here for our quarterly marketing meetings? I would like to have you serve on our marketing council."

"Of course. I would be honored." Maybe she would be able to migrate that function over to Lucy or Maria in time.

"And the spokesperson. Approximately how much out-of-pocket expense, for fees and travel, would she incur?"

"Or he, Mr. Mangold; now we're thinking of a man. Maybe an opera singer. In any event, he or she would probably require a fee of twenty thousand dollars, with another twenty or so for expenses."

She heard some scratching in the background. "Hmmm. I'm considering the budget. Could we sign the spokesperson up for a six-month trial and start her, or him, in January?"

"Of course."

"*Sehr gut.* Congratulations, Mrs. Morgan. You've got the job."

Sandrina called Lucy and Maria. Then she called Claudius and Christoff. Then she called Michael and got his mobile phone voice mail. It was her own voice; she had programmed it for him last Christmas vacation: "Hi, you've reached Michael Morgan's mobile phone."

"Michael, it's me. I'm home."

Sandrina went into the kitchen to make a sandwich. Warren had called, finally, exactly one week later. Where had he been? She had been to Paris, she had lost her mentor, and last night she had been to hell and back. And where was he while all this was happening to her. Who knew? But he wasn't there for her, that was for sure.

It had been Michael who comforted her and cared for her, although she knew now that no one could be there all the time. And she knew Diana was right. Michael would forgive Sandrina anything, while Warren was busy trying to figure out what it was he wanted out of life.

So what was it that had made her stray? What void existed in her life? Michael and work couldn't fill it up. Maybe the baby would have, but now she'd never know. Her instincts told her that while a baby—or an affair—might provide a temporary fix, the void could be filled only from within, not without.

Resolved, she went to her study and sent Warren an e-mail: "Warren, I can't do this any more. S."

The phone rang. It was Beth.

"Sandrina, it's almost three. Arnelle, Lucy, and Joseph are in the conference room waiting to talk to you about the opening. Who are you taking with you to Hawaii?"

"I was planning to go alone, but I might want to take someone else." But who? Not Isabel. "By the way, we got the Brenner's account. Can you send around an announcement from me and draft a contract?"

"Congrats! I knew we would. What's the fee?"

"Fifteen a month."

"Consider it done. I've rescheduled Mr. Aiken for Monday. Same place, same time."

"Thanks. Anything else?"

"Mr. Waterhouse called again. He said it was important and that he was a personal friend. I told him to call you at home. Hope that was okay."

Before Sandrina had a chance to answer, Beth switched her into the conference room. Her heart wasn't in it, so she listened perfunctorily for a few minutes and used the ringing of the other line as her excuse to cut the call short. She could see from the caller ID who it was.

Chapter Eighteen

"Hello?" she answered.

"What the hell did that e-mail mean? What exactly can't you do any more?" he yelled, still a lion but a growling one this time.

A chilling pain shot through her when she heard his voice like that, as when the dentist hits a nerve with the drill. "Warren—"

"Don't say anything. Let me talk."

She was quiet. Tears welled up in her eyes.

"Sandrina. I need to see you. I've been thinking. About us. I—"

"Warren. Where have you been? A week and no word. A lot has happened—"

"What do you mean?"

"It's just that, I don't know, I'm confused. It seems whenever we get really close, you disappear—"

"What? You're crazy. Do I have to remind you that you were in Paris with your husband? I have things…happening. I've been trying to work everything out—"

"It's just that I'm out on a limb, Warren. Emotionally. Joshua died."

"I know. I saw it in the paper. I'm sorry—"

"I need you—"

"You have me. You could have picked up the phone yourself, you know. It's not as though, under the circumstances, I can reach you whenever I feel like it."

"The limb, Warren. I feel like the branch is cracking." She paused, listening to him breathing. "I think Michael suspects something."

"Listen, Sandrina. We can't talk about this on the phone. Can we meet? Come here, to the Essex House. Come now."

"I can't."

"You can't or you won't?" This time the lion's growl was fierce.

"I can't. I have to stay here. In case Michael calls."

"Are you going to the office tomorrow?"

"I must," she said.

"Good. I'll come to your office at ten thirty as planned for the meeting, and afterwards I know a place where we can have lunch and talk things out."

When Warren arrived promptly the next day, Sandrina and her team were assembled in the conference room waiting for him. As soon as he walked in, a flush of desire spread through her body and a deep rush to her heart. Sandrina had briefed Isabel and Lucy thoroughly and then let Isabel do the talking; if she had tried to speak she was sure her words would come out as a choke.

Sandrina watched her protégé make the presentation with an acquired finesse that impressed her. Isabel was clever enough to openly credit Sandrina's reputation in the industry, and she even slipped in a flattering comment about how much better TravelSmart was than any of the competitors. It was an inch short of overkill.

Sandrina looked for warning signs or missteps, but Isabel performed perfectly; she was bright, articulate, prepared. To everyone else, Isabel must have appeared sweet and sincere, but Sandrina was beginning to see through her. Isabel was trying so hard to please Sandrina that she came off as cloying, with an aftertaste like artificial sweetener.

Warren thanked them and said he looked forward to working with them, the modulation in his voice different in a business meeting than when they were alone. Sandrina walked him to the elevators to show him out, and they arranged to meet in the lobby ten minutes later. As soon as Warren and Sandrina were out of sight, Isabel asked Lucy, whom Sandrina had asked to supervise the account, "Did you notice anything unusual between them?"

"Them whom?" Lucy asked, genuinely perplexed.

"Sandrina and the client."

"Isabel, what ever could you mean?"

"Didn't you see the sparks flying? Are they—?"

"Isabel. Stop there. Sandrina would never do that. I've known her for years. She —"

"Of course," Isabel said, retreating. "I've been reading too many romance novels."

Warren and Sandrina walked around the corner to a small French restaurant with a patio in the rear. Although it was warm, the patio had a trellis rooftop covered by amethyst wisteria, whose copious blooms and leaves provided shade from the sun. The tablecloths were a lime-green and soft pink Provençal pattern, and instead of flowers the centerpieces were arrangements of dried herbs. After Warren ordered a bottle of cold, fruity white wine, Sandrina looked into his eyes and lost her misgivings about his disappearances. He touched her cheeks gently with his strong fingers, and very slowly kissed her, first the lids of her eyes, then the parts of her face abandoned by his loving touch just seconds before, then her neck, more urgently, and, at last, her lips.

Sandrina remembered all the harsh judgments she had made about other people's infidelities. She understood now that being in love wasn't the result of weak character or mal-intent but rather a small spark that was struck inadvertently and could eventually make a whole forest burn. Especially if the forest had been left too dry too long.

Her eyes stayed fixed on his face, reregistering every detail, from the liveliness of his gold-flecked eyes to the male ruddiness of his skin.

"For a second, yesterday, I thought I had lost you," he said.

"It's not easy…" she began.

"There may be nothing easy about our circumstances, but you can't deny how easily things flow between us. Words, feelings, our bodies. I can love you passionately — for the tender, sweet woman I know you to be under those sharp outfits and business talk. I know how vulnerable you are."

"What about your needs? What do you want?"

"Sandrina, I love you. I want to change my life. Our lives. I want to be with you. I need no one, that's the truth. But I want to feel you leaning on me…" Then with a cockeyed smile: "Even if you knock me over on the floor once in a while."

She had tears in her eyes as she thought about the people who leaned on her, Michael, and her mother. Warren sat across from her representing the promise of the real thing at last, of being understood, but crossing the chasm would be perilous and the casualties dear.

The waiter interrupted. Warren ordered for her, something that made her feel taken care of — a salad and steamed mussels. She wasn't hungry anyway.

As he focused on her eyes, he said, "On the flight home I ruminated over the sudden shift in my perception of beauty. I thought back on all the women I desired before I met you. They paled by comparison. I am beginning to understand that the kittenish types I chose in the past viewed sex as a strategy, a bargaining chip of power, a means to an end."

"Do you mean marriage?" she asked.

"Sometimes that end was marriage, sometimes a promotion, or a play for position, money, or status. And sometimes..." He paused. "It was the power of conquest, a course of conduct I had previously attributed only to men. I used to think sexual encounters with beautiful young women were favors granted; I realize now that they were, in fact, debts incurred."

"Yes, but youth is hard to compete with. I look in the mirror —"

"You will always be beautiful, no matter what age," he said. "And, more important, you possess that very quality I sought from and thought was the exclusive right of younger women — the ability to live in the moment."

For a second or two, she knew that she would never love another man that way again. But she was committed elsewhere, to Michael and their life together. Her relationship with Warren was a solar eclipse, she the hot sun and he the moon of many faces. She felt her sun moving on.

As if reading her mind, he said, "I wonder if you would ever leave your husband."

She answered: "I could never hurt him like that."

Then, a rabbit out of a hat, he asked: "Would you have a child, Sandrina? With me?"

That was it—the tipping point. A child, a love child, what she had thought she wanted all along. The irony triggered a sad laugh.

"Yes," she said. "Yes, that's what I want too—"

Her cell phone rang.

"Sandrina, where are you?" Beth said.

"At lunch."

"For Christ's sake, it's four o'clock. Max and Jason are freaking out! You were supposed to be there at two."

"Oh, my God. Call them; tell them I had an emergency. I can be there at six or first thing tomorrow morning. Apologize for me. Let me know when you've reached them."

"Warren, I completely forgot a client meeting." Neither had touched their lunches; they were halfway through the second bottle of wine.

"I'm sorry. Was it important?"

"Never mind. It's more the timing than the urgency."

The phone rang again. It was Beth. "They want you on the new hotel site at six tonight *and* at eight tomorrow morning. Sandrina, they are really pissed."

"Okay, Beth. I'll be there. Send Lucy ahead."

"Lucy is out. She had a meeting with the photographers."

Sandrina was torn. She looked at Warren looking at her. Against her better judgment she said, "You had better send Isabel then. Make sure you tell her that I'll be there soon."

"Where were we?" she asked Warren.

He sighed. "You know what? I want to spend the rest of my life with you. Concentrate on your business now. You had better eat something, especially as it sounds as though you won't be getting dinner tonight." He smiled and brushed a lock of hair out of her eyes with the back of his hand.

Sandrina walked in just in time to hear Jason say, "You're a smart girl, Isabel."

"Yes, she is, isn't she," Sandrina agreed. "Max, are you all right? You look awfully flushed."

"He's fine," Jason said. "Let's get to work. We don't have a minute to spare."

After a grueling, seemingly endless meeting with Max Sharf and Jason Rothstein, Sandrina was nearly dead. They had hunkered down with nothing to sit on but wooden crates in the middle of what would be the lobby of the Millennium Universal Hotel, reviewing every detail of the extravaganza planned for the following evening. Because Max and Jason used to own comedy clubs, they understood the importance of timing, buildup, and the delivery of an effective opening line.

To see the place, any normal person would never believe that in twenty-four hours it would be ready to receive 500 guests. The construction crews were still working, and would be straight through the night in rotating shifts. There were pizza cartons and cigarette butts strewn about. The marble flooring was still covered with a white plastic film that had been heat-applied to protect it from scratches made by equipment and furniture being dragged across. Electricians were tinkering with the circuit breakers so that the wiring looked like spaghetti gone awry. Sandrina knew, having driven the same road many times before, that by Friday at eight p.m. everything would be perfect.

After reviewing each detail with excruciating precision, Max and Jason finally let her go at midnight. As soon as she got home she went to the bedroom. Michael was propped up on their bed reading *The Economist*.

"How're you doing tonight?" she asked.

"Better," he said.

She didn't know what she should say. The night before he had slept in the guestroom. At least now he had moved back into their bed. "Honey, I was at a meeting, for the Millennium Universal opening tomorrow night."

"Uh huh."

"You believe me, don't you?"

"Sandrina, I want to read. It helps get my mind off our problems."

"Okay, honey, good night." The cheek she kissed was cold and unresponsive.

That night she dreamed that she and Warren were walking on a beach. They were holding hands. It was a perfect sunny summer day. Warren hadn't shaved and she noticed that all the whiskers on his face were growing in exactly the same direction, and were soft, like the nap on velvet. They were completely alone. Then a black cloud came out of nowhere, around the bend, and under it, as if the cloud was his parachute, she saw Michael. She saw him before he saw them. And she didn't know what to do.

She woke up from her dream to find that Michael had wrapped his arms around her, and she could hear his breathing, choppy and uneven. Sandrina felt confused by how little had really changed in her relationship with Michael, despite her feeling, being, in love with Warren. Michael filled some profound need in her; she wondered what she would miss most about him if he were gone.

Warren's spicy erotic aroma, a mingling of nutmeg, wood shavings, and hyacinth, had stirred her senses, and she realized that she had long ago forgotten the way Michael smelled. Her senses blocked his imprint now for reasons she didn't understand. His smell, taste, and touch neither turned her on nor off. What she felt when she was with him now was comfort, and what she felt for him was sympathy.

"Good morning," he mumbled in her ear. Sandrina turned to face his dawn beard, so sparse and splotchy, with gray, black, and light brown hairs growing every which way, so unlike Warren's beard in her dream.

"Michael, I've got an eight o'clock with Sharf and Rothstein. The opening is tonight."

"Do you want me to come to the opening?"

"I'm touched that you would. But better not. I'll be too busy to pay you any attention."

"Then I might go to Southampton tonight. Thomas and I have our big powwow first thing in the morning, and you can work undistracted."

"That sounds like a good plan. I'll take the Jitney out tomorrow afternoon."

"You look tired, 'Drina. And worried."

"I guess I'm a bit of both."

"It's almost over," he said, but she wasn't sure which of their problems he was alluding to — the hotel opening, the *Finance Journal* story, or their marriage.

Sandrina knew she would have to look smashing that night, so she left a message for her hairdresser to stop by her apartment at six to style her hair. She splashed some water on her face and threw on a pair of black cotton pants and a sleeveless t-shirt. To dress up her casual outfit, she put on her lucky earrings, the black enamel with the diamond crosses, and a pair of Jimmy Choo sandals.

In the cab to East 42nd Street, where the new Millennium Universal would soon be open for business, she called Arnelle at home to get an update on the RSVPs. Then she made a quick stop at Starbucks.

The makeshift, on-site office that Max Sharf and Jason Rothstein had been using during the construction supervision phase consisted of two rooms in the basement of the hotel. The only natural light snuck in through slivers of windows at the tops of the walls that were eye level with the sidewalks outside. There were architectural drawings everywhere, documenting the hundreds of changes the development team had made during the process. To Max and Jason, they weren't building a hotel but creating a lifestyle. They had traveled the globe in search of creative details they could pilfer, resulting in a rich broth of ideas not unlike the stone soup of fairy tales.

Max had had leukemia for ten years, hanging on through remissions and reoccurrences by sheer force of will, and Sandrina had gotten used to the peculiar devastating symptoms of his disease. A couple of years earlier, Max had lost all of his body hair from chemotherapy and it never grew back, giving him the appearance of a baby. His body temperature had changed too. He was always freezing, even in the middle of summer, so his desk was surrounded by electric space heaters, glowing orange day and night. He had an insatiable craving for sweets, even though he was rail thin, so when she arrived the morning of opening night she brought with her a box of Starbucks pastries.

"Aren't you having one?" he asked. She toasted him with her grande latte.

"No, they're for you," she replied.

Jason arrived a few minutes later. "I didn't leave here until four a.m.," he said apologetically.

"The place looks great," Sandrina said. "Congratulations."

"So where do we stand?" Max asked.

"As of half an hour ago, we have a hundred and forty-two media acceptances," she reported.

"How many from foreign publications?" Jason asked.

"About thirty-seven," she estimated.

"It's the foreign buzz that I think will make us or break us," Jason said.

"How about the travel press?" Max asked.

"All accounted for. Not a single one declined," Sandrina stated.

"I would hope not. This is the most exciting hotel opening in New York City this century," Max said. Considering how young the century was, it was clear he hadn't lost his comedy club humor.

"We invited some off-beat press as well. The art publications are covering the opening, because of the giant Damien Hirst painting in the lobby."

"Did you know the staff has nicknamed it Herman?" Max said.

"As in Hesse?" Jason asked.

"And the Jeff Koons's on the walls. Of course the design magazines will be here. I've invited the downtown media, and have the technology editors and bloggers coming to cover the cutting-edge personal area networking set-ups in the guestrooms," Sandrina said.

"Inventive. Anyone else?" Max asked.

"The fashion media is coming to cover the outfits of the hoi-polloi," she said.

"What are you wearing tonight, Sandrina?" Jason asked.

"A sequined cat suit by Dolce & Gabbana," she said. "I was thinking of putting it on your bill."

Neither Max nor Jason laughed.

"It was a joke," she said.

They both emitted a sigh of relief.

"We called the *Wall Street Journal*. They're sending someone to do one of those quirky center-column stories. "

They talked a while about the security, food, music, and celebrity RSVPs. Angelina Jolie and Brad Pitt were expected, as well as Eliot Spitzer and Michael Bloomberg.

"In the same room?" Jason asked.

"It's a big place," Sandrina responded. "Big enough for two extra-large egos."

The Australian contingent had been invited, including Hugh Jackman and Nicole Kidman, but they never RSVP'd to anything. They just came if they felt like it.

At eleven, Arnelle, Joseph, and Isabel arrived to start getting things ready. They would set up the press tables; supervise the caterers, musicians, decorations, and security. Sandrina said goodbye and promised to return at seven p.m.

"Sharp," Jason warned.

The entire office was engaged in one way or another to pull off an event with 142 press people and 400 other high-profile guests. Last-minute changes to the highly controlled access list, special requests for lighting or exclusive interviews, particularly from the television media, timed releases of information so that everyone got what they needed before deadline, and the coordination of logistics occupied the whole staff so intensely that the day flew by and most other projects got put on hold. Sandrina was preoccupied, but Warren drifted in and out of her thoughts throughout the afternoon.

At four, the car service picked her up at the office and fought its way through traffic to her apartment on Fifth Avenue. She had an hour before her hairdresser was due to arrive.

For at least ten minutes she sat in front of the phone and stared. All day the plot had been hatching in her mind. With a crowd of anonymous strangers and security so tight it would keep out its own, the setting couldn't be more perfect. The question was—would he take the risk? Would he come if she begged him to? Without further hesitation, she dialed Walter Schneider, and caught him in his office on his way out the door.

"Walter, it's Sandrina Morgan, Michael's wife."

"I know who you are."

"I'm calling about the letters."

"They're safe and sound in our safe."

"I know. But we need them too. We need proof that my husband is innocent. Can we meet somewhere?"

"I'm afraid I can't help you. Besides, I'm sure I'm being followed. We could never meet without being seen."

"I know a place where it's possible..." Sandrina said, thinking of the airtight security she could count on for help. "Walter, you don't mind celebrities by any chance, do you?"

After hanging up, Sandrina was trembling so hard in anticipation that she turned on the TV to calm herself down before she undressed and stepped into the shower to wash the fine construction dust from the hotel out of her eyebrows and hair. The water pooled around her feet while she looked for a towel, feeling troubled and unsure about how she could reconcile the feelings she had for Warren and the love she felt for her husband. Proud Michael, how vulnerable he was just now.

Ritchie, all punk-blond hair and multi-pierced nose, arrived and styled her hair. Struggling into her skin-tight black sequined cat suit, she finished off the ensemble with an exquisite pearl choker and earrings from Harry Winston. Marcus Lippincott, public relations director for Harry Winston, had called her earlier that afternoon to offer the set, insured for a quarter of a million dollars, and delivered by armored car. It was a perk of the business that Sandrina took advantage of on special occasions to add sparkle to her allure, but tonight the jewels hung uncomfortably on her ears and throat.

Absentmindedly, she fondled her engagement ring while she looked in the mirror. The apartment was silent, with Michael gone, and she could hear Warren's voice reverberating in her ears: "Will you have a child with me?" Then the doorman rang, breaking her trance, to say that her car had arrived.

The police had cordoned off East 42nd Street in anticipation of a big crowd. Due to the Millennium Universal's proximity to the United Nations, and the continuing threat of terrorist attacks in New York City, cars were only permitted to drop off passengers but not to stand or wait within a four-block radius of the hotel. Several of the rich and famous were angered by the inconvenience. Many chose to walk, because it was a lovely summer evening, creating the atmosphere of a pedestrian zone found in the old-town sections of European cities like Heidelberg and Milan once past the guard checking people in.

When Sandrina's car pulled up in front of the hotel, it was still light outside. The sky was striped magenta and orange and dotted with wispy-white clouds. Max and Jason were conferring upstairs in a guest room. After double-checking that Walter Schneider was on the VIP list, she let her clients know that she was there and then went to check with her staff on the details.

All was in order as the guests began to arrive. At around eight, the Park Avenue socialites popped in, on their way to the Hamptons or Litchfield County. The women were dressed in summer silks and chiffons by Gucci, Prada, Valentino, and other, mostly European, designers. Closer to ten, the younger chic set, mostly traders who worked on Wall Street or the children of former real estate tycoons and investment bankers, wearing Ralph Lauren, Dolce & Gabbana and Chloe, passed through to be photographed for *W* or *In Style*. By midnight they went on to private parties in penthouses or late dinners at Aureole or Daniel.

At midnight, the downtown crowd began to make their appearances. In summer leather by Roberto Cavalli and outré frocks by Stella McCartney and Alexander McQueen, with barely a body untattooed somewhere, with spiky hair in orange, cranberry, lime, and raspberry sorbet, they spent their days as artists, designers, performers, restaurateurs, and observers of the netherworld.

The constant flashing and popping of the paparazzi cameras, desperately trying to capture a celebrity glimpse, was blinding. Every time Sandrina opened her eyes she thought she saw Warren, in the crowd, at the bar, drifting between rooms. But as soon as the bright light dispersed, he was gone.

At four a.m., when the last of the revelers had gone home, Max, Jason, and Sandrina were splayed and spent on the ballroom carpet. They were drinking coffee, although they hardly needed the caffeine.

"What do you think?" Jason asked. As he spoke, his eyes were bright. Sandrina had always thought it odd that he spoke only out of one side of his mouth—like Popeye without the pipe.

"All the right people were here," Sandrina confirmed.

"Was that accountant-looking guy you spent so much time talking to, you know the one who handed you that envelope before drooling on Madonna, from the financial press?" Jason asked, pointing to the white vellum envelope Sandrina guarded in her lap.

"Oh, him. No, he was…an accountant."

Jason scratched his head.

"How many working media actually did show up?" Max asked.

Sandrina leafed through the papers Arnelle had given her before she left. "Every network was here, as well as CNN, Fox, ZDF, and BBC. You guys pulled off fourteen one-on-one interviews. The wire services and syndicates were in full force with photographers and everything. The gossip columnists—"

"Speaking of which, did Donald Trump really show up with Melania and Monica Lewinsky?" Max asked.

"None other," Sandrina replied.

"I thought he liked thin blondes," Max asked.

"He likes free ink," Sandrina stated.

"Can you leak that to the press?" Jason asked.

"I'm not sure that's necessary. I brought Marc Malkin over to meet them. By Monday, the tidbit should be everywhere. On second thought, I'll do a limited release to the Washington media tomorrow. This old story might take on a short second life now that Hillary is Secretary of State," Sandrina said. "Max, Jason, I'll send you a complete report on Monday after I have a chance to confer with the team. Right now, I'm going home."

By the time she got to the apartment and changed, it was morning and she couldn't sleep. On impulse she picked up the phone.

"The Essex House," a voice said.

"Mr. Waterhouse, please," Sandrina requested.

"How did it go last night?" Warren asked, his voice groggy and slow.

"I kept seeing you. Were you there?"

"No. I didn't know I was invited."

"I thought you came anyway."

"Would I have gotten past the army I saw on TV?"

"No."

"Do you want to come over?"

"Now? I haven't slept."

"Come now. We can have breakfast."

Sandrina showered and brushed her teeth, all the time feeling as though she were moving in slow motion. Deep shadows the shape of half-moons had appeared under her eyes. She hid them with cover-up and quickly brushed her lashes with mascara and put clear gloss on her lips. Then she tied her wet hair back in a ponytail, put on her khakis and a t-shirt, and tossed her sunglasses and a book into a backpack, prepacked with the dinner clothes she intended to take with her on the Jitney to Southampton later that afternoon.

In the taxi on the way to the Essex House, she realized that she did not know his suite number. She pulled out her cell phone.

"Warren, it's me. How do I find you?"

"I'm in Suite 302. But, Sandrina, this place is a dump, and I have a bachelor's refrigerator. In other words, empty. The dining room opens in ten minutes. I'll meet you downstairs."

"Better hurry. I'm here."

Sandrina was waiting in the lobby for five minutes when Warren sauntered out of the elevator. He looked like an oasis in the desert to her, and she couldn't take her eyes off him as he moved toward her; his hair was wet, accentuating the variation in color, and he had a small nick on his chin where he'd cut himself shaving. Intertwining his fingers with hers, he kissed her on both cheeks, brushing noses as he transported his lips from one side of her face to the other.

The lion's roar of a laugh as he said, "You look seventeen."

"I feel ninety," she replied.

They sat at a table with a view of the horse-drawn carriages lined up on Central Park South. It was feeding time, before the tourists descended on the Park, and the long coppery bay and sorrel and dapple-gray faces disappeared into dented chrome buckets filled with oats.

Sandrina entertained Warren with stories about the night before. The cast of characters, costumes, interactions between people.

"Donald and Melania and Monica? What a threesome. Who would have thunk it?" he said, signing the check before they wandered back into the lobby of the hotel. The Essex House had a block-long thoroughfare that ran the length of the building between Central Park South and 58th Street. At each end was a revolving glass door. In the middle, a hallway that housed the elevator bank intersected the long strip. Warren and Sandrina stood there, at the crosswalk, nuzzling, touching, with every part of their bodies and faces except their hands and lips. They wavered. Should they go upstairs, should they not? Finally, Warren decided.

"Not now. There's not enough time," he said again. "Come on. I'll take you to the Jitney."

Chapter Nineteen

Michael met Sandrina at the Jitney stop in Southampton with a worried frown. Groggy from sleeping deeply on the bus, she had nearly forgotten the treasure she held in her purse. "The plot sickens," he said. "Let's go to the Golden Pear for coffee. We need to talk."

She patiently sipped her delicious frothy cappuccino and waited for him to speak.

"'Drina, there's been an interesting development. Thomas has offered me a deal."

"What kind of deal?"

"He's agreed to put in writing that I had no knowledge of any wrongdoing and that any liability resulting from a potential investigation would be his—"

"Michael, he's not doing this out of the goodness of his heart. What's the catch?

"I would have to walk from my shares. And sign a gag agreement," Michael explained.

"If you are subpoenaed, you'd have to talk. He wouldn't expect you to perjure yourself, would he?"

"What do you think?"

"Anything else?"

"He's offered me the subsidiary that develops and manufactures specialty chemically treated papers."

"Does it have potential?"

"I've always thought so, but it burns cash like crazy. All that R&D expense —"

"Why would Thomas be willing to make a deal now?"

"That's what I've been wondering."

Sandrina was suspicious that Thomas had been having her tailed. Otherwise, how could he have guessed about her rendezvous with Walter Schneider? Unless he'd had Walter followed as well — all the way to the Millennium Universal. "You think he's worried you'll get the letters Walter has in his safe?"

"Naw, then what incentive would I have to leave all that money behind?"

Michael was right. And for one tiny second she considered giving him Walter Schneider's envelope with the exonerating evidence so he could slug it out in court. But then it might be years, more likely decades, more of Thomas. "Good point."

"He's greedy, 'Drina. Our business is very asset intensive, and with the legal bills looming, he needs to raise capital. The industry is in the midst of consolidation. I'm thinking that maybe he's in talks with one of the biggies — International Paper, Georgia Pacific, Mead-Westvaco, maybe Weyerhaeuser. He knows I'd never agree to be acquired."

"So if he has a buyer, the *Finance Journal* brouhaha blows over, and you're out of the picture—"

"—Thomas gets it all."

"So he shuts you up and picks your pocket at the same time. Sounds like a true Thomas deal. Michael, despite the inequity, my instinct tells me that this is an opportunity for you to come out of this clean."

"If only I had those letters, 'Drina…if I knew for sure I could come out of this clean."

"Would you still take Thomas's deal?"

"Yes. For us."

Sandrina reached into her purse and pulled out the white vellum envelope. "The originals are home in the safe upstairs."

When he realized what she had done, he said: "Sandrina, how did you do it? You're a…" She held her breath, expecting him to say *bruxa*. "…magician! Can you pull another rabbit out of your hat? Come up with my next act? I can't see walking away from all that money without seeing the forest through the trees."

She laughed. "Was that a pun?"

"Not an intentional one." He laughed too.

Sandrina had been thinking about a plan for Michael's situation for weeks. Since he had told her about the federal investigation, upping the ante, her wheels had been turning more urgently, and as soon as they arrived at Thomas's house she plugged in her laptop and started researching her idea further—the idea she had ironically gotten from a conversation with Warren. It had to do with commodities.

Michael sat across from her on the other side of the large partners desk in Thomas's study. Sandrina could see him, and he her, but neither could see what the other was doing on his laptop. She saw him read his e-mail, look up at her, and smile. She noticed him hit the delete key in an exaggerated gesture before moving on to read the rest of his messages.

They worked until five and then went upstairs to change. Sandrina undressed and Michael came up behind her, running his hand up the curves of her body and through her hair. He made love to her so sweetly and gently that she felt as though he had sung her a lullaby instead. They lay in each other's arms for a long time, listening to the fierceness of the waves, and she thought how people are like seawalls: they take the storms and the pounding that life dishes out, and just keep on repairing and strengthening for the next round. They carry on.

A long table had been set for the dinner and placed by the pool out back. Pamela's decorator had had slipcovers sewn from tissue-weight Irish linen that made the hotel standard banquet chairs look exotic and ephemeral. A heavier fabric, the color of beach sand with a pattern of fleur-de-lis, covered the table. Each place had a different setting of china, in pastel colors mirroring the ocean's hues, from sea-foam green to turquoise blue.

There were many other guests invited to dinner, which Sandrina had not expected considering the tension of the situation. She sat between Thomas's dentist, who told dirty jokes all night, and Pamela's jeweler, who, after a few glasses of wine, told her how Thomas had negotiated brutally for every necklace and pair of earrings Pamela owned. The broker who sold them the house was there, with his pregnant mortgage broker wife, as were Thomas's doctor and Pamela's tennis pro.

"Don't they have any friends who aren't on the payroll?" Sandrina whispered to Michael when she left her seat at one point during dinner.

"Would you be friends with Thomas unless you got paid?"

"Good point," she agreed.

Time had only exacerbated the mutual dislike between Thomas and Sandrina because Sandrina refused to allow Thomas to control her and she thought he was a boor. It had been nearly thirty-six hours since she had slept but for a short nap on the jitney, but she was alert. The instincts of a guerrilla fighter charged her, and her adrenaline was pumping as if she were at war and the enemy at camp.

Sandrina used her lack of sleep as an excuse to leave the party early, signaling for Michael to follow her upstairs so they could be alone. They heard the crowd talking, and the music playing, as they whispered.

"'Drina, I looked into starting another U.S. paper mill when this all started a couple of months ago, but Thomas would squash me like a bug."

"Don't be afraid of Thomas," she said.

"I'm not like you. You're afraid of nothing," he said. Warren had told her the same thing. "But even if I weren't afraid, the fundamentals don't work. When our great-grandfather started Morgan Paper, it was a healthy, competitive business with high margins. It costs two billion to build a mill these days, and paper has become a commodity."

There was that word again—commodity.

"You're smart and connected," she said. "How about Europe?"

"In Europe, Thomas could cut off the supply of raw material with a few phone calls before we manufactured a single sheet," Michael said. "We need a new idea, a proverbial needle in the haystack."

"Michael, I have an idea," she said. It was now or never. She sucked in her breath.

"An electronic paper exchange. A couple of weeks ago, I read a report from Goldman Sachs predicting that online exchange transactions will exceed six hundred billion dollars in a few years. You know everyone in the industry, you'll have instant credibility, and Thomas will need *you* —"

"You're onto something, Sandrina. The paper industry has so many intermediaries — converters, cutters, distributors, paper merchants — between the manufacturer and the customer. It's always been inefficient. And there are fluctuating imbalances between supply and demand."

"Exchange-based hedging tools could help smooth that out as well," Sandrina added.

"Cool. So how does it make money?"

"There are really three ways. I think you could do them all. First, you can charge a membership fee. If a company doesn't pay the fee, it can't trade," she explained.

"Like a seat on the New York Stock Exchange."

"Right. But virtual seats are unlimited — the more members, the better. Second, you can charge a transaction commission. The standard on other exchanges seems to be around three percent. How big is the market?"

"Last year the world paper market, in the seventy-five countries that count, was around three hundred billion dollars."

"How many players?"

"It's the old eighty-twenty rule. About twenty percent of the players—say, two thousand global corporations and a few hundred buyers and sellers—drive eighty percent of the revenues."

"Piece of cake. You could call them all on the telephone."

"That's true; I know most of the players personally."

"The third revenue model is to charge posting fees to the sellers, like eBay does, " Sandrina said.

Michael was warming to the idea. "What do we call it? E-PAPER? P-Bay?"

"Nah, that's too unoriginal. We'll think of something."

Chapter Twenty

When Sandrina got to the office on Monday morning, Isabel presented her with a 30-page PR plan for Chaucer Suites that she had worked on all weekend. "Well, Isabel," she said. "No grass can grow under your feet."

"I learned that from you," Isabel replied. "The best, I might add."

"I'll need to look this over carefully before sending it to the client. Has Lucy seen it?"

"Not yet. She's still not in."

"I see one problem already — the contract isn't even signed yet."

"Not a chance that won't happen. Mr. Waterhouse was sold. I have confidence you can handle him."

Sandrina did not want to stifle the girl's enthusiasm. "Okay, thanks."

"I'm going down to Starbucks, Sandrina. Can I get you something?"

"That would be great!" Sandrina reached for her purse. "I'll have —"

"I know. A grande latte with vanilla and cinnamon and two equals. And put your purse away. It's on me."

Well, that was a first.

Sandrina entered the Four Seasons through the 52nd Street entrance so she could stop in the ladies' room before meeting Ralph Aiken. The scene she encountered in the downstairs lobby was rather comical; four men in suits on Blackberries placing that last frenzied text before lunch, as if the world couldn't wait another hour and a half for them to finish eating.

Ralph Aiken was standing by the reservations desk with his hands in the pockets of his gray flannel suit. His shirt was white and his tie a conservative solid blue. He rested slightly more on the heels of his wing-tip shoes than on the toes, giving the impression of impatience rather than anticipation. He was slightly jowly but still handsome, especially when he met Sandrina's green eyes with his seen-it-all blue ones.

Sandrina shook hands with Ralph Aiken.

"Strong handshake," he said.

"Thank you," she replied.

Although Sandrina preferred the crisp businesslike atmosphere of the Grill Room, the maitre d' led her and Ralph Aiken across the vestibule to the left, past the Picasso tapestry, into the more formal Pool Room.

"It is more private here," Aiken offered.

"Mr. Aiken—"

"Ralph. Please call me Ralph. Care for a drink?"

"Iced tea, please."

Ralph ordered two iced teas from the waiter.

"Ralph. To what do I owe the honor of this invitation, shrouded in mystery as it is?"

"Sandrina, I represented Joshua Baum for over twenty years. We became friends. He was very fond of you."

"He was a great man. I loved him very much," she said. "I miss him every day."

"I had an unusual relationship with him," Ralph explained. "I'm really a corporate lawyer, you know, contracts, M&A. But we're a big firm, and over the years I gradually took over all of Joshua's legal needs. His estate, real property closings, tax planning, small litigation matters, eventually confidential personal issues as well."

"Is this leading somewhere?"

"Sandrina, please be patient. This is difficult, and I'm not even sure ethical, because my client is deceased. But I know he would want me to have this conversation. So I'm here more as his friend than in an official capacity."

The waiter returned. Sandrina ordered Dover sole meunière. Ralph asked for the Four Seasons burger. Sandrina buttered a mini-croissant that she fished out of the big silver bowl full of bread.

"I'm sorry," she said. "Please go on."

"The Monday before he died, Josh called me and asked me to contact a Ken Larkin, editor of the *Finance Journal*. You see, there was a problem that needed to be fixed."

"Does this have to do with my husband's business?"

"No. It has to do with you —"

The food was served. They took a few bites in silence.

"The *Finance Journal* is going to publish a series of investigative reports on Morgan Paper. But they had planned to run a box along with the story about how Michael Morgan's powerful publicist wife tried to bribe the *Journal* into abandoning its investigative tack."

Sandrina remembered how she had pushed the envelope of ethics in a last-ditch effort to help Michael by offering to trade information with Larkin. "How did Josh find out?"

"Somehow Joshua knew everything."

Sandrina could only smile at the bold truth of Ralph's statement. "That type of article would ruin me."

"That's why Joshua had me threaten a libel suit."

"And Larkin backed down?"

"He admitted he was the only one who heard the 'bribe.' It would've been his word against yours."

"I had no idea—"

"Josh was sure you knew nothing. He said he had to call you right away."

"He did. But, as I told you before, I was out of the country. When I came back…he was gone."

Aiken shook his head. "Did you know about the Klimt?"

"No, that was also a complete surprise."

"Beautiful drawing. I've always admired it." He cocked his head to the side and remarked, "Now that I think about it, Sandrina, I can see a resemblance."

"Ralph?"

"Yes?"

"How does it work? Do I owe you anything for your services?"

"Not a penny. It was covered under Joshua's retainer."

The waiter interrupted again to take their orders for dessert. Blackberries for Sandrina and chocolate velvet cake for Ralph.

"I guess that's what Joshua was calling to tell me," Sandrina said.

"Actually, there's more. When he couldn't reach you, he called me to say that if anything happened to him before you returned to New York I should give you a message. He said, 'In a relationship, one person always loves more. Stay with that person, Sandrina.' That was Joshua's advice."

Michael would forgive you for anything.

Her knees were shaking under the cloth but her body from the tabletop up was as poised as a nun.

"Sandrina, shall we stop by and pay a call on Esther now?"

"You were right, Ralph. I'm not feeling up to it right now. But I promise to see her this week."

When Sandrina was upset, she walked. After her lunch with Ralph Aiken, she felt as though she desperately needed the salve of nature and Joshua to talk to, but her only choice was to walk the gritty, noisy streets of Manhattan and talk to herself.

She headed west on 52nd Street, almost getting clipped by a limo with blacked-out windows because she was preoccupied and had crossed the street against the light. Heading south on Madison Avenue, she hit 23rd Street and then cut over to Fifth, taking a detour over to ABC, an emporium of unusual gifts and household items, because she wasn't ready to go back to the office yet.

Finally, she circled back to her office building on lower Fifth Avenue, where three silent Venuses greeted her.

Sandrina booted up her computer. Beth's voice came over the intercom. "Michael's on the phone."

"How was your lunch?"

"Interesting. Joshua's lawyer took me to the Four Seasons."

"How come?"

"Josh left me the Klimt in his will. The blue drawing, *Woman in Profile*."

"Wow! You have any idea what that's worth?"

"Does it matter? It's priceless to me."

"Listen, 'Drina, we have dinner with the Gaspars tonight. I just noticed it in my calendar. Where should we go? I thought Daniel."

"That's a great idea."

"Let's meet at home at six," he said. "And thank you again...for the weekend."

Sandrina felt a pair of eyes drilling into her back. She turned around in her chair, expected to find Beth. It was Isabel.

"Nice suit," Isabel said, and walked away.

Lucy came in a moment later for a scheduled meeting. "What was that about?"

"Isabel was just admiring my suit," Sandrina reported.

"She did a great job on this plan," Lucy said, leafing through the document. "It is ambitious, but she seems capable and willing to execute."

"Good. Tell her to send over bound copies, and I'll call Warren to set up a meeting."

"I thought you knew," Lucy said.

"Knew what?"

"Isabel was over there today, at twelve-thirty. She delivered the bound copies in person to Mr. Waterhouse. They met for two hours."

"Alone?"

"I guess so. I couldn't go, and she said you couldn't either—"

"Beth!" Sandrina shouted through the wall. Beth came in. In a low voice Sandrina asked her, "Did Isabel check my schedule with you regarding a meeting today with Chaucer?"

"Yes. She came by yesterday and asked if you were free today at 12:30 p.m. I told her, 'No'."

"What did she say?"

Beth thought for a second. "She said, 'What a shame.'"

"Beth, please ask Isabel to come in here right away." Sandrina waited restlessly, thinking about what she should do next, trying not to overreact. This could be nothing more than being on edge. She was not objective, not when it came to Warren anyway. Or Isabel.

"Sandrina?" Isabel said from the hallway just steps outside Sandrina's office. "You wanted to see me?"

"Sit down," Sandrina commanded, trying to keep her cool. "I hear you had a meeting with the new client today. How did it go?"

"It went well, I think. I was nervous because you weren't available during the only time Mr. Waterhouse was. A couple of his clients were here from England. He wanted to take advantage of their presence to garner support for the effort. You should have heard him, Sandrina. He went on for twenty minutes about how smart you are, how successful, how well-connected."

"Uh-huh. And what did you do?"

"Why, I agreed of course. You're not mad at me, are you? I'm only doing my best for TravelSmart. I know how busy you are." Isabel smiled that ingratiating fruit-slice smile.

"Any other plans I should know about?" Sandrina asked.

Isabel hesitated, as if she were trying to remember. "Oh yes, there's a Chaucer Suites board meeting in London next month. Mr. Waterhouse wants me to present the plan to the Board. Can you make it?"

Sandrina felt her flesh crawl. And what if she couldn't make it? Did Isabel plan to go anyway? "I'll check and let you know if you can confirm the meeting or not," Sandrina said, unyielding.

"I just want to tell you how much I admire you, Sandrina. In the year I have been here I've learned so much. You're just the best there is. Thank you for all you've done for me."

"Anything else?"

"Oh, one little thing. I almost forgot," she said. "Do you mind if I take my vacation after London? If we go, that is. My Dad lives in Dublin, and it would really save me a lot of money if I could pop over and visit him while I'm already in the U.K."

"Sure, no problem," Sandrina said, secretly hoping that Isabel would find a reason not to come back.

Chapter Twenty-One

Daniel, on 65th Street, had an understated elegance that attracted an upscale New York crowd. Sandrina was still reeling from her couched confrontation with Isabel. She wanted to discuss it with Michael but feared that he would find her behavior paranoid, or somehow catch on that there was something about this new client that rattled her cage. After all, on the surface, Isabel was just doing her job.

Walking arm in arm the few blocks between their apartment and the restaurant, Michael and Sandrina arrived on time but the Gaspars were already waiting. A bottle of Taittinger Compte de Champagne rosé was chilling, and Sandrina noticed that every table in the room was full.

They all warmly embraced. "We were lucky you were in town. Still traveling so much?" Beatriz asked Michael.

"I'm leaving for Chicago in the morning—" Michael looked at Sandrina and smiled "—to meet with the Commodities Exchange, and I won't be back until Thursday."

"You would have missed us then," Beatriz said. "We're going to a horse auction in Kentucky tomorrow."

Flavio looked around at the crowd. "I thought there was a recession in America?"

They all ordered chilled fresh pea soup, followed by canapés of salmon roe, with fat beads like salty Tic Tacs that popped in the mouth. The ladies had farm-raised squab and the men short-ribs braised in red wine, accompanied by the chef's special potatoes, pan-crisped with chives, parsley, and black olives. They were so stuffed they skipped dessert and settled for the lemon meringue tartlets and chocolate drops that were served with coffee after the meal.

Sandrina had an overwhelming feeling that this was where she belonged — not in a fancy restaurant in a designer dress but with her husband and old friends. She was overcome with gratitude, for her success, Michael, her loyal clients and acquaintances. But deep in her heart, she was still conflicted over what she really wanted from love.

Michael beamed at her across the table. He would never hurt her; of this she was sure.

Catching her attention he said, "Sandrina, wake up. Flavio is talking to you."

"What did you think of our Copacabana, Sandrina?" Flavio repeated his question.

"It was even more spectacular than I imagined it would be."

"Did you enjoy Rio?" Beatriz asked.

"Very much. Has business been picking up since we launched the new marketing strategy?" Sandrina asked, shifting gears.

"So-so," Flavio said. "We still cater mostly to business travelers, but their numbers are way down — the economy and a greater reliance on video conferencing, I'm told. The leisure clientele has all but vanished so the net result, in terms of profits, is negative."

"I know we have big articles scheduled to appear in *Departures* and *Journey*, in time for the winter holiday season and Carnival. I'm sure that will help," Sandrina replied.

"Ah, that is when we make sure we are not in Rio. It's so hot," Beatriz said.

The thought of hot Rio made Sandrina shiver.

As they were about to leave, Flavio pulled Sandrina aside.

"I received the strangest phone call from a Ms. Isabel Riley," he said.

"She called you?" Sandrina couldn't believe her ears.

"Yes. The woman requested a meeting, claiming she thought there were a few things I should know — about your 'character.' How did she know I was in New York? And that you had been in Brazil?"

"What did you say?" Sandrina asked, willing herself to keep calm.

"I told her I did not have time to meet with her on this trip, assuring her that I knew everything about your character that I needed to know. After thanking her for her concern, we ended the conversation."

"Thank you for telling me, Flavio."

"Sandrina, we have a saying in Brazil: *Te cuida.* It means 'watch your back.'"

"I thought that was Italian," Sandrina said.

"Unfortunately, Sandrina, every language needs a version, and its meaning is universally understood."

Diana opened the door with a coat of chalk-white Clinique face masque at least half an inch thick spread all over her face. She was wearing a paisley silk bathrobe and smoking a cigarette from a mother-of-pearl holder that she had had for as long as Sandrina could remember. In her hand there was a paperback copy of Michel de Montaigne's *Essays*.

"Back again?"

"Is that any way to greet your only daughter?"

"It's seven thirty in the morning."

Sandrina plopped down on the cantaloupe-colored couch. "This is serious."

"Being in love with one man while you're married to another is very serious," Diana said. She sat next to Sandrina and put her cigarette out in the ashtray.

"Believe it or not, that's not my only problem."

"So? I'm waiting."

"It's Isabel."

"That girl is like a cancer, Sandy. Cut her out of your life before her poison spreads."

"I'm afraid it's too late. She's metastasized."

"It's never too late. Trust me. Cut your losses and move on."

"It's not that simple. It takes time and thought to extricate the clients from her clutches. She's managed to ingratiate herself with my oldest and biggest client," she said, referring to SH. "Losing them would be almost as bad as losing Josh. They're like family; they've been with me from the beginning."

"Yes, I know how much they mean to you. Still, they're only one client."

"I suspect she's moving in on some others too." Chaucer and Gaspar Hotels came to mind, and she wondered if there were more as well.

"Don't frown. You'll get permanent lines," Diana said, smoothing Sandrina's furrows with her thumb.

"I have to go," Sandrina said. "I'd kiss you, but…"

"I understand. Going to the office?"

"Eventually, but first I have an important stop to make."

It was rush hour as Sandrina emerged from the air-conditioned lobby of her mother's apartment building into the madcap intersection of Park Avenue and 58th Street. She stood there for a few minutes to gain her bearings. People whizzed by in both directions, nearly knocking her down. She felt the motion of their rushing past like a too close encounter with a speeding truck.

She turned left on 57th Street, and walked east. She crossed Sutton Place and walked toward a patch of green, Sutton Garden, noticing the townhouses that lined the mews and the sheet-of-postage-stamps pattern they made. She sat in the park, and closed her eyes. The cool morning breezes from the river made her feel as though she were on a catamaran, drifting away from her problems.

A tugboat horn let her know it was nine o'clock. Esther's house was around the corner and she rang the bell to see if Esther would see her unannounced. Stewart opened the door and smiled broadly, out of character for the normally dour houseman.

"Mrs. Morgan. So good to see you," Stewart said.

"Is Mrs. Baum at home?"

"Yes. Come in. She's having coffee in the garden. I'll let her know you are here."

As she waited, she drank in the unforgettable scent of eucalyptus and old cedar. She noticed a mark on the wall along the stairwell, a blank square about a foot on all sides, accentuated by the rim of slightly darker paint around it. It was the spot where the Klimt used to be.

"Come this way. Mrs. Baum is delighted you are here."

Stewart led Sandrina through the giant living room through the French doors onto the garden patio, where Esther sat, looking very small, wrapped in a crocheted blanket despite the season. The purple, lavender, and mauve shades of the wrap reflected the hues of the irises and phlox and catmint in full bloom nearby. Stewart pulled a chair close to hers so that the two women could talk. Sandrina kissed Esther's hair and held her hand.

"Hello, dear. It's so good of you to come," Esther said.

"I am so very, very sorry Esther, for not coming sooner—"

"I know, dear. Ralph explained everything to me."

Esther did not look well. She had lost weight, but that wasn't it, Sandrina thought. The sparkle in her eyes was gone, and her voice had lost its authority; it became fainter, like someone who is talking to you while they are moving away.

"Esther, I am so grateful for the Klimt. But if you want to keep it—"

"I wouldn't think of it, Sandrina. Josh wanted you to have it. It reminded him of you; he always said there's another half of you the world has never seen."

Sandrina thought about this. "What do you think he meant by that?"

"I'm not sure. But when we bought the drawing at Sotheby's, he said that the half of the drawing that the artist did not reveal was the part he wanted to keep to himself. That what you see is what he was willing to share, the rest being his alone."

"How awful for the woman in the picture, Esther. To be unfinished. Don't you think?"

"Not unfinished, Sandrina. Unrevealed."

She wondered if Warren had found her hidden half, if that was the part of her that responded to him—the vulnerable part, the part unprotected by money, success, and brand-name clothes. It was the part of her that she had hidden from Michael all these years, the part she had denied.

Stewart returned with fresh coffee for them both. Sandrina noticed Mata Hari's nose and paws pressed up against the plate-glass window and Elizabeth, or was it Elizabeth II, both English shorthair mixes, curled up on the Queen Anne chair by the black-lacquered Napoleon III piano, under a portrait of the Battle of Waterloo.

"Sandrina," Esther said. "I have a favor to ask."

"Anything."

"It's a big one."

"Just ask."

"Well, I'm not long for this world —"

"Esther! Don't say that."

"No dear," Esther said, holding up her hand as if to stop the platitudes she knew were coming. "The truth is I'm not that interested in living any more."

"Oh, Esther. I'm sure your feelings are just natural. You have just lost your life partner. Things may not be the same, but your grief will pass. You have your children, grandchildren, the cats," Sandrina said, gesturing toward Mata Hari at the window.

"True, Sandrina. Life goes on, but not for me. How can I explain it? It was as if Josh and I were grafted, like a branch to a tree —"

"That's exactly how Joshua explained your relationship to me when I last saw him."

"Funny. He and I never discussed it in those terms, but that proves my point, doesn't it?"

Esther took a fragile sip of coffee. Her hand was shaking as she brought the delicate porcelain cup to her thin, dry lips.

"Was Joshua the love of your life, Esther?"

"Yes." She paused.

"Did you know it right away?"

"Yes," Esther replied. "But it wasn't always smooth sailing. You know, I left him once."

"You did?" Sandrina was astonished by Esther's confession.

"Yes. I was about your age, I guess. Our children were grown and gone—we started earlier in those days. I was a virgin when I married, I felt my beauty fading, I was aimless, and felt neglected. Josh was so absorbed in his business. I met a man in a poetry class at the 92nd Street Y, and I thought I was in love. I moved into his studio in Carnegie Hill."

"What happened?"

"I thought he understood me. He would read poems he wrote for me—on the roof, under the stars. And cook for me. Things Josh never did."

"Why did you go back?"

"I realized this man, odd that I can't even remember his name, never really loved me. It was a lark for him. And he was flattered by my rapture—I was the famous Joshua Baum's wife. After a while, I felt like a fool."

"How long did it last?"

"We were together only three months, but the memory lasted for years. I went back to Josh, he forgave me—he would have forgiven me anything he loved me so—but I couldn't release the longing for poetry until... Come to think of it, I don't know what made it finally go away. But it did."

Esther looked very tired and old. A faint blush fanned across her cheeks, and her eyes lit up when she spoke of her long-ago lover, but it faded so quickly Sandrina wondered if it had ever really been there at all.

"I had better go, dear Esther. And those are storm clouds rolling in — you should be getting inside. What was the favor you wanted to ask?"

"Sandrina, when I go, will you take my cats? It is a big burden to impose, but I know you will love them as I do. All of my children have dogs. I can't think of anyone else."

Sandrina smiled visualizing those world leaders of the feline world roaming around her Fifth Avenue duplex. "Of course, Esther. I'll put the litter box right under the Klimt."

Chapter Twenty-Two

An enormous bouquet of summer flowers was delivered as soon as she arrived at the office.

"When will I see you again?" Unsigned.

Beth walked in with her daily call list and a printout of her calendar. "It's a busy one," she warned.

"Good. I need to be busy today."

"Flowers from Michael?"

"Uh...yes."

"You have thirty-one calls to return, the most important are follow-up calls from Oprah and Katie Couric's producers. They both want to interview Max and Jason."

"Fabulous! I'll call them myself."

"Heads up," Beth said. "They both want an exclusive."

"Uh-oh, that is a problem. I'll think of something," Sandrina said. "Next?"

"Jason wasn't too happy about the delay in your trip to Hawaii. He called several times. He wants to meet with you about something very important."

"I want to meet with him too," Sandrina said. "There are a few changes I need to make."

"Sandrina, Isabel's over there all the time. She's basically taken over the account, relegating

Arnelle and Joseph to menial tasks, shutting Lucy out, pulling rank with her fancy new title."

"I know." Sandrina used her long fingernails to tap out her frustration on the desk.

"And she's pulling the same thing with Chaucer. She has met with Mr. Waterhouse several times without your knowledge."

That annoyed her, but she brushed it off. "I'm less worried about Chaucer than I am about SH. I trust Mr. Waterhouse to be loyal — the account is still in the honeymoon phase — but Jason is another matter altogether. If he thought he could get a better deal, he wouldn't hesitate to jump ship."

"Sandrina, when are you finally going to get rid of Isabel?" Beth sounded exasperated.

"Soon, but I don't want to jeopardize the accounts. I need to think things through. I want to get Hawaii and this whole SH foray into the resort business settled before I spring the news that I intend to move Isabel out. I need to reestablish my value to them, and my commitment. Then I'll be in a position to make the staffing changes that I need to."

"What about the meetings she's scheduled to attend?" Beth asked.

"Say nothing. We want to strike first. If she has any clue she might get fired there's no telling what she would do. Plus I need grounds; if you know of anything, write it up in a memo and put it in her HR file. It's so different now, Beth. You used to be able to fire someone more easily. But she shows up, works long hours—until I have proof of something, we might get sued for wrongful dismissal. Even with proof, I need to give her a warning. It'll be hard to do, considering I just promoted her

"I have a bad feeling about her. How long will it take?"

"It'll take a few weeks at least," Sandrina said.

Lucy stuck her head in and said, "Everyone wants to know what time the creative meeting will be today."

"Do I have a lunch?" Sandrina asked Beth.

"Not one that you've told me about," Beth said. Sandrina knew she was being mildly scolded for last week's lost afternoon.

"Let's call the creative meeting for noon to two today. Tell everyone lunch is on me. Order a few pizzas," Sandrina said to Beth.

"Here's your mail," Beth said, handing her a folder.

In the mail folder, Beth had included the draft of the contract for Chaucer Suites. Sandrina fingered the edges of the paper while she read the first paragraph for the fourth time. She couldn't concentrate, thinking how awkward and potentially dangerous this could be, co-mingling a business relationship with her adulterous one. Wouldn't everyone pick up on the chemistry between them?

For instance, she should call him today to discuss the meetings he had had with Isabel. And to tell him she was planning to ease Isabel out. But the import of their relationship eclipsed both her professional responsibilities and her better judgment. She removed the contract and decided to think about it for a few days, to see how things progressed.

The Excel spreadsheets in the folder confirmed how well her business was doing. There were two Requests For Proposal, from the Cancun Tourist Board and Harrah's Casinos. She was invited to speak at the American Hotel Association's annual meeting in Dallas, and Reg McIntyre had asked her to guest lecture during the fall semester at Columbia Business School. Ralph Aiken had sent a letter to all the beneficiaries of Joshua Baum's estate, notifying them that the will was in probate. And Claudius had sent a fax saying that he would be in New York during the last week of July on his way to Newport for the regatta. Would she and Michael be free for lunch?

She logged on to respond "yes" to Claudius and saw the messages from Warren, flagged in red: "Can you meet me at Pesce tonight at six?"

And one from his secretary inviting her and Isabel to a steering committee meeting on July 6th.

"You are requested to present your plan at 11:00 a.m. to the steering committee at its regular quarterly meeting in New York for comments prior to the final presentation to the Board in London on July 13. Attendees from Chaucer: Mr. Warren Waterhouse, Chairman; Mr. John Sharp, Director; Mr. Trevor Horn, Director; Mr. Gerald P. Dempsey, Director; Mr. James Waterford, Director

Kindly provide the names of those who will be attending from your organization.

Sincerely,

Emily Poole

Assistant to Warren Waterhouse"

So this was how he intended to do it. A split personality. How could men compartmentalize the different aspects of their lives? Sandrina couldn't. Everything and everyone she loved was mixed together in a stew.

"Emily, Unfortunately I will be out of town on business on July 6th. Lucy Loving will be attending the meeting in New York in my place. I'll be in London for the final presentation. Please extend my apologies. Sandrina. CC: wwaterhouse, lloving, iriley."

Then she responded to Warren: "Yes. See you at six. And the flowers are beautiful."

She clicked on the agenda for the creative meeting, making notes near the items she thought she could help with. Arnelle had gotten wind of a special section on the Hawaiian Islands in an upcoming issue of the *New York Times* and wanted to strategize on angles to ensure a presence for SH's new venture.

Victoria wanted to invite a few of the travel bloggers to Gary Brent's Alexander Valley Spa as well as the wine press who had already accepted. She needed suggestions for names. The first press junket to Baden-Baden—beauty editors from *Vogue, Glamour, Harper's Bazaar, W,* and *Vanity Fair*—was scheduled for mid-August, but Maria was having trouble gaining the cooperation of an airline to comp the air despite the earlier assurances by Lufthansa.

The smell of pepperoni wafted down the halls of the TravelSmart offices. It was commingled with something else: Isabel's perfume.

"What's the fragrance?" Beth asked her.

Sandrina and Lucy were listening to the exchange.

"It's Gucci's new scent," Isabel answered.

"What's it called?" Beth asked.

Lucy answered. "It's *Envy*, isn't it?"

"You've been perusing the Duty Free," Isabel said.

"I'd recognize that smell anywhere," Lucy said wryly.

"Who wants to go first?" Sandrina asked when they were all seated.

Maria jumped in. "I can't get complimentary air to Frankfurt," she said. "August is the peak travel season, and the carriers are loathe to lose revenue by giving away seats. Maybe if the list included travel writers, but beauty editors? They all turned up their noses."

"We've never had trouble before," Sandrina said.

"Their business is way down because of terrorism fears. August is a big vacation month, and they actually think they can sell all the seats they have," Arnelle answered.

"Who have you tried so far?" Sandrina asked.

"Lufthansa, Continental, and Delta. They all said, 'No.'"

"Try American and U.S. Air," Sandrina suggested. "And, if that fails, call Christoff Peipers to pull strings with the airlines from his end."

"Isabel, anything new on SH?"

Isabel looked up startled. "Status quo."

"Jason wants to meet with me. Any idea why?"

"Not a clue," she said. "Maybe to go over your trip to Hawaii?"

"Okay…let's see. Who's next? Arnelle?"

"There's a July 15 deadline for the winter travel special in the *Times*. It will be devoted to Hawaii this year," Arnelle said.

"Who's editing it?" Sandrina asked.

"H.P. Weinstock. Do you know him?"

"It's a her, Arnelle. And, yes I do. She was actually in Rio covering the conference. I saw her in the audience during my presentation. I'll give her a call. By the way, I would like you to go over there next week. The special section is a good reason for you to precede me," Sandrina replied. She saw Isabel jump.

"No problem," Arnelle said.

"Arnelle, what did you think of the reviews of the Millennium Universal?"

"Fantastic! Only *The Observer* panned it. They said the style was trendy and the bathrooms small," Arnelle said.

"We're trying for a follow-up on the high-speed Internet access from every room and the state-of-the-art executive services center. It seems that business travelers spend more time online than in the bathroom anyway," Joseph added.

"Try the *Wall Street Journal*'s Friday section," Sandrina said.

"And the *Finance Journal*?" Joseph asked.

Sandrina paused. "Skip that one for now," she replied. "Lucy, Isabel? What about Chaucer?"

"Well," Lucy started. "We've got that upcoming meeting with the steering committee on July 6. Isabel is working on the presentation now."

"I need to see it before next Friday. After that is the long weekend. I'm leaving for Hawaii right after, on Wednesday the fifth to be exact. Isabel, how'd your meetings with Mr. Waterhouse go?" Sandrina asked.

"How'd what go?" Isabel replied, reddening.

"Making progress?"

"Sure. I'm working with him on the presentation to the steering committee and to his board. Those are important meetings. We need to get buy-in," Isabel said.

Lucy's cell phone rang, and she stepped out of the room to answer it.

"Mr. Waterhouse has invited Lucy and me to join the steering committee for dinner after the meeting," Isabel slipped in.

"Oh, really?" Sandrina asked. "What did you say?"

"Why, yes, of course. Shall I pick up the check?"

Every pair of eyes in the room seemed to be staring at Sandrina. "I suppose so," Sandrina replied.

Lucy reentered the room, visibly excited. "Sandrina, great news. That was my friend Sara, who works at American Express. Amex is interviewing agencies, and she got us on the list."

"That is great news! When?"

"Well, that's the thing. Our slot is July 6 at 11:00. But, don't worry, I can handle it," Lucy said.

Sandrina noted a smile creep across Isabel's face.

"Anything else, Sandrina? We've all got a ton of work to do," Lucy said, glancing at her watch.

"Who ended up getting the Monarch Hotels account?" Sandrina asked.

"I haven't seen any announcements in the trade press yet," Joseph said.

"Follow up on that one, please. It would be good to know who the competition is," she said.

Warren liked to sit at bars, the noisier the better, whereas Sandrina preferred private banquettes in quiet cocktail lounges. She arrived before he did and paced up and down the street a few times before deciding to freshen her lipstick and lay early claim to a couple of choice bar stools. When he walked in, he looked distracted. He kissed her chastely on the cheek.

She was wearing the same outfit she had had on the night they visited the *candomblé* temple in Rio. If he recognized it, he didn't say so.

"How was your day?" Warren asked.

"Except for the flowers, nothing out of the ordinary," she said.

He looked around, as if he expected to see someone he knew. "Ever been here before?"

He had forgotten, or at least it seemed that way to her, that Pesce was where their relationship had escalated from an offshore escapade to a tempest that threatened her marriage. She looked at him quizzically, but decided to move on with what she had to say.

"Warren, I'm a little concerned about the business relationship between Chaucer and TravelSmart."

"Really? Why?" he asked.

"I don't know. It makes me uncomfortable. Love is justifiable—it's precious because life is so short."

"Are you saying that the end justifies the means?"

"I guess so. But there isn't any justification for mixing business and—"

"Pleasure?"

She looked at him. Was this pleasure? Passion, yes. Pain, for sure. But she would not have chosen the word pleasure; that was too trite and transitory a word.

"But the business part is problematic. It could undermine my professional reputation, my credibility, if people find out."

"They won't—you own your business, I own mine. We can do what we want."

She thought she would try another line of reasoning. "It could damage our relationship, yours and mine. What if TravelSmart doesn't live up to your expectations?"

"No chance of that. You're the best—"

"But I'm not day to day on the account. Isabel Riley is. I'm not sure about her yet. She's young and new to the position. And then there's us—see what I mean? It's a muddle."

"We can handle it, Sandrina."

"What about Isabel? How does she behave in meetings?"

"Very professional and enthusiastic," he replied.

"She's attractive, don't you think?" Sandrina regretted asking the question as soon as the words left her mouth. She squirmed while she waited for an answer.

Warren took a sip of his martini. He pursed his lips and looked over her shoulder, at something or someone Sandrina knew wasn't there. He shifted his weight and shrugged his shoulders slightly. She had her answer before he said anything, so that by the time he finally replied, evasively, she already knew the truth.

"Isabel? She's a kid. I mean she's perfectly okay to send out press releases, but she's no threat to you."

"I guess not," she said, trying to regain her dignity. "Anyway, how is your apartment search coming along?"

"Progressing. These things take time. Especially as my needs are changing."

Sandrina thought about telling him about her conversation with Ralph Aiken, especially Joshua's caveat that one person in a relationship always loves more than the other. Yes, Joshua had meant Michael and her, but she wondered how vulnerable she would be with Warren if she became the lover instead of the lovee.

As if he could read her mind, he laughed his lion's roar and said, "You worry too much. Come on, let's go."

They left Pesce and decided to walk up Seventh Avenue toward the Essex House. Warren covered her bare shoulders with his jacket. It was wrinkled and dusty, not crisp and fresh the way Michael's would have been. When they got to the Essex House they went up to Warren's suite.

"I apologize, Sandrina," he said. "This place is a bit of a dump. When I bought it seven years ago for my hotel clients to stay in when they visited New York, I never dreamed that I would someday be living here myself."

The back-facing one-bedroom condominium had become extremely rundown from repeated and transient use. The many layers of paint had caked, and the steam heat had caused it to peel and chip away. Swirls of New York soot had flown in from the airshaft, leaving circular smudge prints on the undamaged sections of the porous plaster walls. The bathroom toilet leaked and the saggy mattress on the bed should have been replaced ages ago. The draperies, bedspread, and carpeting were a worn but coordinated brownish-red, originally purchased with an eye toward hiding stains.

"Nothing a little decorating couldn't fix," she said, noticing the waterlogged ceilings.

"I've got an appointment with a realtor to look at apartments. Will you come?"

"Sure," she replied.

She wondered what he had in mind. How big would it be? Was it for him alone or for them? Sandrina walked over to the bureau and examined the framed photographs that she found there.

"My daughters," he explained.

"They're beautiful."

"Thank you. I can't wait for them to meet you."

They sat on the sofa holding hands. So different than being with Michael. She felt no pressure to be strong, have answers, make decisions, perform.

They talked for a long time, he recounting for her all the happy moments he could remember about his daughters.

"I failed them, though. It was as if the feelings I had for them were locked inside. When I felt them welling up I would suppress them—"

"How so?"

"I'd go on a trip. Not show up for family events. Shut them out. I was so happy to see them, but had no idea what to do with them, and so relieved to be alone again."

She thought she had better tell him, clear the air. "Warren, I can imagine how they felt. I think I love you. But I feel desolate when you disappear from my life. Are you aware you do the same thing to me that you just described doing to your daughters? I feel like I'm speeding along with an infinite horizon ahead of me, and all of a sudden I reach the edge of a cliff. I have to jam on the brakes, or fall off."

"Are we breaking up?" he asked.

She hesitated. "No, I think we're just getting started. It's just that if I'm going to blow up my life for us, I need to know it will work. I only know you care for me when we're in the same room."

"I know. I know you feel that way."

"Then why do you keep pushing me away?"

He shrugged his shoulders. Sandrina felt the side of his body that was pressed against hers tense up.

"Old habits die hard," he said. There was an edge to his words. "Sorry. I don't mean to be flippant. I'm just not sure I can do it, Sandrina. I never believed that happiness could exist. I'm terrified, but I'm going to try. The *italero* told me that you were my last chance — this is the real thing, Sandrina. I know it."

He stroked her cheeks with his fingertips, and then he walked over to the makeshift bar on top of the stereo console. He poured her a glass of Merlot and put on a CD with haunting love songs that she had never heard before.

"Edith Piaf," Warren explained.

"Nice," she said. She was feeling relaxed from the music and the wine. She stood by the photographs again, rolling her neck from side to side to loosen the muscles.

"Where's your husband?" Warren asked.

"Chicago." She felt a pang of guilt.

Warren came up behind her. His hands were like hot stones, pressing against her contracted muscles. He kissed her neck, and she felt the coarseness of his beard prepare her skin to receive the suppleness of his lips. He turned her around and continued to kiss her throat, using his thumbs to lift the gold chain that trespassed there so that he wouldn't press it into her flesh as his mouth searched the erogenous zones of her neck ever more urgently. As his cheek rested on her chest he slowly unbuttoned each tiny pearl on her blouse until he could slide the wisp of cotton off her shoulders. He tossed it on the sofa behind her.

He took a step back and looked at her full breasts. She was stimulated now, and her nipples were erect under the veil of lace her bra created. He removed one, and then the other, from the cups, and buried his nose between them, inhaling deeply. He pressed up against her and she could feel his tumescence through her clothing.

Sandrina stood there transfixed as he slowly unhooked her bra and let it slide down her shoulders. He circled his tongue around her areolas and sucked gently while he cupped her breasts in his hands. Her bra tethered her arms to her sides rendering her helpless as his tongue traced the line on her abdomen.

When his mouth met the waistband of her skirt, he reached an unwelcome impasse, and, less patient now, he tugged at the snap with enough force to separate the zipper halfway without being pulled. The skirt fell to her ankles, in a way that would allow her to open her legs a few inches, but not move her feet or run away.

Warren finally removed the binding bra and tossed it on top of her blouse. She was moaning now and she reached her hands down between his legs to return his caresses, but he took her wrists and placed them behind her waist. He fell to his knees and probed her navel with his restless tongue while he slid his hands into her lace panties and pressed her forward to him.

Breathing heavily now, he let the swatch of cream lace that covered her buttocks ride down her thighs until they dropped onto her coffee-colored skirt. He pressed his nose into her soft mound of hair and stayed there, as if in prayer, for what seemed like an eternity.

Sandrina bent over to kiss his hair, and let her hands glide up and down his back. She managed to unbutton his shirt halfway and to run her fingers through the thick carpet of hair on his chest, before he made her stop and returned her long arms to her sides.

"This is for you, Sandrina." She started to argue, but he said, "Shh," with such decisiveness that she uttered not another sound.

He held her hands tightly by her side, her diamond engagement ring cutting into his palm, as his tongue probed her hidden opening seeking the spot that would give her the most pleasure. She was moving her hips faster and faster now, in exact synchronization with his accommodating tongue. Just as he felt her start to come he released her hands and pressed her into him, where he rocked her hips from behind and consumed her as a starving man would a jar of sweet honey.

When it was over, she stood there like a weeping willow. Her damp hair and long limbs were so loose and spent that a sneeze could have made them sway. He held her up by the waist as he unbuckled her shoes and removed the bunched articles of clothing from around her feet. He picked her up and carried her into the bedroom, where he lay down beside her naked body, with all his clothes still on. She could see the bulge in his pants that was still there and tried once again to reciprocate his love, but he rolled her onto her back and lifted her arms over her head so he could see her in full face, a woman in profile no more.

"Stay, Sandrina, stay. Please stay."

"I can't. I have to go."

"To what? An empty apartment?"

She knew that Michael would call. "Yes, an empty apartment."

"Then stay here tonight. I need you. I want to feel you, breathing in my arms, all night." He kissed her forehead, her nose, and her lips.

She was so moved by his passionate pleas that she almost gave in. "What time is it?"

He rolled over to read the digital clock on the night table. "It's one in the morning. The night is practically over. Stay here," he said. "With me."

Sandrina propped her head up on her hand while she leaned on her elbow and looked into his eyes. Her hair fell forward, hiding half her face.

"I'd better go home," she said. "I will be missed."

Warren took Sandrina home in a taxi. She told the driver to let her off on the corner of Fifth Avenue, and she looked back to see Warren waiting there, in the shadows of the taxi's back seat, until the doorman unlocked the brass gate and let her in. He was looking up at the imposing limestone residence with its picture windows overlooking Central Park as the taxi sped away. She missed him already.

As soon as she returned to the Essex House the next day at noon, as she'd promised she would, she could sense that his mood had changed. Warren was dressed in faded shorts, an old t-shirt, and a pair of Teva sandals; so far he had been more careful about his appearance.

He described to her how he had taken his clothes off when he returned the night before and left them piled in a heap at the foot of the bed; she could see that they were still there through the open bedroom door. He told her how he had wrapped his body, still aching for her, in the bedspread where she had lain, and how he had covered his face with the pillow still moist from her perspiration and smelling sweet like her.

"When I woke up, the bedspread was soaked through with my sweat. I still feel as though a jackhammer cracked open my skull. Let's go out—I need some Advil," he said.

"As close as I feel to you, I still don't know what would make you feel better," she said. "How do you relax?"

"I cook," he said.

"Really cook? Or smolder?" Her questions had been serious, but Warren thought she was joking; at least she had made him laugh.

"Cook—as in chop, sauté, and bake. I haven't done much of it since moving here because the kitchen is so small."

Sandrina noted that the Pullman kitchen was indeed cramped and inadequate; she peered into the half-refrigerator, separating from its top hinge, to find only booze. The oven was a cheap, mass-market brand, the color of goldenrod. There were pots and pans, barely used, and a few utensils.

Warren sighed. "Better than nothing I suppose. What do you say? I'll cook you dinner—it will be fun."

As soon as he decided on the menu he sprang into action, checking the cupboards against his list. "I have none of the ingredients I need, except the most basic spices and staples," he said, looking defeated.

"We have to go out for Advil anyway; we can pick up what you need at the store," Sandrina suggested.

They went to the International Spice Market for a container of black Kalamata olives, buying dried black beans, clam juice and beef stock, baker's chocolate, nuts, and vanilla there as well. At an Italian fish store on Eighth Avenue they bought a pound of black squid, with the ink. There was a butcher shop nearby where they picked up the meat and a vegetable stand on the corner for produce and herbs. As an afterthought, and because they were sweating from the excursion in the intense midday heat, Warren bought a six-pack of frosty Corona beer to swill while he worked.

Once upstairs, Warren turned his attention to the task at hand with an intensity that made Sandrina feel ignored. She declined the offer of beer, so he drank alone. She pulled a chair up to watch him pick over the beans, discarding every blemished and imperfect one, then rinse them and set them aside to soak.

"What can I do?" she asked.

"Pass me another beer."

She stroked his back while he minced the onion, garlic, cilantro, and thyme. When the seasonings were ready, he let her add the stock and other ingredients and then he told her to let the soup simmer for three hours.

"Now what?" she asked, fascinated.

"Especially for you, *matinta Pereira*, devil's food fudge brownies!"

She was getting aroused as she observed the passion with which he chopped two ounces of bittersweet chocolate and put the pieces in a saucepan with the butter to melt. He relentlessly beat the resulting marble mixture into the sugar, eggs, and vanilla extract until the substance looked like melted tar. Then he folded in the walnuts and slid the pan into the oven to bake.

Sandrina pressed her body against his back as he closed the oven door. She wrapped her arms around his waist. Her voice grew sultry; she said his name, "Warren."

But he pushed her away and said, "Not now."

As he meticulously prepared each dish, he continued to drink the icy beer. Despite the coldness of the liquid, she could see Warren getting hotter and hotter. The perspiration gathered under his arms and on his forehead. Sandrina borrowed a washcloth from the bathroom and mopped his face; she turned the thermostat down to its lowest possible temperature while she watched him prepare the steak.

While Warren readied the marinade with extra-virgin olive oil, brined peppercorns, capers, mustard seeds, and dry red wine, Sandrina thought how like an artist he was. He painted the sauce on the steak with a bristly brush he found in a kitchen drawer, and then he coated it with a layer of coarse, crushed black pepper so thick that not a hairline of the blood-red flesh showed through. Finally, he covered the plate with foil and put it in the refrigerator.

"To allow the meat ample time to absorb the flavorings," he explained.

Warren took a sniff of the garlicky olives and set them in a cracked bowl in front of Sandrina. She didn't eat any but watched him munch on them while he drank and prepared food, spitting the pits into the sink while he cleaned the baby squid, slicing the bodies cross-wise and halving the tentacles. He put the cleaved chunks in clam juice and poured in the ink to give the sauce its black color. Finally, he told Sandrina to add the basil, garlic, and other herbs to the pot and let the squid simmer for an hour and a half.

While the pots rattled under their covers, Warren joined Sandrina on the living room couch. She took his sandals off and massaged his feet, and then she put the washcloth, now soaked with ice water, over his eyes. She turned off all the lights in the suite, in an effort to reduce the heat. The only illumination came from the candles on the dining room table where she had set two places. Warren played Wagner's *Die Meistersinger* on the stereo, with its dark and threatening sounds blowing through the rooms, a breeze without air; Sandrina was displeased but said nothing.

A shrill sound cut the dense atmosphere; Sandrina's cell phone was ringing. It was Michael.

"I'm home – where are you?"

"I'm on my way," she hung up. She gathered her things as she said, "Warren—"

"I know,"he said. "I heard. Go."

On her way out she noticed the steaming pot of black bean soup, as inappropriate as it now seemed for a summer's day, reminding her of Brazil. She registered the black squid, the pepper steak, and the brownies, and she realized that Warren had unconsciously created an entirely black meal.

Sandrina looked back one last time from the open doorway. He had thrown the washcloth on the floor, and was pounding his fist on the table, making the dishes clatter and shake.

"What will you do?" she asked him, noting the brooding look on his face.

"Seems a shame to waste all this food," he said.

"Will you be all right?" she asked, thinking of his father.

"Don't worry—I can take care of myself. Go."

As soon as Sandrina shut the door, he picked up the phone and dialed. Then he turned off the burners for the squid and the beans and, slamming the door as he left his suite, he went down to the bar for a martini—and to wait.

Chapter Twenty-Three

Michael was electrified when he greeted her, explaining that he had decided definitely, following an encouraging meeting with the Commodities Exchange in Chicago, to pursue her idea to start an Internet paper exchange. He was ebullient with hope.

With the prospect of the end of Michael's problems pushing them like a tail wind, they made love as a reunion, full of memories and shared experience replete in the event. They stayed entwined, until the sun fell behind the buildings across the Park, casting leaf-shaped shadows on their bedroom wall.

Slipping from a sleeping Michael's embrace, Sandrina reluctantly packed her bags for Hawaii, which she would drag with her to Southampton, where Monday had been reserved for the "big one" with Thomas.

Only then did they leave to catch the last Jitney out on Sunday night.

By Monday afternoon, in Southampton, they successfully hashed out details of an agreement with Thomas. Fortunately, the lawyers for both brothers also had houses in Southampton, so they were available to draft the paperwork, and on the morning of July 4 — Independence Day — Michael forfeited his shares of Morgan Paper in exchange for total protection from all liability or persecution related to the company's misdeeds.

Then Michael and Sandrina celebrated at Florence Fabricant's beach barbeque before Michael took off for Paris to lock in what he hoped would be his first anchor client for his New Freedom Paper Exchange.

"I wish you could come with me," he said.

"I know. But I'm in some trouble myself, and I've got to try to save the SH account."

It was an inferno-like July day, and she paced up and down the corridor of the United Airlines terminal before she decided to try Warren one last time before her flight took off for Honolulu. She left him a message that she was off, and she guessed she would see him next in London, but if he felt like calling her in Hawaii she had sent him all her numbers by e-mail. She was perplexed at his disappearance, but she had so much else on her mind that she let it slide, especially since it seemed to be his way — to be out of touch when it suited him.

When Sandrina arrived at the Aloha Regency Waikiki, in Honolulu on the main island of Oahu, she began to formulate her theories of how the new SH venture, which they had named The Lomi-Lomi

Hotel, could take on an established market leader like Aloha. She knew that the problems they would encounter — an already existing glut of hotel rooms, a slow economy, and fear of terrorism — were nearly insurmountable. She wanted to study Aloha, find the holes, and create points of difference for the Lomi-Lomi that would attract a greater share of the diminishing number of vacation travelers.

It was their only hope for success — to identify the existing market leaders' serious gaps in customer service, to design a package of services that offered everything the competition lacked, and to take advantage of the sad reality that the traveling public was a fickle crowd.

The 1,100-room Aloha Hotel looked more like an office park than a fantasy resort. Sandrina knew that current tastes preferred small to big, unique to chain formula, intimate to boisterous, the unexpected to the tried and true. The colossal atrium lobby, was an embodiment of noise, from the squawking birds, bustling tourists, and crashing waterfalls to the verbal volley of business transactions taking place in the glass-fronted shops and service establishments. Even the plants that cascaded over the atrium-facing balconies seemed to have something to say. It reminded her of the Brooklyn Botanical Garden on a public school holiday.

Three undulating natives, dressed in hula skirts and petal-covered bras, attempted to assuage the ruffled feathers of the new arrivals with Dixie-cup portions of mai tais, flower leis that they draped seductively around the tourists' necks, and brochures about island attractions. These items were distributed assembly-line style. At the reception desk, Sandrina and the others were told that their rooms weren't ready.

"Look," Sandrina tried to reason with the front desk clerk. "Look at all the people here. What are we supposed to do?"

"Tsk, tsk," Cindy Harmony, from Park City, Utah, said wagging her finger at Sandrina as if she were an errant child. "House rules prohibit check-in before noon. You should have planned your arrival time better."

"But that's when the scheduled flights land!" Sandrina said, throwing her hands up in exasperation.

"Sorry. We don't schedule the flights," Cindy said.

"Listen, I'm exhausted. Is the room occupied?" Sandrina said, making an attempt to negotiate.

Cindy glanced at her computer screen. "No, the previous guests have checked out."

"Couldn't you have housekeeping make up the room early?"

"Oh no, Madam. The rules don't permit out-of-sequence maid service. It would mess up the cleaning queue," Cindy said.

That little tidbit went right into her notes.

Sandrina wandered around the hotel's Hawaiian craft museum, and in and out of the restaurants and shops. She couldn't decide whether the Chinese/Italian Ciao Mein and the Southwestern/Japanese Rock 'n Roll Sushi Bar restaurants were corny or cute. Finally she settled into a canvas sling-back chair on the beach and ordered a frozen piña colada to cool her body and her nerves.

It was muggy and ominously overcast, with a heaviness in the air usually associated with the Kona trade winds and more typical during the winter months than in July. She saw a column of rain over the ocean, like a stream of pepper being shaken into an angry soup, that disappeared almost as immediately as it had come, leaving behind a multi-colored lollipop of a rainbow.

Sandrina's suite was finally ready. The rooms were standard-issue Aloha, predictable and neat, with sliding glass doors that opened out to the walkway along the atrium. She fell onto a Polynesian-print comforter, thin and glossy from wear. She was completely drained from the eleven-hour flight, not-including the two-hour layover in San Francisco, and emotionally exhausted from the

upheaval in her business and private lives. She
calculated that she had been sitting upright or in
motion for seventeen hours, and she craved nothing
more than stillness and a supine position.

On the coffee table in her suite, on the VIP
floor, she found a welcome letter from Daisy Hana
propped up against an amenity basket, compliments
of the Aloha Regency Waikiki Sha Na Na Spa. In it
were a comb, sponge, mirror, toothbrush, and Aloha
shower gel. She pulled out her pad and made some
more notes. What self-respecting spa goer would
need or want these things? What percentage got left
behind? How much money did they cost to
assemble? Where, she wondered, was the "value-
add"?

Arnelle had left her a folder at the front desk.
In it were drafts of pre-opening fact sheets about the
Lomi-Lomi, detailed research on the Hawaiian hotel
industry and the history of the islands themselves,
and a bio on the general manager, Kevin Clark, who
had already been hired, and with whom she would
be meeting during her stay. Arnelle had also left
her information about Daisy Hana's small local
public relations agency with which they would be
working on pre-launch publicity and the hotel
opening for the Lomi-Lomi. Sandrina started to
read. Dinner would be in four hours, and she
needed to finish her homework, nap, shower, and

dress before meeting Daisy in the lobby at seven for her briefing.

There were 120 hotels on Oahu alone, representing a fair cross-section of the more than 200 hotel brands in the marketplace. Each one eroded the Lomi-Lomi's hope for success. It made Sandrina think about how she had heard that the *tsunamis*, Hawaiian tidal waves, ate away at the black sand beaches of Hilo. She was tired, and her head ached, but she read on.

The land was so scarce and so valuable that if you placed a hundred dollar bill down on Waikiki Beach it might not pay for the cost of the patch it covered. She was intrigued by the mystical explanations Hawaiians seemed to have for everything, and she read that the island of Oahu, which boasted such expensive property, was thought to be one of the six island children of the goddess Papa and her lover, Lua. Papa made love to Lua to exact revenge on her philandering husband, Wakea, who impregnated the young goddess Hina while Papa was away. *Some things never change*, sighed Sandrina.

At some point she realized she wasn't concentrating. The statistics about room nights and occupancy rates were giving way to fatigue. She fell asleep with the papers strewn about her on the bed, falling into a dream where she lost everyone and everything she had; she was pushing a shopping cart filled with trash down Fifth Avenue. Warren saw her but didn't recognize her, so he walked by. Only Isabel knew it was she and snickered with joy at Sandrina's misfortune.

When she woke up, she felt as though someone had dumped a bucket of icy seawater on her while she slept, salty and cold at once. The air-conditioning was blasting frigid air on her sweat-soaked body. She couldn't wait to get out of the room. When Daisy arrived at seven sharp, a shaken Sandrina had been waiting in the lobby for some time.

"*Aloha*, Sandrina. *Komo mai*! Have you had a chance to walk around?" Daisy said.

"Actually, I've seen a lot, and taken copious notes," Sandrina replied.

"That's good, because I'm taking you off-site this evening. We're going to drive by some of the other competition, so that you know what we're up against, and then we'll have dinner at the Halekulani Hotel's La Mer Restaurant. It's delicious!"

As soon as they entered the *porte cochere* of the Halekulani Hotel, Sandrina knew what the Hawaiian experience was meant to be. The most extraordinary profusion of tropical flowers—orchids, anthuriums, protea, hibiscus—filled the space around her with color, scent, and contrasting textures. Ukulele music played softly in the lobby, creating an aura of tranquility.

"The flowers are sensational, Daisy, don't you think?"

"Oh yes. A famous florist, Kanemoto-san, arranges them. This is the *sogetsu* style of *ikebana*. In this combination, the blooms have spiritual significance."

"And the music? Does it have spiritual meaning too?" Sandrina asked.

"More traditional than spiritual. Uku means 'flea' in Hawaiian dialect," Daisy explained. "And 'lele' means jumping. 'Uku-lele' technically derives from the quick finger movements on the strings, but the happy, lighthearted sounds that the instrument makes have come to symbolize the spirit of the Hawaiian people."

Sandrina thought how different the two hotels were. The Halekulani an oasis in a desert of sameness, the Aloha an American suburban shopping mall with bedrooms. She had to find the niche between the two for the Lomi-Lomi.

They toured the hotel property, Sandrina admiring the vast immaculately trimmed lawns and gardens. The Orchid swimming pool had a mosaic flower of such artistry built into its bottom that it looked as if it would float there forever, in homage to the perpetuity of nature.

Daisy got the front desk manager to slip them into a bungalow, where Sandrina noticed that the amenity gift was a china plate with homemade chocolates and sweets from the hotel's pastry chef. The treatment was vastly superior to a basket of mass-market toiletries, Sandrina noted. She counted six shades of white in the color scheme of the pristine room, which she felt contributed to the mood of peacefulness. On the pillow were a seashell and an orchid, and in the bathroom a five-foot deep Japanese soaking tub.

The La Mer restaurant was housed in the main building of the Halekulani Resort. It looked like a Southern plantation mansion one might find in Mississippi or Georgia, with a deep lanai connecting the building to the outdoors. But the roof of the dining pavilion distinguished it as uniquely Pacific, because its slope was patterned after a Polynesian longhouse, perfectly angled to capture the breezes and divert the island squalls.

They sat at a table outdoors with a view of Diamond Head. Although it was late, the July sun was still setting. They each had a mai tai, and Daisy continued filling Sandrina in on local lore. They saw a *honu*, the green sea turtle not long ago nearly extinct, popping its head out of the ocean; it was leathery and languorous, like a big, old ottoman on which to rest your feet.

"It feeds in the waters off Waikiki in the evenings," Daisy explained, while they ate dinner, a delicious *mahi-mahi* wrapped in edible seaweed called *limu*. "Sandrina, what are you thinking?" Daisy asked.

"You'll laugh when I tell you," Sandrina replied.

"Try me."

"When my husband was little, before he could say Mommy, he used to call his mother Mahi-Mahi. It's silly—"

"No, I like that story, Sandrina. It makes you more human, less intimidating."

"Thank you. And thank you also for dinner. The food is really great."

"La Mer is one of the few restaurants on the islands to enjoy the highly coveted AAA five-diamond award," Daisy said.

"Do you really think anyone cares about those ratings any more, Daisy?" Sandrina asked. "I mean, they seem kind of dated. At least on the mainland the Zagat's type of rating seems more credible. Diners rating the establishments, guests rating the hotels, customers assessing value. It's more empowering and more believable."

"You may be right. I never thought about it that way. These rating systems have been around since the fifties."

"That may be the problem," Sandrina said.

"What do you mean?"

"Well, I think the value proposition for the traveler has changed. He has to be motivated by something special, unique, or fabulous— more like the Halekulani, something worth taking a risk for. Four stars or five diamonds, or even a second dose of something just pleasurable, isn't enough any more."

"What does that mean for the Lomi-Lomi?" asked Daisy.

"I'm not positive just yet, but I have a hunch that what used to be a competitive advantage, namely that the customer always knew what to expect—consistent service, lagoon pools, Sunday buffet brunches—Aloha's offering, could now be a competitive disadvantage. It's not enough any more merely not to disappoint. Why should a vacationer go to all the trouble, unbearable security lines, for instance, maybe even the risk of getting blown up, just for the Same Old Thing?" Sandrina thought of *Screwtape*, and Warren, and wondered if she was willing to take such a gigantic risk for what might become The Same Old Thing for her?

"I see," Daisy said. "So is there room for one more?"

"Well, it won't be easy. We just have to position the Lomi-Lomi's image in the marketplace. We need to invent a provocative value proposition—to figure out what neither the Aloha nor the Halekulani have that today's traveler can't do without."

"And then?"

"Promote the hell out of it," Sandrina said, raising her glass in a toast.

Daisy laughed. "To look at you, Sandrina, one would never expect such fighting spirit from such an elegant package. I'd better get you back to the Aloha. You're going to have a long day tomorrow."

"What's the program?" Sandrina asked.

"Tomorrow morning at eight Hoapili will meet you in the lobby. Don't be scared when you see him. He looks like a sumo wrestler, but he's as gentle as a lamb. He will escort you to the Lomi-Lomi construction site."

"I'd better wear something I don't mind ruining, right?"

"Right. It's a mess. I'll meet you there and give you the tour; it will be extensive, all day in fact, because the property Max and Jason purchased is four acres along Waikiki Beach. Then I'll take you back to the Aloha—SH is renting space from them until the Lomi-Lomi opens—where you'll meet with our general manager, Kevin Clark," Daisy said. "And then, Friday morning is the big meeting with the senior operations staff—the *kahuna*. They're all on board to get ready for a December opening." Daisy looked grim. "Sandrina, they're expecting you to come in with ideas, solutions even. I like you, so I am going to tell you something I shouldn't."

"What's that?"

"Jason is very angry with you. I don't know if he's talking to anyone else or not, but if I were you I'd pull out all stops on this one. It's just a feeling that I got the last few times I talked to him. The account may be in danger."

"I appreciate your honesty, Daisy. I have the same feeling myself. That's why that even though this couldn't be a worse time for me personally — I've left a lot of things unfinished back home — I'm here. I'll do the best I can."

"Is there anything you need?" Daisy asked Sandrina.

Sandrina reviewed the notes she had made. She needed some drama, a catalyst, a clincher. "Are you friends with the public relations managers at the Aloha and the Halekulani?" she asked.

"Yes, they both used to work for me," Daisy said. "Honolulu is a small town. Everybody knows everybody. And we always help one another."

"Good. Then I need a copy of their operating manuals, or whatever they call the books that state standard operating procedure, dictate the rules, guarantee consistency — " Sandrina said.

"That shouldn't be a problem. I'll phone them tomorrow."

"And Daisy — I need them tonight."

The ringing of the telephone at five a.m. woke her up from a gray-sludge sleep. She had worked until midnight studying the operating manuals for the Aloha and Halekulani resorts.

"Sandrina?" It was Beth.

She could barely answer, as she tried to come back from the twilight zone between unconsciousness and clarity.

"Yup," she said. Her mouth felt like it was filled with melted peanut butter. She stretched her jaw. "Beth?"

"Did I wake you? What's the time difference there? It's ten o'clock in New York."

"It's okay. I have to get up anyway. What's up?"

"I hate to bum you out, but I thought you should know. SH Hotels just terminated our services. The letter came certified mail a few minutes ago. It is dated July 1."

Sandrina was shocked. "What does it say?"

"The letter is very formal, and form-letter like. 'Official sixty days notice according to the contract dated —"

"What does the cover letter say?"

"It says that they expect a report from you on your Hawaii trip, and a plan for pre-opening publicity, or they won't pay for the sixty days. It says that they had wanted to tell you in person but that you never responded to their request for a meeting from two weeks ago."

That was true. She had dodged and avoided that meeting, thinking she could fix things with a brilliant showing in Hawaii. Sandrina felt as though she'd been sideswiped by a hit-and-run. Cancellation of the contract would be a loss of not only $250,000 in annual fees but a 19-year relationship as well. She knew the relationship was strained, but the speed and severity of this action, without even a warning, took her by surprise.

"Is Isabel there?"

"No. She called in sick today. She said she'd probably be out tomorrow too. Summer cold. She told me to tell you when you called in that she needed to rest up for the big Chaucer meeting in London next week. She's leaving Sunday night."

"What's her home number? I'll call her there."

"It's 772-1650. Sandrina, I don't think the timing of this letter or her 'illness' are coincidental."

"I know what you mean. Neither do I. Beth, do me a favor? Get the locks changed before the weekend." It was a feeble attempt at precaution, a day late and a dollar short, because she knew that Isabel would have long ago removed anything of value pertaining to the accounts she intended to steal.

"Should I distribute new keys?"

"To everyone except Isabel—if she happens to show up, that is."

While Sandrina showered, she cursed herself under her breath. All the warning signs had been there, and she had pooh-poohed them. When she had hired Isabel, she thought she saw promise, a younger version of herself. But an honest mind can never anticipate a devious one, she knew, and she saw now that she had been duped and used.

One thing was for sure—it had to stop. Isabel would not go to London; she'd call Warren and warn him about Isabel. Dripping wet, shampoo still in her hair and unequivocally naked, she dashed for the phone and dialed Isabel's number. It was eleven o'clock in the morning in New York. After four rings the machine answered.

"If you're getting this message it means I'm not home. In fact, I'll be out of town until late July. You can try me back then." Not much information there, except confirmation of what she already knew—the only illness Isabel had was mental.

When she tried Warren's office, Emily picked up the phone.

"Mr. Waterhouse's office."

"Is he there?"

"Mrs. Morgan? No. He's left for London. He's on personal holiday until Sunday; then he'll be staying at Brown's. He's meeting you there on

Tuesday, isn't he? I don't have his weekend number. He's very private, as you may know. But if I hear from him I'll tell him that you called. Why don't you send him an e-mail?"

"Maybe I'll do that." She looked at her watch. No time for e-mails, and she knew better than to react. *She needed to think, that's what. Give it a day. Rome wasn't destroyed in a day. Or was it 'built in a day'?*

Sandrina was mulling over her troubles while she dressed. Grabbing her laptop case, she flew out the door with less than a minute to spare.

The logistics went smoothly, and Sandrina tried to absorb as much about the Lomi-Lomi as she could in a short time. She had known Max and Jason for nearly two decades, and she knew that it would do no good to call and wheedle. If she wanted to win them back, she would have to prove that she was still the best person for the job.

Max and Jason had purchased the oceanfront property from a local developer who had fallen on hard times. The hotel had an atrium lobby, around which the 815 guest rooms were wrapped. The rooms were gutted, the swimming pool drained, and the lobby an empty pit that looked as if it had been struck by a missile. Daisy Hana took her for a quick lunch at a nearby beachfront café, where she got to see a family of humpback whales spouting geysers in the distance, and then she shuttled her back to the Aloha to meet with Kevin Clark.

Sometimes in the international world of public relations, Sandrina came across an odd duck. A person who ran toward adventure, or away from the banal, and settled down in a milieu so foreign that he or she became like a mutant species.

When she met Kevin Clark, she knew he belonged to her odd-duck club. He could have been anywhere between 30 and 50, with bright blue eyes and a nondescript hair color and cut, typical of men who were raised in the Midwest. In fact, there was nothing especially unusual about him from his appearance and, until he talked to her, Sandrina wasn't impressed.

He spoke like a courtly gentleman, infusing funny word inversions into his speech that made Sandrina laugh. Kevin invited her to "tea-spots" on the Seaview Terrace with its beautiful panorama of the ocean. She laughed out loud at his charming twist on the pretentious English expression "a spot of tea."

"So tell me about yourself, Ms. Morgan," he said, over a vanilla custard dessert called *haupia* and Earl Gray tea. "And, I don't mean the sales pitch."

"What do you want to know?"

"Where are you from?"

"Born and bred in New York City. And you?"

"Born in Fairfield, Iowa. My parents were meditators."

"I didn't know you could do that as a profession."

"You can't. I saw my life sun-setting—"

Sun-setting? "Is that a verb?"

"It is now. Anyway, all I heard when I was growing up were mantras. The same three words, chanted over and over again. Ohm-Ohm-Ohm. So I took an inordinate interest in language—I have a Ph.D. in linguistics from the University of Arizona—and went to work for Ramada. They're domiciled there, you know."

"Why the hotel industry with an advanced degree in linguistics?"

"Very good question. I wanted a career where I could meet thousands of new people, from different cultures, who speak in different tongues. Most people choose to live in Hawaii for the weather; I requested this assignment because it is a cultural crossroads, a Pacific melting pot, Pele's Melee I call it—"

She laughed again. Kevin Clark was weird but endearing. He was cheering her up. "And, may I ask, of all the tongues you've heard spoken, which one is most intriguing?"

"The forked one," he said. "It is also the most prevalent."

"Yes, I would venture to say it is the new international language of business," Sandrina replied.

"So, what would you like to see?" he asked.

"What have you planned?"

"I Arnold Palmer'd the beaches tour, they're all the same—sandy. And Hawaii's got a bunch of restaurants, but everything you need to know about them is in the Oahu tourist guide. There's a Pearl Harbor Memorial and a mock-Hawaiian wedding...are you married?"

"Yes. I am."

"Well, we'll skip to my Lou that then. I know...in thirty minutes you can catch the Archeology and Dune Walk. Then I've organized a luau in your honor, followed by the torch-lighting ceremony. Sound goody-goody?"

She smiled. He actually made her forget her problems. "Sounds great."

After the most extraordinary luau, where the *kalua* pig was roasted in a fire pit built into the sand and a show with dancers twirling poi balls of fire, Sandrina slept like a lava rock. The fire dancers had given her a great idea for her very important meeting the next day.

Max was there. Sandrina had not expected to see him. He sat at the head of the table with two small space heaters by his sides. With a nod of his head, he signaled for her to begin. Flustered but determined, Sandrina decided to give it all she had. *Hell, what did she have to lose that she hadn't lost already?*

"Let me preface my thoughts by saying that opening a new resort hotel in this anti-travel environment is going to be tough. It will take excellence on your part and creativity on mine." *If I'm still here.* "I will give you one hundred percent of my creativity and commitment. But if you don't agree, or see holes in my balloon, tell me. Okay?"

All heads bobbed.

"Do you have sprinklers here?" Sandrina asked.

The room full of managers looked at one another, again heads rising and falling in unison.

"OK then...let's get started." She held up the operating manuals Daisy had given her and lit them on fire with an Aloha Regency Waikiki match. She was careful to douse it with water once the effect had registered.

"Let's forget the standard operating manuals. At least the customer service sections," she said.

The operations manager opened his mouth to speak but was stopped by Max, who shushed him with a finger to his lips.

"I'm going to be blunt," Sandrina continued. She looked straight at Max when she spoke. "The Lomi-Lomi will not have the best location or facilities. SH is a "hot" brand, thanks to years of hard work..." She paused to let the message sink in. "... but it is synonymous with trendy style and downtown urban locations. To most of its existing customers, a resort offering will be a disconnect. Overall tourism numbers are down, Hawaii is perceived to be a foreign country by many Americans and not exotic enough to others."

"Sandrina," Max said. "Cut to the good news."

"This is just my opinion," she said. "But it is an educated opinion, and I have the advantage of a global overview and inside information from many of your counterparts in the industry." She hoped she drove home the breadth of her contacts and experience.

"We are always interested in what you think," Max said. He smiled warmly, putting Sandrina at ease.

"It's really sociological and has to do with changing psyches and societal trends. In the 1950's, many think as a reaction to wartime uncertainty, customers wanted standardization. They wanted to know what they were getting, and they wanted it to be reliably the same every time they went back to a service establishment. Aloha, Marriott, McDonald's, to name a few, are brands that were developed in response to customer desire. These companies, as you know, were rewarded with exponential growth. They were successful in becoming household names."

"But the baby-boomers, our largest socioeconomic segment, are the children of the fifties generation. They grew up with Aloha and McDonald's," said the director of operations.

"True. But do you know any children who don't rebel against their parents?"

"So what *do* they want?" he asked.

"We need to do specific research to find out exactly what the customers want. And then give it to them. That's called being customer-focused," Sandrina explained.

"We can't knock down or move the building," said the director of operations.

"Certainly not. You need to concentrate on customer service offerings."

"Tell them some of your ideas," Daisy said.

"I propose we found the Lomi-Lomi Hawaii Customer Research Institute. We do trend studies and use the data as the basis for customer strategies. Then we can publicize select results to gain media coverage."

"That not only gets exposure, because original findings are newsworthy, but it also sends the message to the public that the Lomi-Lomi is customer-driven," Daisy said.

"And that SH is listening!" the director of operations added. He was, Sandrina decided, a politician of the wind.

"Look around you at successful companies in other industries. The way Sephora merchandises cosmetics. How Starbucks sells coffee. Even Nike with its 'Do It Your Way' tagline. What they seem to have in common is the recognition that today's consumers see themselves as individuals. The Internet has created an environment where every customer is a market segment of one. This 'mini-me' mentality expects customization, not standardization," Sandrina said.

"It's true what she's saying," said Kevin Clark, who had come in late. "I'm willing to pay three-sixty for my Kona-latte because I can put in just the amount of vanilla, cinnamon, nutty-meg, and sugar that I like."

"You use all that stuff?" asked the vice-president of marketing.

"Remember that scene from *Harry Met Sally*?" said Daisy. "Meg Ryan goes into a restaurant and she wants her apple pie with strawberry ice cream hot, but if they only have vanilla ice cream then she wants it cold, but if —"

"If we let every customer do that," interrupted the vice-president of food and beverage, "we might as well close down before we open."

Sandrina directed her words to Max again, "SH is a great name. Everyone knows it. They trust you. Trust is important. We don't want to lose that." She hoped she had made her point about trust.

"Are you saying that we can maximize our brand advantage and give each customer what he or she wants individually?" asked the vice-president of marketing.

"Exactly!" Sandrina exclaimed.

"But how?" asked Max.

She was prepared. "Take a cue from the Internet. It's open twenty-four hours, seven days a week, three hundred and sixty-five days a year. It's fast. It's efficient. I know I can get whatever I want, whenever I want it." *Except a response from Warren,* she thought. "Why don't you offer twenty-four hour check-in? Why should a tourist have to wait for two hours, hot, tired, and cranky after a long flight from the mainland, because his room hasn't come up in the queue for cleaning?"

"But late morning/early afternoon check-in has been de rigueur since Ellsworth M. Statler invented the hotel," said the director of housekeeping.

"So change it. Starbucks changed the way coffee shops serve coffee. And now they have forty-seven hundred of them." She hoped Max would give her extra credit for creativity.

Sandrina's ideas were well received; at the end of the meeting the managers gave her a standing ovation.

After the others had left, Sandrina said to Max, "Beth called me this morning. I know about the letter."

"Sorry about the timing, but the contract said it had to be sent on the first," Max said.

"It's not the timing; it's the content. After nineteen years—"

"It's business, Sandrina. Not a marriage. Deliver or you're out."

"I would say that I have delivered." She remembered how hard she had worked on the Millennium Universal opening. "Over and over again."

"But lately you haven't been...engaged. Missing meetings, not returning phone calls, distracted."

He was right. She had been distracted. "I've had some personal issues. But they seem to be coming to a head."

"I'm more sympathetic. I've got some personal concerns too, as you know, but Jason, well, he's unforgiving."

"Max, you're right." She was getting an idea. "I wasn't listening carefully about your plans to expand into the resort business. But I know I can help you. I have confidence in your vision, and if you reconsider, I promise to give you the kind of support you'll need to pull this off."

"I believe you."

"Max," Sandrina said. "Why did you come? I was told that neither you nor Jason could make it."

"I came because I needed to see for myself if you really didn't care any more or if something else was going on. I came because in my heart I didn't believe—" He stopped.

"Isabel?" Sandrina asked.

"Yes. Sandrina you were terrific in the meeting this morning."

"Can anything be done, or is it too late?"

"I'll talk to Jason on Monday. I'll let you know."

Chapter Twenty-Four

Sandrina had never before felt such an overpowering need to be alone and think. She was glad she had the weekend and its promise of distance and solitude to gain perspective. Although Daisy had offered her a complimentary stay at any of her other hotel clients on one of the other islands, she knew she needed to be away from civilization, telephones, Internet access, fax machines, and the other distractions of her circumscribed universe.

The events of the last few weeks had engulfed her, clouding her judgment and reordering her priorities. She knew she had to decide between Michael and Warren, and refocus on her responsibilities to her clients. She had been sorely wrong about Isabel; now she wondered what else she might have misread.

Scouring the guidebooks that she'd brought with her, she was intrigued by the description of the raw beauty and geological grandeur of Hawaii Volcanoes National Park on the Big Island. When she told Daisy about her plans to go there, Daisy recommended that she stay at a small inn near the park.

"I've got to warn you though," Daisy said. "It gets cold at night. And there aren't any phones, or a pool, or TV. I doubt your Blackberry will work."

"Just what I want," Sandrina sighed.

"If you stayed here, in Waikiki, you could see the Arizona Memorial at Pearl Harbor and Iolani's Palace. It's the only Royal Palace in American," Daisy said.

Sandrina smiled. "Thanks. I promise, next time. It's not that I don't want to—"

"I understand," Daisy said. The two women embraced.

Sandrina went back to her room to pack. Neither Warren nor Isabel had returned her calls. Warren was probably out of touch, and Isabel, she suspected, was ducking her. Michael had sent her a fax that things were going well in Paris and he expected to be back in New York by the middle of the next week. She sent him one back, "Good luck! Off to rest. I'm exhausted. Contact may be difficult. Will call Tuesday from London."

She looked in the bathroom mirror and saw her image tinted green by the off-putting light cast from the fluorescent bulbs. She impulsively removed all of her makeup, scrubbed her face hard with a washcloth, and then tied her hair back with the ribbon from the hospitality basket that Daisy had sent upon her arrival. Symbolically, she was off-duty.

Sandrina left after lunch on Friday afternoon and flew Aloha Air 35 minutes from Honolulu International Airport to Keahole on the Big Island of

Hawaii. She rented a Chevy Blazer and drove past small villages through a rain forest along the mountainous winding road to the Kilauea Lodge in Volcano Village. On the way she stopped in a Wal-Mart and bought hiking boots, woolen socks, a rain slicker, and a t-shirt with a picture on it of a large *pueo*, the brown-and-white Hawaiian owl, famous in Hawaiian mythology for its protective powers.

When Sandrina arrived at the Kilauea Lodge, with its vaulted, open-beamed ceiling and blazing central fireplace, she knew immediately she had made the right decision. She felt an empowering thrill begin to creep up her spine.

Sandrina checked in and went to the bar. She ordered a Blue Hawaii, made with vodka and blue curacao, which she sipped while admiring the stone and timber fireplace mantle, embedded with coins and mottos from all over the world. After cocktails she was escorted to a one-bedroom cottage nestled in the forest of *hapu* and *amauanau* ferns behind the main lodge. It was rustic but lovingly renovated: it had its own fireplace and wood-burning stove, a locally hand-crafted wooden rocking chair, and a collection of vintage photographs of the Hawaiian queens from the Kamehaneha line.

The Blue Hawaii knocked her out, so she decided to skip dinner, go to bed, and get an early start in the morning.

On Saturday morning, after a workman's breakfast of scrambled eggs, poi, breadfruit, guava juice, and Kona coffee, Sandrina climbed into her Blazer and headed to the 11-mile Crater Rim Drive that encircled the Kilauea caldera. The Kilauea volcano was one of the most active volcanoes in the world. It was still on top of a "hot spot," apropos, Sandrina thought, for the situation she found herself in.

She was mesmerized by the natural wonders she passed on the road—sulfur fumaroles, caused by surface water leaking into volcanic fissures, which smelled like rotten eggs; breeching fault lines that appeared about to split and swallow her car; rift zones and craters; and, steam vents so hot she felt as though she had driven into a sauna. It looked and felt as she thought Hades would.

A small sign shaped like an Indian arrowhead pointed down an overgrown path. She decided to follow it, parking the car and continuing on foot, passing the Hawaiian Volcano Observatory, disappointed to find that is was closed to the public. Peering over a railing into the heart of the Halema'uma'u crater, which she had read the Hawaiians believed was inhabited by Pele, goddess of fire, she saw it splutter and belch.

It was cold and had started to rain. She pulled the slicker up around her and slugged through the rapidly forming puddles of brown water along the lava-paved path that led to Devastation Trail, which was like something out of *The Night of the Living Dead*, with hollowed gray tree stumps lined up in a field, cemetery-style, where everything that once was alive now stood dead.

A little further along she was in a structure like a naturally formed utility pipe, where her own light footsteps echoed loudly. She found a sign that identified the tunnel as a "lava tube," formed by cooling lava as it cascaded down the volcano's side. Lava ash is fertile, proof to Sandrina of Pele's feminine presence, so at both the entrance and exit to the lava tube she found lush effusions of greenery — furry moss and fiddlehead ferns — the latter so named because they looked like the scrolls on the heads of violins. There were *ohia* and *koa* trees, and even wild blackberries, their thorny branches pushing through the righteous orchids that had grown there first.

Once the rain had stopped, Sandrina was drawn back to the Halema'uma'u crater by the melodious warble of a fluffy red *apapane* bird, which briefly lit on her backpack and then flitted toward Pele's crater. Sandrina followed the bird to the edge of the crater, where she sat on a rock and drank the water they had given her at the lodge. She pulled out the guidebook and read about Pele's predicament.

In the Hawaiian legend Sandrina had read, Pele had a handsome lover from Kauai, whom she wanted to live with. Her jealous sister, Namakaokaha'i, goddess of the sea, would flood every home Pele and her lover tried to build. Pele finally escaped her sister's reach on top of the mountain, and claimed the crater as her home.

But Pele bore a grudge, and every time she got mad, she would spew a little 2000° lava around to let everyone know her fury. The patterns formed by droplets of lava were called Pele's tears, and the molten rock drawn into fine strands by the rushing wind was called Pele's hair. Legend had it that Pele would appear sometimes as a human, a beautiful woman with black hair.

The rain had stopped and the gases from the volcano mixed with the water vapor to form a filmy, view-obscuring haze called *vog*. The showers had erased the changeability, leaving behind a steady warm temperature in the mid-seventies. Sandrina centered herself on the flat lava rock and planted her feet on the ground.

She closed her eyes and remembered first what her mother had said, about there being no lack of love in her life, and she knew that it was true. First, she touched her heart with both palms, and thanked the goddesses of the world for filling her existence with so much love and success, because she knew that above all this was no small thing, and she wanted to declare her appreciation for these blessings. Then she thought about the dilemma she was in, and decided not to budge from that rock, even if the volcano started to erupt, until she had resolved it, although she admitted to herself that if she heard rumblings she might rush her decision a bit.

Sandrina had worked very hard for many years to get where she had gotten in life. She had always been true to her friends, loving to her family, and honest with her clients. But she had fallen from grace of late, and she wanted to know why. More important, she needed to fix it—this mess—before those people she loved, and who loved her, got hurt even more.

If only Joshua were here, what would he say? She knew he would advise her to fire Isabel immediately. That was easy. And not to do business with Warren's firm—"conflict of interest" he would say. Done deal. It was true, she knew, what Joshua always said about not mixing business and personal matters. But she had already decided to settle those scores, as soon as she arrived in London on Tuesday.

What would Joshua have said about Michael and Warren? Nothing more than he had already said. It was just like Joshua to recognize the imbalance in the scales of Love—Justice's alter ego. He would have only asked her the right questions, not forced her choice. But he had sent her that prescient message through Ralph Aiken. There was more to that message than Ralph could ever understand.

Sandrina wondered if she had ever really been fair to Michael. When she met him she was ready to get married. And Michael had been so in love with her. He had nurtured her wounds and made her scars fade, the ones inflicted by her father. He allowed her to have what she thought was unimaginable for her—a stable home life. And, he had defied his family to marry her. He had provided the launching pad for her rocket; without his encouragement, support, and contacts she might never have become who she was.

When she thought about it, she was immensely grateful to him, but she wasn't fulfilled. He didn't even approach knowing her, reaching the depths of her mind, her spirit, or her sexuality. He hadn't tried. Could he, would he, change? Had she ever given him the chance? Maybe the fault lay with her, not him.

Then she recalled what Esther had told her. It reverberated in her ears like a warning signal. She too had strayed due to some inner lack of fulfillment, causing her to bolt from stability in search of passion and poetry.

And Warren. Did she love him? She was beginning to wonder. He was enigmatic and she was physically drawn to him as she had never been to anyone before. Was she confusing sex for love?

Sandrina closed her eyes and clapped the heels of her hands to her temples, like cymbals. A minor eruption exploded, geyser-like, from Pele's crater just as the sun started to set. All the people she knew she loved occupied her mind, working at odds and in tandem to help her solve her conundrum. She felt the wind direction shift dramatically and the *vog* clear as suddenly as it had appeared, revealing the last remnants of a sky the color of a robin's egg. The sun continued its final descent, melting into the feisty crater atop the volcano as it erupted into a fiery display.

Suddenly Sandrina knew exactly what she had to do. The peacocking Halema'uma'u crater sang to her as it did its dance, like the splashing a band of children make as they clap their hands in a swimming pool. She interpreted the musical sound, and her vision of red rubies and yellow sapphires tossed into the air, to be affirmation of Pele's approval and the ultimate show of feminine solidarity. She felt lighthearted and relieved at last.

Chapter Twenty-Five

Once Sandrina had a plan, there was no time to lose. She had driven back to the lodge fast, packed her belongings, checked out, and made the last connections back to the mainland, enabling her to catch the red-eye over the North Pole from San Francisco to London.

She made one phone call from the airport in San Francisco as she waited for her connection to London. It was to Gary Brent.

"Can't join the junket tomorrow, Gary. Something urgent came up. Tough cookie business. I'm sure you'll understand."

Burning to get to London faster, she would arrive only 24 hours before he expected her, but she would need extra time to say what she had on her mind.

When she arrived at Brown's, an anachronistic hotel a short cab ride from Chaucer's offices, the front desk manager looked her up and down as if she were a squatter, so she realized she had better check in and freshen up before letting Warren see her again. Those superficial trappings meant nothing to her now; she would greet him clean but stripped of makeup and seductive clothes. She asked for his room number, as well as Isabel's, so that she could let them know she had arrived. It took her most authoritative tone, and a 20-pound note, to get the information. It also helped that her name was known.

"Oh, forgive me, Mrs. Morgan," Nigel behind the desk said. "I didn't realize it was you."

He was flustered as he scooted from behind the counter to help her with her bags. "Is there anything else I can do for you?"

"Actually, Nigel, there is. Please transfer the charges on Isabel Riley's bill to mine and check her out. She'll be leaving within the hour."

"Of course. As you wish."

In her suite, Sandrina quickly peeled off her clothes, pulling herself together with as much haste as she could muster and putting on the only clean outfit that she had left, a red ensemble. It had broad shoulders and a slightly revolutionary air.

Isabel's phone didn't answer, so Sandrina went to Warren's room. Before knocking, she drew a deep breath, not sure how he would react to what she'd come to say. Rehearsing her words under her breath: *You have touched me in my molten core, but it's Michael I choose. It's Michael I love. We weren't meant to be.* She closed her eyes and knocked three times, softly. There was no response. She tried again, louder this time. Still not a sound. Her heart was thundering in her chest.

She stopped in her own room briefly to think what she should do next. Dialing the number for Chaucer's London office, she was informed by a clipped voice that Mr. Waterhouse had left an hour before. She pulled a crisp clean sheet of Brown's stationery from the drawer, with its chocolate ink and little derby logo, and wrote a note to Isabel: "You're fired." She then inserted her business card into an envelope with the note, left her room, and slipped the envelope under Isabel's door.

It was the cocktail hour, and she hoped that Warren could be found in the bar she had spotted to the left of the front entrance when she came in. The St. Georges bar was very dark. The walls and furniture were all the same heavy wood and leather, the color earth looks like after a heavy downpour. The bar counter itself was long and narrow. One had to squint to see down to the far end, the only natural illumination coming from the Victorian stained-glass window spilling color across the shadows. As she approached the double doors, with crosses on them, she felt a chill up her spine; only this time it was an unpleasant sensation, like an electric shock or a jag of ice.

First, she saw Warren's back facing her covered by the sleek gray sweater, like wolf's fur, that he had worn in the bar in Brazil. The dim light coming through the window caught the brilliant highlights in his hair. His hands and arms were animated as he spoke to someone hidden from her view by his massive upper body. She could see his martini, and a wine glass nearby. She heard him laugh, his lion's roar, as she took a step closer toward the bar. And, then he leaned slightly to the right, just enough for her to make out Isabel's face, as he adjusted his arm so that he could slip his hand in between her thighs.

The sense of déjà vu overwhelmed her. A different country, a foreign bar — but the scene familiar. She could imagine the conversation so exactly that she could smell his spicy scent and martini-laced breath and taste the words he was whispering in Isabel's ear, so sweet on his tongue.

She had never doubted her decision, but now she wondered how she could have ever made such a disastrous mistake.

The bile rose to Sandrina's throat, but she swallowed it down. She felt dizzy but remained standing. She backed out of the doorway, staring at the scene, hoping that they hadn't seen her. She bolted out the front door of Brown's and ran down the block, toward Bond Street, then past the boutiques she knew so well and somehow no longer had any interest in. Suddenly she heard heavy footsteps catching up. "Wait!" he shouted. "Sandrina —" And then she felt his hand clasp her arm.

They stood frozen, staring at each other, not knowing what to say. She saw the amber flecks in his eyes taunting her and watched the muscle in his jaw twitch with tension. She felt her body go slack as something left her forever—trust in her own judgment, her vanity and self-absorption, her belief that there could be something better than what she had.

How could she have been so wrong? But then she played their tape in reverse and realized that he had told her all along what he was, what she should expect. She chose to ignore his caveats, heeding the urgings of her sexuality and deep emotional need to be seen, to be known, to be loved, and to be taken care of. It was true that these needs had been buried beneath the familiarity and complacency of a mature marriage, but she realized now what she had taken for granted too long—that Michael was trustworthy, faithful, honest, and exclusively in love with her.

She kept trying to jerk her arm from Warren's grip, but with each pull he held fast, tightening his clutch, hurting her. She reflexively made a fist with her free hand and socked him right in the jaw. The diamond engagement ring left an inch-long gash on his chin. He grabbed her other wrist to keep her from hitting him again.

"I almost gave up everything for you!"

Suddenly it began to pour cold, hard rain. Several women had gathered in the windows of the shops to watch the escalating performance on the street. The ladies were cupping their hands around their mouths. Sandrina was sure she heard one of them shout, "Give it to him again!"   Warren wrapped his arms around Sandrina in a bear hug. He looked in her eyes. The color of optimism had given way to something else, fury.

"I knew you never would," he said.

They were both completely soaked through as the rain kept falling. Warren pulled her into a doorway for shelter. He had the same expression she had seen that first night in the bar in Brazil. His eyes were lustful, his smile was gentle, and his body language was wary. But this time she knew he was the one who was confused, not her. She struggled to get loose, but he was too strong.

"How could you know?"

"I have a fable to tell you: A scorpion asks a frog if he can ride on her back across the river. The frog is very smart, so she says, 'If I give you a ride, then you will sting me and I will die.' The scorpion says, 'If I kill you, then we would both die, because I would drown.' She trusted him, and the frog swam to the middle of the river with the scorpion on her back. The scorpion stung the frog, and as she was dying she asked, 'Why did you do that? Now we will both perish.' And the scorpion said, 'Because it's my nature.'

You, Sandrina, are much smarter than that frog."

Isabel boldly approached in time to hear Warren's story. She appeared bemused, standing naturally under a broad Brown's umbrella. She offered Warren cover under her umbrella, but he would not let go of his hold on Sandrina. The crowd of female shoppers emerged as soon as Isabel arrived.

"I could relate to that fable as well," Isabel said, nonchalantly, to Sandrina.

"Yes, Isabel, a scorpion is a good description for you," Sandrina said. That comment elicited snickers from the crowd, which had begun to swell.

"Before you get all high and mighty, did it ever occur to you that I did nothing more than what you would have done?" Then she raised her eyebrow and pointed her chin at Warren. "Excuse me — did do," Isabel said.

"And what's that?" Sandrina asked.

"Used your brains and looks to get what you want in life."

Sandrina went weak in Warren's grip; he instinctively let go of her wrists. She saw in Isabel everything that she had always fought against becoming — selfish, calculating, and cruel — a woman operating alone in the jungle, living by predatory rules. She realized at once how dangerously close she had come to putting aside the very qualities that differentiated her from Isabel — loyalty, honesty and the capacity for love.

"There are worlds of difference between us, Isabel." Sandrina took several steps toward her, but Isabel backed away. "I have earned what you want to steal. I am honest about my intentions while you are duplicitous. You don't know the first thing about love." She looked briefly but longingly at Warren.

"Oh please, Sandrina, save your mud-slinging for someone who cares what you think—"

Before Sandrina could respond, a London bus had pulled close to the curb, spraying Isabel with muddy water and backed-up sewer slime. She lost her footing and fell off the curb into a puddle glistening with green disinfectant. The crowd of ladies, now grown to a throng, broke into applause.

"Help me!" Isabel cried.

Warren looked at her and shrugged his shoulders. "Sandrina, can we stay friends?"

The last thing she said to him before she walked away was "Sorry, it's not my nature."

As she trudged through the rain back to Brown's, she realized that she was who she was—good and not so good, a package. The irony was that Michael did love her for who she was; that was why he depended on her so. There were many types of love, she supposed, and each had its price. The passion she had felt for Warren carried with it a counterpoint of pain. But the lasting love she felt for Michael, with its bearings of loyalty and trust, friendship, companionship, and constancy, had its merits. The Same Old Thing was looking pretty good to her now.

The first thing Sandrina did when she got back to her office was tear up the Chaucer Suites contract that she had had the good sense not to sign. Then she called every client she had. She had just hung up with Jason Rothstein, the last and most difficult of her client conciliation calls. He and Max agreed to renew her contract for another year, at which time they would review her performance. If things went back to the way they'd been before, as Max was sure they would, then she could be reasonably sure that the relationship between TravelSmart and SH Hotels would continue indefinitely.

As she was confirming with Beth that Isabel's credit card, cell phone number, e-mail address, and profit-sharing plan had been canceled, she noticed a new nest on the ledge of a building across the street and its occupants, a red-tailed hawk and chicks.

She took it as an omen.

Chapter Twenty-Six

There was a cacophony of pots and pans and shouting coming from the kitchen of the restaurant, as Michael watched Sandrina sweep in. She was breathless and eager; as all heads turned to look at her the kitchen noises rose to a crescendo. Michael had ordered her a Cosmopolitan. She managed to glide into her seat, brushing up against his arm seductively as she did so, and take a first sip of the flamingo-colored cocktail, all in one elongated graceful gesture.

"Happy birthday, darling," she said. "I'm so sorry to be late. It was impossible to find a taxi. I had to walk from my doctor's appointment." She held her glass up to offer a toast.

"To you," she said.

"To us," he replied.

The pink liquid cast a rosy glow on her face. Michael gazed at her adoringly but with a dollop of reserve that had not been there before. "You still look like the twenty-five year old I married, especially with no makeup," Michael said. "You are softer and more supple. Like a girl again. You've lost that sharp edge that I watched you hone these sixteen years. How is it that I love you even more deeply than before?"

Sandrina had changed during the past year. They both knew it. The things he spoke of that made him love her more were there. Passion, pain, choice, and betrayal had changed them both.

"Thank you. For always loving me—no matter what," she said.

"That's like thanking the sun for rising. It couldn't be stopped if one tried."

"Two grilled salmon au poivre, please. And, a bottle of Wild Horse Cabernet, 1997," Michael said to the waiter without consulting her.

"I'm so glad your trip went well," she said when the waiter left.

"It was wonderful, 'Drina. Hachette Publishing signed on for five years. They're one of the biggest purchasers of paper in Europe. I got both the English and Swiss governments to buy in to your idea to set up a secure boutique exchange for currency paper."

"That's great, Michael. Congratulations," Sandrina said as she began to think about the recent past.

"What are you thinking, 'Drina?"

"I was thinking about how circular life is. Hachette publishes *Journey* magazine. That's where I started my journey, and now we are back at the beginning—"

"Or maybe finally near the end." He gave her a profound look. "Hey, while I was there I did some snooping. *Elle* is about to fire their PR firm."

"But they're not in travel."

"So what? Here's your opportunity to expand."

"Why not?" she asked. The idea appealed to her.

"Did you read about Thomas?" he asked.

"It's all over the news. How sad. And to think it could have been —" she said.

"—Me. I'm thinking about it all the time. Let's not talk about such depressing subjects now. Tonight we are celebrating, are we not?" he asked.

Thinking of the baby that she was going to have, the one they both now desperately hoped for, she wanted to say, "In more ways than one." "Michael, I have a special gift for your birthday."

"Everything I need and want is right here," he said.

That wasn't exactly the response she had hoped for. But he was different now. Maybe that was why he thought he loved her more, because now he was willing to.

"Would you marry me again," she asked him, "with everything you know now?"

"Yes," he said. "In a minute — but this time I wouldn't expect perfect bliss. There are apt to be bumps along the way."

"Joshua once said that people change only when it becomes more painful not too," she said.

"Joshua was wise," he said. "Would you marry me again?"

One thing she had learned from Warren was that to be in love she had to be vulnerable and open enough to get hurt. She had been deeply hurt before she met Michael, by her father, and she didn't like it one bit. It was much more comfortable, safer, to have been on the receiving end of the love spectrum during the early years of her marriage to Michael—now she was ready to give her husband the love he deserved.

Michael leaned over and took her hand, looking into her green eyes for the answer to his question.

Satisfied by what he saw there, he turned his lips to hers, but she had already pressed them to his ear, brushing her chin with his as she did so. The scent that was uniquely his—mown grass and talcum powder and ginger—the one she'd nearly forgotten, washed over her like a warm bath.

"Come closer," she whispered.

"How come?" he asked.

"I have a secret I want to tell you."

Made in the USA
San Bernardino, CA
10 June 2014